TWO LAST FIRST DATES

COZY COTTAGE CAFÉ

KATE O'KEEFFE

WILD LIME BOOKS

ISBN-13: 978-1548465148
ISBN-10: 1548465143
Edited by Chrissy Wolfe at The Free Every Chance Reader
Copyright © 2017 Kate O'Keeffe

Wild Lime
Books

❀ Created with Vellum

ABOUT THIS BOOK

To Paige Miller Two Last First Dates sounds like a disaster waiting to happen.

Paige is a hot mess. She's stuck in a job she hates, the guy she fell for is in love with someone else, and she's agreed to a dating pact to marry the next guy she dates. Talk about being in a jam. Now, she has to figure out what to do professionally and personally... Life as a spinster with fifteen cats doesn't sound too bad, though.

Deciding to give up on love, Paige begrudgingly befriends Josh Bentley, the friendly coffee delivery guy, while helping out at the Cozy Cottage Café. His T-shirts make her eyes roll, but their runs have become an important part of her day and a blessing to her waistline, because Bailey's cakes are too good to pass up.

Meanwhile, her best friends offer to find Mr. Right for her, and all Paige has to do is let them. But when the man of her dreams walks through the door, any thoughts Paige had of being alone with those fifteen cats fly out the window. Now, she just has to hope her friends choose him as her Last First Date.

But in the end, are Two Last First Dates enough to find The One?

ALSO BY KATE O'KEEFFE

It's Complicated Series:

Never Fall for Your Back-Up Guy

Never Fall for Your Enemy

Love Manor Romantic Comedy Series:

Dating Mr. Darcy

Marrying Mr. Darcy

Falling for Another Darcy

Falling for Mr. Bingley (spin-off novella)

High Tea Series:

No More Bad Dates

No More Terrible Dates

No More Horrible Dates

Cozy Cottage Café Series:

One Last First Date

Two Last First Dates

Three Last First Dates

Four Last First Dates

Wellywood Romantic Comedy Series:

Styling Wellywood

Miss Perfect Meets Her Match

Falling for Grace

Standalone titles

CHAPTER 1

I COULD NOT BELIEVE we'd done this. Again. I glanced at my friends, chatting excitedly, sipping their glasses of champagne, smiling and laughing as though they had no cares in the world. I let out a long, deep sigh. I mean, how many pacts to marry the next guy you date could a girl reasonably make?

Two, it would seem.

You see, we'd done this before, my friends Cassie, Marissa, and me. A year ago, around a bonfire much like the one I was standing beside now, on this very beach, in fact. And it had turned out just nicely for Cassie—well, not exactly in the way she intended, but it had worked out all the same.

And now we'd gone and done it again, this time with our good friend Bailey replacing the loved-up Cassie. We'd agreed to One Last First Date. Only, I'd already been on my One Last First Date, and considering I'm single and alone, it's fair to say that hadn't exactly worked out the way it was meant to for me.

"Hey, Millsey!"

I turned to look at the man approaching me. My heart skipped a beat and my tummy knotted into an elaborate rug as I took in his

1

chiseled jaw, his dark, scruffy hair moving in the gentle breeze. The chatter from the others on the beach faded into nothing.

There he was, Will Jordan, the man of my dreams. Shame about his girlfriend. And just to add further agony to an already heartbreaking situation, she was one of my closest friends. Naturally.

"I just wanted to say thanks for this." Will smiled, gesturing at the bonfire and the picnic blanket. He raised his champagne flute and clinked it against mine, smiling, the edges of his dark eyes crinkling in a way that sped my heart rate up. "Here's to you. You're awesome, you know that, right?"

"Thanks." *Just not awesome enough to want to date.* I put the flute to my lips, took a large swig, and swallowed. The bubbles tickled my nose. I tore my eyes from Will's handsome face and looked down the beach and out to sea.

He wrapped his arm around my shoulder and my legs instantly turned to jelly. "You mean a lot to her, and to me."

Against my better judgment, I looked up into his eyes. I nodded, not trusting myself to speak. Why did his arm have to feel so right around my shoulders?

"And we're . . . good?" he asked, hesitatingly.

"Oh . . . um . . . yes. Absolutely." I shot him my hundred-watt smile I knew could fool anyone, anytime.

He gave me a squeeze. "Great. I'm really glad."

Anyone looking at the two of us would think we were the perfect couple, standing beside a bonfire on a perfect summer's evening, the sunset over the horizon casting a beautiful, warm glow over us.

Cassie sidled up to our little group of two, grinning like the cat who got the best flavored cream in town, and considering she had Will, I guess she did. "So, how did I do on the swim?"

I smiled at my friend. Although she was dressed in dry clothes now, her hair was damp and had begun to curl. She still looked beautiful. Damn her. "You did great."

Will let his arm drop from my shoulder, stepped toward Cassie, and collected her in an embrace. "Hey," he said, all gooey-eyed, as though he hadn't seen her in weeks rather than mere moments.

"Hey," she replied, smiling back at him.

I tried to swallow the lump in my throat.

Without letting go of Will, Cassie reached out and took my hand in hers. "Thanks for this, Paige. I'm so happy you're okay with . . . everything."

By "everything," she meant her and Will. Oh, and the distinct lack of Will and *me*. But what else was I going to do? As I'd lectured myself countless times since Cassie had told me they'd fallen in love, the heart wants what the heart wants. And I was powerless to change that.

Still, it should have been me.

"It's fine. I'm happy for you both." I swear I didn't nearly choke on the words. Suddenly cold, I wrapped my arms around myself, watching Will out of the corner of my eye.

I shook my head. I needed to give myself another stern talking to, that was for sure.

"Hey, Paige!" Marissa called over to me. "Get over here. The fire's toasty warm."

I shook myself out of my reverie and flashed her a smile. "Sure." Glancing at Cassie and Will, I said, "See you two lovebirds soon."

I joined Marissa and Bailey by the fire. It worked its magic, warming me up immediately.

"You okay?" Marissa asked in a hushed tone as she leaned in to top up my glass with more champagne. "You look like you've seen a ghost."

"I'm . . ." What was I? Well, I'd gone on my One Last First Date with a guy who had about as much interest in me as I had in quantum physics, rejected me, and was now loved up with someone else. "Heartbroken" seemed about the best way to describe it.

"Hold on, if you look like you've seen a ghost, it's not that Goddess of the Beach, is it? I mean, she's not . . . *here*, is she?" Marissa's eyes darted around nervously.

I let out a chortle, shaking my head. "I didn't think you believed in the Goddess of the Beach?"

Marissa was my hard-nosed friend who never took any crap from anyone. In some ways, she was the opposite of me: cynical, skeptical, always taking things with several pinches of salt. Right now, I could do with being even just a little more like her. She would never choose a guy who didn't choose her back.

Marissa bristled. "I don't believe in it. It's just, you can never be too sure, right? And we did just make a pact, supposedly in her presence, right?"

I let out a sigh. Ah, yes: The Pact.

I looked over at Will, standing next to Cassie, looking so totally in love, you could almost touch it. I sighed. Bailey and Marissa followed my gaze.

"Oh, honey," Bailey said, giving my arm a rub. "He wasn't the right one for you, that's all. You'll meet him some day."

My shoulders slumped. I used to believe it. I used to think there was one perfect guy out there for me, and that, somehow against the odds, I would find him and we would be together, happy forever. I guess I believed in the fairy tale. Now? I wasn't so sure.

I studied Bailey's smiling face. She seemed so certain, so hopeful. "How do you know I'll meet him?"

"I just do." Her certainty was impressive—and a little aggravating.

"I thought Will was the guy for me. And look at how wrong I got that. He was in love with Cassie the whole time. The. Whole. Time."

Bailey smiled sympathetically at me. "You weren't to know. He didn't tell anyone he was in love with her, right?" Bailey looked at Marissa for confirmation.

Marissa shook her head. "It came as a shock to everyone, to be honest. Even to Cassie."

Cassie, who'd been dating the guy she thought she was going to marry for almost a year, until Will dropped his "I'm in love with you" bombshell and changed everything.

I took another slug of my champagne. This stuff was going down rather too well tonight.

"You'll find him," Bailey repeated with conviction.

Tears stung my eyes. "Actually, do you know what? I don't think I will." My voice had a definite quaver to it. I hoped my friends didn't notice.

4

Marissa and Bailey both protested immediately. I raised my hand to silence them. "Hear me out, okay?" They both nodded. I sniffed back the tears and continued. "I've always been the kind of girl to like a guy for a long time, right? I don't rush things, I get to know him, and, to be fair, I kind of worship him from afar, too nervous he'll reject me to do anything about it. And then, when I finally do something about it, it goes horribly, horribly wrong."

We all glanced over at Will and Cassie, who were now sitting, huddled up together on the blanket, looking out to sea, totally oblivious to the rest of us in their new love bubble for two.

"What are you saying?" Marissa asked, narrowing her eyes at me.

"I guess I'm saying . . . I don't think I make the right decisions about men. In fact, I'm terrible at it. So, you two can go on your One Last First Dates and I'll just . . . not."

"You're giving up on finding The One?" Bailey asked, her brow furrowed in concern.

I pursed my lips together and shook my head. "What's the point? It'll only end in heartache. For me."

"You can't give up on it, Paige!" Marissa protested. "We only agreed to the pact ten minutes ago."

I drained my glass and squared my shoulders. The alcohol had gone straight to my head, emboldening me. "I don't think I have any alternative. I've shown you I can't choose the sort of guy who's right for me, so there's nothing for it but to forget the whole thing."

I could see my life flash before my eyes. Watching all my friends fall in love and get married, becoming godmother to a cast of thousands, living in my little cottage with climbing roses along the path. And cats. Lots of cats, clearly. What self-respecting spinster doesn't have cats? Perhaps a goat, too. Why a goat? I don't know, but somehow a goat who would eat all the roses I worked so hard to cultivate seemed appropriate in my current state of mind.

"Paige, come on," Marissa objected.

I crossed my arms, resolute. "No, I've made up my mind."

Actually, until that very moment, I'd had no idea I would make such an outlandish declaration tonight. I'd always been a romantic,

5

always believed in love, in the possibilities it could bring. And now? I could blame it on the champagne, but something had changed.

After it became obvious to my friends I wasn't backing down, they gave up trying to talk me around and we stood in silence, listening to the crackle of the fire and the rhythmic waves on the shore.

"I have an idea," Bailey said with a smile, punctuating the silence. "Do you want to hear it?"

"If it'll knock some sense into Nun Paige here, be my guest," Marissa scoffed, her arms crossed, clearly annoyed with me.

"Paige. If you could choose the right man, one who would love you back and want to be with you for the rest of your life, would you?"

I looked over at Will once more. Choosing the right man wasn't exactly my strong suit. "The point is, I'm no good at it," I replied.

"Just answer. Please?" Bailey was as persistent tonight as she was sweet.

I shrugged. "Sure."

She gave a curt nod. "Okay. That's all I wanted to know."

"Why?" Marissa asked, looking confused. "Is this going somewhere?"

"It is." Bailey leaned in closer to us both, her eyes flashing. "I have an offer for Paige."

An offer? My interest piqued, I raised my eyebrows in expectation.

When nothing was forthcoming, Marissa exclaimed, "Well, what is it, then?"

Bailey looked from Marissa to me, her face beaming. "*I* will choose the guy for Paige."

I recoiled in shock. "You'll do *what*?" I shook my head with vigor. "No no no no no." I might be terrible at making the right decisions in the romance department, but I wasn't desperate.

Was I?

Marissa clapped her hands together in excitement, *her* interest now piqued. "Ooh, and I can help, too!"

"Sure! Great idea! We can be the two matchmakers, right?" Bailey replied.

"Yes! We could even come up with a snappy name, you know,

something like 'The Cute Cupids,' or 'Two Hot Chicks.' Oh, wait, Cassie might like to help out, too, so maybe '*Three* Hot Chicks'?"

Bailey laughed. "We're not trying to self-promote here, we're trying to find someone for Paige."

"Hello? We need to go on *our* One Last First Dates too, remember?" Marissa chimed.

"I know, but let's focus on Paige first. She needs our help," Bailey replied.

I watched, agog, as my two friends discussed me and my predicament as though I wasn't there, my feet in the sand, right next to them. "Excuse me?" I said. They continued to talk between themselves, plotting and planning my fate. "Hey, you two?" Still, nothing. "Oi!" I shouted.

They both stopped in their tracks and looked at me in surprise.

"This"—I gestured to them both—"is not going to happen. Not. So, you can forget what you're going to call yourselves or anything else for that matter. I've made up my mind; I'm giving up on men."

"Listen to her, Paige. I think she's onto something here," Marissa encouraged.

My eyes darted between them. They were actually *serious* about this?

Bailey pursed her lips. "Look, you said yourself you want to be with someone but you no longer trust yourself to make the right choice."

"Yes, but—" I was totally exasperated by these two.

Bailey put her hand on my arm. "If you do what we're suggesting, you won't have to make a choice. We will find him, vet him, do whatever needs to be done, ready for you. All you have to do is go on a date with him."

"One Last First Date," Marissa added.

I chewed the inside of my lip, my mind racing. I was being honest when I said I didn't feel capable of making good choices when it came to romance, but this? This was a giant leap for womankind.

"I know it sounds crazy, Paige, but it might just work," Marissa said. "Right, Bailey?"

Bailey nodded. "It might. It's worth a shot."

"What's worth a shot?" Cassie slunk up to us with Will in tow.

Immediately, I looked down at my feet, muttering, "Nothing. It's nothing."

Cassie and I had been friends for years. I loved her, and I trusted her with my life. But the whole "Will-and-Cassie" thing was too raw, and tonight was meant to be about me accepting them. The last thing I wanted was for them to know I had sworn off love. It was . . . humiliating.

"Oh, okay," Cassie replied, wounded. "I guess I don't need to know."

I bit my lip, my chest tight.

Bailey pulled her phone out of her pocket and checked the time. "Wow, I have to go. I've got to be up early in the morning. My café waits for no woman."

Seeing my chance to escape from an awkward situation, I said, "I'll come with you."

"Sure." Bailey flashed me her beautiful smile, and I couldn't help but smile back at her. She may have come up with a totally harebrained idea I wasn't going to touch with a ten-foot pole, but she had my back.

After collecting my things, saying goodbye to Marissa, and sharing an awkward hug with the couple of the moment, Bailey and I headed back up the beach toward her car.

So, that was that. I'd given up on love. No more men, no more dating. Just me, alone.

CHAPTER 2

I CLOSED THE FRONT door behind myself and stood in the darkened hallway for a moment, collecting my thoughts. Bailey had asked me again to think about her idea before she'd dropped me at my house. Again, I'd thought about it for a nanosecond. And, again, I'd decided it was quite possibly the craziest idea I'd ever heard.

Other than me asking Will out on my One Last First Date, that was.

"Is that you, lamb chop?" a voice called over the sound of the television from down the hall.

"Hey, Dad," I called. I slipped my wedges and vintage seventies jean jacket off and padded the short distance to the living room, where my dad was sitting in his favorite chair in prime position in front of the television. A commentator was droning on about a cricket match being played in some far-flung part of the world. He sounded about as bored as the people watching the game, and I hardly blamed him. Cricket—a sport my dear old dad once played professionally—is the only sport on the planet where two teams can play one another for five whole days and end up in a draw.

I leaned down and kissed him on the forehead. "How's the game, Dad?"

He shook his head and tutted. "Not good. We're down by five wickets with three hundred and fifty-eight to get. It's a huge target. Huge!"

I smiled at him, flopping down in an adjacent chair. "If you say so. How was your day?"

"Oh, it was okay. Work's work. You know how it is."

That I did. My work was . . . well, *work*, too. I had a job in marketing at AGD, the telecommunications company Marissa and Cassie worked at. In fact, that's where I met them. And Will. He'd left recently, but I'd had a crush on him from the moment he'd joined the company, over two years ago. *Two years?* Oh, my god. What a waste of my time.

Maybe I did need Bailey and Marissa's help?

"How about you, honey? Did you have a nice time with your friends tonight?"

I thought about making Cassie swim in the cold sea to "reset" our One Last First Date pact so she could date Will, telling her it was the Goddess of the Beach who had set the terms. I almost laughed. There was no Goddess of the Beach, *obviously*—I just wanted to make Cassie do something she didn't want to do. I know it was kind of harsh of me, making one of my best friends dive into the cold, dark, foam-capped waves in the dead of night, fully clothed. In fact, it was probably a solid eight out of ten on the revenge-o-meter. But it had felt good. And it wasn't like I'd had her pull her own fingernails out or anything.

"It was fun," I lied. "Fancy a cup of tea?"

"I would if you're offering one of those chocolate chip muffins you made to go with it?" Dad said, looking at me with hope in his eyes.

I shook my head. "Dad, you know what the doctor said: cut down on your sugar."

"I would, honey, only those muffins were so good! Where'd you hide them, anyway?"

Hi, my name's Paige and I'm a bake-aholic.

It's one of the reasons I love Bailey's café so much; the cakes and cookies there are out-of-this-world amazing. I'm always asking her for her recipes, but like Colonel Sanders himself, she keeps them a safely guarded secret. I've been through all of them: the orange and almond syrup cake (Marissa's favorite), the raspberry chocolate cake (Cassie's favorite), settling on my beloved carrot cake with cream cheese frosting. Really, you should try it. So. Darn. Good.

But my baking habit is not quite so darn good for my dad. It's not just that he's carrying a few extra pounds—okay, more than a few—but the sugar is a problem for his diabetes. He was only diagnosed six months ago, and it explained a lot: his constant thirst, his tiredness, his blurred vision. I had been living in my own apartment up until then but moved back in with him after his diagnosis. Someone had to keep an eye on him and make sure he stayed on the straight and narrow.

"'Occasional treats' is what she said. Remember? I don't think that means every day."

He shrugged, grinning. "It was worth a shot."

I shook my head good-naturedly. "Well, you need to take good care of yourself, Dad. I don't want to be an orphan, you know."

"You wouldn't be. Your mother—" He stopped himself. "Well, I don't have any reason to think she's not still alive."

Ah, yes. Celine Miller. Mother of the frigging Year. She walked out on my dad and me when I was seven, and I haven't heard head nor tail of her since. It had been Dad and me for as long as I could remember. We were a close-knit team. We needed to stick together.

"Oh! Six!" Dad yelled at the screen, making me jump. "Did you see that?"

I looked over at the TV. A couple of lanky men, dressed in white, were fist-bumping through their padded gloves, broad grins plastered on their faces.

"We need a few more of those."

"That's great, Dad." I stifled a yawn. "I'm going to head to bed. It's been a long week." I pushed myself up and kissed him on the forehead once more. "Night."

"Night, honey. Have a good sleep."

As I climbed the stairs to the childhood bedroom I lived in once more, any energy I had left seeped out of me. Will had made his choice, and it wasn't me. I needed to move on. Tonight had been a watershed moment for me—if you'd excuse the pun.

Now, I knew what my future would bring: me and Dad, watching TV in the living room together, not eating chocolate chip muffins, and definitely no husband for me.

* * *

ON MONDAY MORNING, I trudged into work, dumping my things on my desk with a heavy sigh. I *had* to break out of this funk. It was diffi-cult enough to get through the day in my job without adding being down in the dumps about my nonexistent love life into the mix.

"Morning, Paige. Or should I say, afternoon?"

I looked up to see my boss, Portia de Havilland, her eyebrows raised in question, peering at me through her designer glasses. I shifted my weight. Sure, I didn't exactly race into the office this morn-ing, but it was a good few hours before the afternoon. Two, at least.

"Good morning, Portia." I pasted on my biggest fake smile, the one that gets nowhere near my eyes. "Sorry I'm late. I had an important meeting this morning I couldn't get out of," I lied. The truth was I *did* have an important meeting this morning: with my lovely, warm, and comfy bed. And the truth also was I really couldn't get out of it—well, not until Dad made me, that was. Monday mornings were hard.

"Is that so?" Portia responded, smoothing her perfectly bobbed hair behind her perfectly-shaped ears, adorned with her perfectly expensive pearl earrings. "Well, you're here now and that's what matters. I need the results from the fiber campaign, like yesterday." She raised her eyebrows at me in expectation.

"Sure. No problem, Portia. Give me five?" I said, smoothly. I searched my brain. Had I done the analysis?

She looked at her expensive Longines watch with its diamond trim and solid gold strap. I felt sorry for her; it must be so tiresome to have to drag that heavy thing around on her wrist all day. "You'll need to be quick. I have a meeting with *Juan Felipe* this morning." She gave me a self-important smile, pronouncing his name with the correct guttural Spanish accent.

Inside, I did a massive eye roll. Juan Felipe Velez was about as far up the ladder as you could get at AGD. He and his business partner started the company ten years ago, and now he was a regular in the media and on the talking circuit in New Zealand and around the globe. He was one of the country's success stories. He also looked like Antonio Banderas's better-looking, much younger brother. Life could be cruel, couldn't it?

Portia loved to drop his name in wherever she could, like we would all just collapse on the floor in admiration for her or something.

"Oh, lucky you," I cooed. Okay, I'm not proud, but I knew how to play the Portia-name-dropping game.

She beamed at me. See?

She began to drone on about who she'd seen at a telecommunications industry event on Friday evening and my mind began to wander. You know that expression "all good things must come to an end"? Well, as I sat there, my eyes glazing over, I began to seriously doubt Portia's soliloquy would ever actually end. Not that it was good, you understand. Well, not for me, at any rate.

As though answering my silent prayer, her phone rang and she glanced at the screen, pausing mid-sentence. Holding a finger up at me, she turned her back as she answered, her voice ringing out in the large room as she walked away.

I let out a puff of air as I plunked myself down heavily in my seat. I powered up my computer. I needed to find the info Portia wanted— and hope she was happy with it. But therein lay the problem. Portia was very rarely happy with anything I did. I'm not saying I'm an unappreciated star employee or anything, and I have been known to arrive a little late on a Monday morning on occasion, but I deserved a medal for the amount of crap Portia threw my way every day. Rework this, reorganize that, cut out that, I want it yesterday, covered in purple glitter and pixie dust, and make sure it's written in ancient Greek with love hearts for the dots on the *i*'s. *Argh!*

It was enough to make me want to quit.

"What does Princess Portia want now?" Helena, one of my coworkers and fellow member of the We-Can't-Stand-Portia Club asked, popping her curly-haired head over my cubicle wall.

I shook my head, pursing my lips at her, and we shared a look.

"You know we should just kill her and be done with it, right?" Helena joked. Or at least, that's what I assumed she was doing. Helena had been here even longer than me and had despised Portia with a passion rarely seen in the corporate world ever since she had become our boss.

Really, if she put as much effort into her job as she did hating our boss, AGD might be doing even better than it is today.

Helena nodded grimly. "She must suffer till her last breath."

I shot her an uncertain look. "Helena! You cannot be serious!" I let out a nervous giggle.

"Of course, I'm not," she replied with a laugh. "It's a line from *Kill Bill*. Come on, Paige. You've got to know that movie. It's a classic."

Helena was also a major Tarantino movie buff. She loved nothing more than to quote random lines from his movies, often with a bunch of expletives thrown in for good measure.

I smiled at her, relieved she wasn't serious. "I'll have to watch it some time. Hey, I need to get this info together."

"Yeah, or watch out." She shot me a meaningful look before disappearing behind the wall.

I knew exactly what "or watch out" meant. One of the junior members of the Marketing Team had been fired by Portia only a month ago for "inappropriate behavior." Whatever that was. She'd been forced to pack up her desk and leave, all eyes on her shame-ridden trudge toward the elevators. Poor girl. She had only been here for a couple of months and she wouldn't have said boo to a ghost.

I put my head down so I could concentrate on gathering the information I needed for Portia—and avoid being chewed out by her in her dramatic, look-at-me way. Or, at least, I tried to. As an Email

Marketing Assistant, it was my job to help deliver the company's email marketing campaigns, and then assess how effective they'd been. Only, today I had a problem. With increasing tension across my forehead, I realized I hadn't actually done any analysis on our most recent campaign. I looked and looked but couldn't find a single thing. I glanced at the time on my screen. Nine twenty-seven. She'd given me five minutes but that was just an expression people used, right? I could take longer, long enough to run some figures and get some rough numbers, in the very least.

I opened the marketing information program. *I have time. I can do this.*

"Hey, Paige." I looked up to see Cassie standing by my desk.

"Hey, Cassie. I'm sorry, this isn't a good time." The vice on my head tightened.

"Oh." She looked wounded. "Sorry, I'll . . . see you later." She turned to leave.

Things had been weird between us since she'd told me about her and Will. But I was trying, god I was trying. Shooing her away when she'd come to see me sent the wrong message. It said, "I'm still hurt," and I didn't want her to think that.

Even if it was still true.

"Cassie. Wait."

She looked back at me with hope in her eyes.

"Look, I've got something I really need to do right now, but do you want to grab a coffee later?"

Her face broke into a grin. "That'd be nice. Cozy Cottage at eleven?" she asked, naming Bailey's café. "My treat."

"Sounds great." I said goodbye and returned to my screen. Just as I had begun to extract some results, my phone rang. Portia. I picked up. "Hi, Portia."

"My office, now, please." Her tone was firm.

Knowing the data was rawer than a sushi roll, I sent it to print, bounced out of my chair, and grabbed it off the tray on my way into the lioness's den. I smoothed my skirt and knocked tentatively on the opened door.

Portia looked up momentarily from her screen and gestured to a seat, returning her attention to whatever she was typing. I sat and waited. And waited. She took a call, speaking for several minutes to whoever it was about dog-sitting over the holidays. Still, I sat there, waiting. I could have used this time to polish up the information. Instead, I was here, holding one sheet of crummy, unrefined data. As Portia advised the caller on her dog's complicated dietary requirements, I half stood and gestured toward the door. She motioned for me to sit, like I was the dog with the oversensitive belly.

Eventually, once I knew more than I ever cared to know about Chantelle's daily routine, Portia hung up and fixed her gaze on me. "Now. Give me the low down on the campaign. I've only got thirty seconds before my meeting with Juan Felipe, so make it snappy."

I narrowed my eyes at her. Not that I wanted to be humiliated by my lack of any real data, but she did keep me waiting an unnecessarily long amount of time, only to tell me I needed to be quick. Do you see what I've got to put up with?

"Well, in a nutshell, the fiber campaign so far has been . . . err"—I glanced down at my sheet—"all in all pretty good."

She arced an eyebrow. "Pretty good?"

"Yes, well, what I mean by that is, we've only got some preliminary figures, but they're looking good. Or, at least, the preliminary ones are. Good, that is. Yes." I was blabbing like a toddler on too much sugar, and we both knew it.

Portia furrowed her brow, studying me as though she was working out whether I was some sort of deranged person, recently escaped from the local looney bin, or just an Email Marketing Assistant trying desperately to pull the wool over her eyes. I think she decided I was a combination of the two.

She reached her hand out and gave a short, sharp nod. I glanced down at the now dog-eared sheet of paper in my hand. Resigned to my fate, I stood and handed it to her.

She perused it, her eyes narrowing, and looked sharply back up at me. "But this is utter tosh. This isn't a report. It's raw data. Where's your report? I told you, I wanted it now." Her face turned pink and I had an image of it exploding all over her office, speckling her white linen jacket with bits of brain and gore. I had to suppress a satisfied smirk. It was a very good image.

I chewed my lip. There was nothing for it but to be honest. I'd been well and truly busted, anyway. "I'm sorry, Portia. I haven't done it. I promise to have it to you later today, with all the bells and whistles. I just need some more time."

I held my breath as she studied me, her jaw clenched. After a beat, she pushed her chair out and stood up, dropping my paper onto her desk. "I have to go. I'll deal with *you* later."

I scrunched my eyes shut as she brushed past me on the way out of her office door. *Good work, Paige. You've unleashed the beast now.*

I spent the next hour extracting and analyzing data, putting it into a presentation with my key findings, and making it look professional and—hopefully—good enough for Portia. In short, I did my job, and I did it well. I hoped it would be enough after this morning's mess up.

By just after eleven, I arrived at the Cozy Cottage Café, Marissa's, Cassie's, and my regular hang out: no men allowed. Well, there are men there, of course, but we don't bring them along. It's been our special place for a long time, and I'm pretty sure, given enough time, we could solve the world's problems over a cup of coffee and a slice of cake here.

Bailey ran the place and I waved at her as I looked for Cassie. She was sitting at the table Bailey reserved for us every day, over by the window, scrolling through her phone. Unlike most cafés in downtown Auckland city, the Cozy Cottage was like being at home—only no dad sitting on his recliner, watching endless cooking shows and live sports. There was no chrome, no mirrors, no hipper than hip baristas here. No way. The chairs were comfy, there were pictures of cats and flowers and fields on the walls, and in the winter, there was a fireplace with an oversized mantle, inviting you in. And the aroma! The Cozy Cottage smelled of coffee and chocolate and cinnamon and, for want of another word, love. It was our happy place.

"Hey, Cassie," I said brightly, taking my seat opposite her. "No Marissa today?"

KATE O'KEEFFE

Cassie turned her phone facedown on the table and smiled at me. "I wanted it to be just you and me. I've ordered your usual."

"Thanks." I smiled back at her. "My usual" was carrot cake with the best cream cheese frosting you've ever tasted. The cake was so moist, it almost melted on your tongue with each delicious bite. If I was the queen of baking, Bailey was the divine ruler, showing us all how it was meant to be done.

I slid my fork into the cake and took a bite. Oh, yes. Sugar. I so needed you today.

"Hey, so I wanted to say how cool I think you've been over this whole Will thing and to say thanks."

I shrugged. Cassie was launching straight at the oversized elephant in the room. "It's fine." I looked down at my cake and took another bite.

She shot me a quizzical look. I suspected we both knew I was having a hard time with it all.

"Good. Now, maybe we can talk about something else?" She grinned at me over her coffee cup.

I smiled back, relieved. "I think that's a very good idea."

"Excellent."

We shared a moment, my close friend and me. It felt like we were back on track, before Will-gate, before I humiliated myself by declaring my feelings for a guy who had no interest in me beyond friendship. Conversation moved to our weekends, Cassie's new job as Regional Sales Manager, and, inevitably, my run-in with Portia this morning.

"So, what happened?" Cassie asked.

I pushed some cake crumbs around my plate with my fork. "I don't know. I guess I just forgot, you know, with everything."

I noticed a grimace flash across her face. "I'm sorry, Paige."

I shook my head. "It's not your fault. I just dropped the ball, and now Princess Portia's going to exact her evil revenge on me. Oh, god." I buried my head in my hands. "She might fire me."

"Oh, I'm sure she won't," Cassie said. "She might not be the most . . . balanced person in the company, but she's not unreasonable."

18

I scoffed. "Balanced?" Cassie was only being diplomatic now that she was in management. She used to rip into Portia as much as Marissa and I did, not so long ago.

"Hey, girls." Bailey arrived at our table. Dressed in her red polka dot apron with a girly frill around the bottom, accentuating her hourglass figure, she looked like the beautiful Nigella Lawson about to present a cooking show.

"Hi!" we chorused. I, for one, was happy for the distraction. The thought that I may be about to be fired wasn't exactly in my top ten topics.

"What's happening?" Bailey asked, taking a seat at the table.

Before I could stop her, Cassie launched into my current Princess Portia woes.

"Well, that sucks," Bailey said.

"I know." I let out a sigh.

"But if you did lose your job, it wouldn't be the worst thing in the world, would it? I mean, you never really say anything positive about it," Bailey said.

I snapped my head up. "What did you say?"

"I said, you don't seem to like your job that much. Sorry if I'm barking up the wrong tree here, it's just you never have anything good to say about it." She looked from me to Cassie and back again.

"Actually, Bailey has a point. *Are* you happy in your job?" Cassie asked.

"Yes, of course I am," I insisted. Wasn't I?

"I must have it wrong." Bailey smiled. She glanced over at the counter where one of her staff was flirting with a customer, holding a growing line of customers up. She pushed her chair out with a sigh. "Sorry to cut this short. I'm going to have to go and sort *that* out."

Once Bailey had left the table, I said, "I *think* I'm happy in my job."

"Okay," Cassie replied, nodding. "It's your life, Paige."

"Yeah, I know."

And Bailey's words rang through my head for the rest of the day.

19

CHAPTER 3

*B*ACK AT MY DESK, I was like a caged animal, constantly poking my head out of my cubicle to check for Portia, half expecting her to dig her claws into my back and drag me, kicking and screaming, into a secret dungeon behind her desk where she would torture me, and then dump me out the window, plunging to the street eight stories below.

I had an overactive imagination.

Deep in thought, staring at my screen, Helena made me almost jump out of my skin when she placed her hand on my shoulder. I swiveled around in my chair, banging my heels into her shins.

"Ow!" she complained loudly.

"Sorry. I thought you were Portia," I said in a loud whisper.

She pulled a face as she rubbed her legs. "Thanks a lot. Do you want to grab some late lunch? I mean, if I can walk after you maimed me."

I rolled my eyes. "Such a drama queen." My tummy rumbled, right on queue. "Sure. Lunch sounds good."

I threw on my cream vintage seventies jacket with the wide lapel I often wore to work. I guess it was my go-to jacket, the one we all have in our closets, despite lusting after other jackets half our lives. As

Helena slipped on her own jacket, I peered in my pocket mirror to apply some fresh lipstick. I paused, holding the lipstick up. Why was I bothering with trying to look good? After all, I'd decided to give up on the whole finding love extravaganza on the beach that night.

I lowered the lipstick and my shoulders slumped. With the anxiety about what Portia was going to do, I'd pushed my predicament to the back of my mind. In some weird way, it had almost felt like a holiday. Wow, that made me sound like such a sad sack.

Lipstick-free, Helena and I lined up to get our lunch at a local salad bar. I listened as she raged on about Princess Portia this and Princess Portia that. The fact the woman had been out of the office most of the day only served to anger Helena all the more.

"I mean, she's hardly ever here. She's always off swanning around up on the exec level in her Chanel suits, 'networking.'" She did air quotes, her face a picture of disgust.

"Yeah," I managed to get in before Helena continued.

"And she's always bragging about who she knows and where she goes and stuff. All those industry events. Why doesn't she ever let one of us go?"

I shrugged as we shuffled forward two feet in the line. "Yeah, it's terrible. But . . . would you want to go?"

"Of course, I would! Are you crazy? All those contacts, hearing what's going on in the industry, what the new innovations are. That would be awesome."

I scrunched up my face. Although I'd have liked the opportunity to get out of the office and do something other than stare at my screen all day, I couldn't say I was too excited about doing it with a bunch of work-obsessed industry types. No. Give me a slice of cake and a coffee with my good friends at the Cozy Cottage over schmoozing any day, thank you very much. "Do you really think so?"

"Yes, I do! Don't you?" She didn't wait for a response, getting back to moaning, instead. "But no, we're stuck in the office, analyzing numbers while *she* has all the fun. Yawn."

Honestly, I never thought I would end up as an Email Marketing Assistant. I'd studied marketing and graduated with a solid degree, moving happily into the workforce, confident I was going to be the best marketing manager, probably best marketing *director*, the world had ever seen. I was full of creative and interesting ideas, inspired by total faith in myself and my desire to market, market, market! But somehow along the way, things had changed. I guess I got stuck. I had lost my mojo.

As I listened to Helena enthuse about all things marketing, it struck me: would it really be so bad if I lost my job?

What?!

I shook my head, trying to dislodge the thought. *That's crazy talk!* I liked my job. Well, not *liked* it, exactly, more . . . tolerated it. Yes, that was it: I tolerated my job. Most of the time, anyway. Except on Monday mornings, and let's face it, who really jumps out of bed with the alarm first thing Monday morning with a "Yippee! I'm off to work!"? Answer: absolutely no one. And perhaps I didn't really like my job on Fridays, either, when it was nearly the weekend and you couldn't wait to get out of that oppressive environment. But otherwise? Tuesdays through Thursdays I was a career girl, pure and simple.

Wasn't I?

By five twenty-seven that evening, there was still no sign of her regal highness. Maybe today wasn't the day Portia would fire me. I logged out of my computer and switched off my screen. I wasn't the kind of marketing assistant who felt the need to stay past five thirty to impress the bosses these days. Oh, no. That particular ship had sailed a long time ago. And, anyway, I didn't want to see my boss, let alone try to impress her.

As Helena and I walked to the elevators, I let out a puff of air. I'd made it through the day without having to deal with Portia's wrath. Now I could head home, whip up a healthy, vegetable-laden meal for Dad, and lose myself in my reality TV shows.

"You know what you should do?" Helena said as she pressed the down button.

"What? Are you going to get all 'medieval on her ass'?" I let out a chuckle, feeling giddy.

Helena's face broke into a grin. "You watched *Pulp Fiction?*"

I nodded, enjoying her reaction. Thanks to the Cassie-Will thing, I had been in the dumps for almost an entire month. I'd listened to sad, soppy breakup music, I'd watched endless rom coms where the girl always got the guy (so nothing like the way it worked in reality, at least not for me), and decided it was time to move on. Time to watch something that might spark something inside of me other than the soul-crushing sadness I'd been wallowing in. And from what Helena had always said about Quentin Tarantino, I knew one of his classic movies would fit the bill.

She nodded at me, still grinning. "*Pulp Fiction.* Oh, yes. You started with the best, Paige, the *best*. It's awesome, isn't it?"

"It's pretty good, lots of great one-liners, angry people, and bad hairdos. Right up my alley right now."

She put her arm around my shoulder, positively beaming. "I'm so proud, *so* proud."

The elevator pinged and the doors slid open. My heart sank. Portia took a step out, looked directly at me, and said, "Ah, Paige. A word?" She walked off without hearing my response.

"Sh . . . sure," I said to her retreating back. I shot Helena a panicked look. I was so close, so close!

She gave my arm a squeeze. "Be strong and don't take any of her crap."

I blinked at her. In a daze, I turned and slowly took the death march to Portia's office. Standing at the threshold, I looked at Portia, already settled at her desk. She looked up at me, her jaw locked, her intention as clear to me as a bright, summer's day.

"Close the door behind you. We need to talk."

I WOKE up before my alarm the following morning and lay flat on my back, staring at the ceiling of my room. I could still make out the contours of the moon and the stars Dad had stuck up there for me when I was obsessed with the solar system at age seven. That and fairies. Oh, how I loved fairies.

The sun peeked through the edges of the curtains, and I could hear Dad puttering around in the kitchen downstairs, brewing our morning pot of tea and setting the table with butter and strawberry jelly for our habitual toast. I smiled to myself. My dad and I'd had the same morning routine since I could remember, though in the winter it was oatmeal rather than toast, and the occasional pancakes or waffles if we were really splashing out for a special occasion.

But today was supposed to be like any other day, so tea and toast it was.

"Hello, lamb chop," Dad said brightly, giving me a peck on the cheek as I sat down at the table. "Nice cup of tea here for you. Good sleep?"

"Hmm?" I looked up at his face. "Sorry, Dad. My mind is on other things."

"That'll be because you're a high-flying executive with important deals to be made, right?"

I smiled at him. "Something like that, Dad."

My dear old dad had never worked in an office a day in his life and seemed to have an image in his head of it as all high-powered, serious meetings between people in expensive business suits who talk about "buy-buy" and "sell-sell." Basically, he had formed his opinion when he watched *Wall Street* back in the eighties, and it hadn't budged since. I admit, I didn't do much to disabuse him of this image, however. He was happy with it and the reality was so much less exciting. Why spoil his fun?

We munched on our toast, sipped our tea, and chatted about the things we always seemed to talk about these days: me telling Dad not to eat any sugar, to get some exercise, and to take his meds. He always agreed, always saying the things he knew I wanted to hear. And then I would often find empty chocolate wrappers stuffed behind sofa cushions at the end of the day. But I knew he was trying, and I knew he found it difficult, so I tried to be understanding, all the while fretting about the state of his health.

"Well, I'd better get myself ready for work," Dad said, putting our dishes in the dishwasher.

Dad's work was at one of the local supermarket chains. For years, he'd stacked the shelves and graduated to the checkout, where he'd stayed, happily chatting away with the customers, indulging his genuine love of people. Then, when I was a teenager, he'd been promoted to managing a team of cashiers. That was a big day in the Miller household. We celebrated with sparkling wine with a fake French-sounding name and the best hot dogs money could buy. He'd been at the same supermarket ever since, happily working, never questioning if it was the right thing for him to be doing with his life— or if he did, never letting on to me.

I had snapped the mold in two when I went to university straight out of high school. No one in my extended family had even attended university, let alone graduated with an actual degree. I was something of an anomaly, my career a constant talking point at family gatherings. It was "clever Paige" this and "our girl with the degree" that. Really, you'd have thought I'd won the Nobel Prize, they were so impressed with me. But of all my family—and with Dad's many siblings, there were a few—it was Dad who was the proudest of me. I could tell by looking at him when he'd be talking to my Aunt Jocelyn or Uncle Barry about me. He'd beam. He'd glow. Usually, it made me all warm inside.

Not today.

I showered and dressed carefully, choosing just the right outfit, preparing myself for what was to come. My wardrobe choices had diminished lately. Not because I'd given my clothes away, but because I'd had no desire to do anything but watch reality TV shows and eat junk for the last month, and consequently, my clothes were a little tighter than they should be.

Finally, dressed in my brown and orange checked wrap dress— because, thank god, wrap dresses can be very forgiving—with my dark hair scooped up into a loose bun, I headed into the office.

I dropped my purse, my jacket, and a box on my desk. I pulled my lipstick out from my purse and applied a fresh layer. I may not be on the hunt for a man any more, but today I needed lipstick. I took a deep breath and walked straight toward Portia's office.

"Paige!"

I snapped my head in Helena's direction. She stood up, took two strides with her long legs, and was next to me within a nanosecond.

"How did it go last night? You didn't return my texts. Did you lay into her?"

It was true, I'd ignored Helena's messages. I wasn't in the head-space. I needed to think, to work out what to do.

"Look, Helena. I've got to do something. I'll talk to you later, okay? I promise."

She gave me a meaningful look. "Sure. You go, girl. I'll back you up, no matter what." She hit her fist against her chest, like she was a centurion, pledging her allegiance to me.

I turned and walked through the line of cubicles to Portia's office, nodding as people said hello. This wasn't the time to be social. I was on a mission, and I wasn't going to allow anything to get in my way.

I arrived at Portia's office and stood, collecting my thoughts. I could see her sitting at her desk, immaculate as always in a pale pink suit with black trim, tap-tapping on her keyboard. I lifted my hand and knocked firmly on her door. Her head popped up, a look of surprise on her face.

"Paige. What are you doing here?" she asked, pushing her chair back and standing up.

Did she look nervous?

I stepped into her office and closed the door behind myself, leaning up against it as my heart raced. "I need to talk to you."

"Okay," she replied uncertainly. She gestured for me to take a seat. I shook my head in refusal. I needed to be standing for this.

"I thought we'd said all we were going to say last night?"

"No, Portia. *You* said all you were going to say. I didn't."

She tilted her head. "Oh?"

I clenched my hands at my side, preparing to launch into the speech I'd practiced on the way here this morning. My mind was made up; I had something to say.

I took a deep breath and looked directly at her. "Portia, I quit."

Okay, so it wasn't much of a speech, and practicing it hadn't exactly taken very long this morning, but I wanted to ensure I hit the right tone. And hadn't I learned in my years in marketing that a clear, simple message was the most effective?

To my unutterable surprise, Portia laughed. "I think you misunderstand, Paige. I fired you."

"No, you didn't. Your exact words were, 'I'm moving you on.' I remember. You never said I was fired."

She shot me a condescending look, as though I was a three-year-old who needed to have the difference between a hug and a punch explained to them. "Paige. We talked about this. Your work has not been up to scratch for some time now. That's why *I* am moving *you* on."

I jutted out my chin, defiant. "But you can't. Because I quit."

She put her manicured hands up in surrender. "Sure. If that's the way you want to play it, fine. Take your petty revenge over whatever it is you think I have or haven't done."

"I will. Thank you." My voice dripped with sarcasm.

As I turned and put my hand on the doorknob, ready to leave, she added, "So, do I take it you don't want that job in Dwight's division, then?"

I pursed me lips. It was true, Portia had fired me—or "moved me on," as she'd insisted on calling it—but she'd also offered me a role in her colleague Dwight Barlow's team, working in product development. She thought I'd be a better "fit" there as she didn't think email marketing campaigns were "quite my passion," as she'd put it. I'd almost scoffed. Of course, email marketing campaigns weren't my passion! Was she *insane*?

My interest had been piqued by the chance to work for a different boss, someone perhaps whose team wasn't plotting to torture and kill him. That never makes for a harmonious working environment, in my experience. So last night, I'd agreed. Getting away from Portia and my yawn-inducing job had been the most important things to me.

And today? Things felt . . . different.

I narrowed my eyes at Portia, with the supercilious look she so often had on her face. Although I'd never shared Helena's Tarantino-inspired depth of hatred for her, this was the last time I ever wanted to lay eyes on her again.

"You know what, Portia? I don't want that job, or any job at AGD. Let's agree I quit and I'll leave right now. I even brought my own box to clear my stuff."

She pursed her lips and stared at me through her designer glasses.

I locked my jaw and squeezed my hands into fists at my sides once more. What was her next move going to be?

Still staring at me, she let out a puff of air and nodded.

I'd won.

I smiled at her. "Good. We're done here."

I could almost hear that old nineties band, singing *I've got the power!* as I flung Portia's office door open and strode toward my desk, people popping their heads over the tops of their cubicles to see what was going on as I passed by. My heart was racing, adrenaline was pumping around my body at a rate of knots, and it felt good, oh so good! *Daa-da, da-da-daa-da . . . I've got the power!*

I reached my desk and began to collect my things. Before I could say "wannabe gangster," Helena was at the entrance to my cubicle. "Oh, my god! What happened?" She glanced at the box in my hands, half full of my personal paraphernalia. "Oh, hell. She fired you, didn't she? That nasty, conniving bitch!"

At Helena's loud exclamation, several more of my colleagues arrived at my cubicle. "Did you say Paige was fired?" one asked. "Oh, my god!" exclaimed another.

It's getting, it's getting, it's getting kinda hectic. Daa-da, da-da-daa-da.

"You cannot take this, Paige! This is wrong, so wrong. You must have your revenge!" Helena exclaimed vehemently, her fist in the air, her face turning purple with rage.

I half expected her to launch into the Samuel L. Jackson Ezekiel vengeance speech I'd enjoyed while watching *Pulp Fiction*. I admit, I'd rewound and watched that speech a few times. But instead, I held my box against my body and smiled at them all. "Actually, I quit."

There was a collective gasp.

"You did? Why?" someone asked as another said, "Good for you!" Helena gawped at me.

"Yup. And . . . I have to go." I collected my jacket and dropped it into the box and slung my purse over my shoulder.

"But . . . don't you have to work your month's notice out?" Helena asked.

"I figured since The Princess doesn't exactly want me around, we'd forget about that whole notice thing."

My—now ex—colleagues stepped aside like the parting of the Red Sea, and I walked through them all. "Bye, everyone! It was great to work with you all. Good luck!"

"Hey," Helena said, grabbing my arm. "Good for you."

I grinned at her. "Thanks. It was nice working with you. And thanks for the tip on Tarantino. I'm not sure I would have done this if it hadn't been for him."

She gave me a knowing nod. "Quentin changes lives."

Usually, I would have thought she'd possibly taken her admiration for the guy a little too far, but in this, I decided she was right.

Stay off my back, or I will attack and you don't want that. Daa-da da-da-daa-da.

As I left, I glanced up between the row of cubicles toward Portia's office. She was standing, watching me, her skinny arms crossed across her chest. I waved and smiled at her, enjoying every moment of my minor triumph.

I was no longer an Email Marketing Assistant. I was out of here. And I was free.

CHAPTER 4

*T*HAT SONG STILL PLAYING in my head, I arrived at the Cozy Cottage Café at just after eight thirty. I hadn't known where else to go. If I'd gone home, it would be to an empty house and would quite possibly lead to more moping about the sorry state of my love life—okay, my total lack of anything even vaguely resembling a love life—and second-guessing myself over my decision to leave my job. I chose being around other people. And, if I was to be totally honest, I was rather impressed with myself and I wanted to share it with someone. I'd had fantasies about standing up to Portia and telling her where to shove the job on quite a number of occasions. Perhaps weekly. Okay, daily. But to actually do it? Man, it felt good with a capital G-O-O-D!

Bailey was standing behind the counter, dressed in her red Cozy Cottage polka dot apron, handing a man in a suit a takeout coffee with her ever-present smile plastered across her gorgeous face. She took one look at me and knitted her brows together in question. I beamed back at her. I was still riding that incredible adrenaline high and could not have contained my happiness if I was paid.

Coffee Guy walked past and smiled at me. I smiled back. Life was good!

"What are you doing here so early?" Bailey asked.

I jiggled from foot to foot. "I just did something."

"Well, you look pretty happy about it, whatever it is."

"Want to know?" I asked like the big kid I was being.

She laughed. "Absolutely. Want a coffee first?"

Coffee could only add to my current state of euphoria. "Yes, please."

"And the usual?"

"It's too early for—" I stopped myself. Of course, eight thirty in the morning was too early to eat cake, but today was one out of the bag. A day less ordinary. "You know what? Yes, I will have the usual. As long as I can buy you a slice, too?"

"Sure. It's quiet here for the next forty-five minutes or more, so we usually get a bit of a breather at this time of day. Go grab a seat." She turned to a new member of staff I'd only seen once or twice before. "Kayla, can you please bring us a couple of lattes, a slice of the carrot cake and a slice of the chocolate mocha, too? Thanks, honey." She noticed me grinning at her. "What? I want to share in your big news and this is late for me. I start work a lot earlier than you."

"No worries."

We sat down at our usual table in the window, the morning sun streaming in. I could hear Kayla clanging and banging about behind the counter.

Bailey glanced over at her, and then back at me. "Don't worry about her. She's having a bad day. Now, tell me your big news." She grinned at me across the table.

"Well . . . I quit my job." I held my breath and studied her face. Bailey was the first person I'd told outside of my immediate team. Telling her made it feel all the more real. And incredible.

Her face creased into a broad smile. "Oh, my gosh. Really? That's amazing." She shot me a quizzical look. "Isn't it?"

I nodded. "Oh, yes. I hadn't realized it until this morning when I woke up. I mean really, really realized it, you know? I hate being an Email Marketing Assistant. I hate it! It bores the pants off me. Plus, I hate my boss. Well, she's no longer my boss, so I guess I hate someone who used to be my boss." I let out a laugh. "Anyway, the point is, I wasn't happy so I left." I beamed at her, impressed by my singular ability to make a decision and act on it. I should write a book about it. *How to Live Your Best Life* by Paige Miller. Yes, I liked the sound of that.

"Wow. I had no idea. I mean, I'd heard you say it wasn't the best job in the world, but I didn't know you hated it that much. Good for you for doing something about it."

Kayla delivered our cakes and coffees, slapping them down on the table in front of us. The coffees spilled over onto their saucers. Bailey shot her a look. Kayla glared at her and stomped off.

"What was that all about?" I asked, my eyes wide.

Bailey shook her head. "Don't ask. Something to do with not wanting to handle food with gluten in it."

I gawped at her. "All your food has gluten in it."

"I know, right?"

I put a large scoop of carrot cake and cream cheese frosting deliciousness in my mouth, savoring the taste, the texture, everything about it. "This is so good," I mumbled.

"Thanks. And, no, you're not getting the recipe."

I chuckled. Bailey had read my mind. I drank my coffee and smiled some more as I thought about how it had felt to simply pack up and leave AGD.

"Now that you've quit, what's next?"

I was midway through my next mouthful. I stopped chewing. What was I going to do now? I had been so focussed on the excitement of finally working out I hated everything about my job, I hadn't thought anywhere near that far ahead. I swallowed and look blankly at Bailey. "I've got no idea."

"The world is your oyster, it would seem."

I grinned at her, my heart full. "I could do anything, couldn't I? Anything at all. I could run away and join the circus, I could become a zookeeper, I could become an artist!" My brain felt like it could pop with the possibilities. Hmm, maybe no more caffeine for me today.

Bailey swallowed her bite of cake and smiled, shaking her head. "Your enthusiasm for life is infectious, Paige Miller."

I grinned at her. My phone beeped. I pulled it out of my purse and looked at the screen. There were messages from Marissa and Cassie, both wanting to know whether the rumors were true. I fired off a group text telling them to meet me here and read the next message. It was from Helena.

You are The Bride!!

I'm the what? I showed the text to Bailey. "What do you think that means?"

Bailey shrugged. "I have no idea. But it's kind of poor taste after . . . you know." She looked abashed. We both knew she was referring to the whole me-Cassie-Will love triangle thing. Only it wasn't a triangle, more two lines melded together inside a huge love heart and me, out in the cold. I ignored the twist in my belly. Helena didn't know about my feelings for Will, so that didn't make sense. I sent a quick text back. A moment later, my phone beeped again.

Kill Bill: Vol 1. Watch and learn

I should have known. "It's from a Tarantino movie. *Kill Bill: Volume 1.*"

Bailey nodded knowingly. "Ah, Uma Thurman. She was 'The Bride.' A total kick-ass assassin." She cocked her head, sizing me up. "You know, you look a little like her. Maybe you could get a yellow jumpsuit?"

I smiled to myself. A hot assassin in a yellow jumpsuit? Now *that* I could get on board with. I wondered whether there were any job vacancies for that?

There was more clanging and banging from behind the counter, grabbing our attention.

Bailey pursed her lips. "I'll need to go and sort that out." She drained her coffee and stacked our plates, skillfully holding everything with one hand. "Another one?"

"No, I'd better—" I looked up at her and grinned. "Yes, please." I had nowhere else to be. I could sit here all day and eat cake. Or not. I could do whatever I wanted. It was a liberating feeling.

Bailey returned to the counter with the plates, and I could hear Kayla and her talking. I returned my attention to my phone and fired off another text to Cassie and Marissa, asking them where they were. I needn't have bothered. I looked up to see them striding through the door and over to the table, where they plunked themselves down in a flurry of questions.

I put my hand up in the "stop sign." They looked at me expectantly. I nodded at them both, plastering a grim look on my face. "I'm no longer at AGD."

Their mouths dropped open, making them look like those clown heads you throw balls into at fairs. I tried to look as serious as possible, pranking my friends. But I couldn't help it. They looked so shocked, I burst into laughter, clutching my sides as I threw my head back. I'd never been much of a liar. I never saw the point. If the truth was so bad, then you needed to change it, not lie about it.

"Your faces!" I managed.

"So, you weren't fired?" Cassie asked, furrowing her brow.

I pressed my lips together and shook my head.

"You quit?" Marissa squeaked.

I nodded. "Yup."

And then they were back to rapid-fire-questions-at-Paige time, both wanting to know what had happened, why I'd done it, how it had felt, and what I was going to do now.

"I guess it's been coming on for a while, but, really, it's because I woke up this morning with my mind made up. You know I haven't been happy for a while. A long while. When her royal highness, Princess Portia, suggested I move into Dwight's team, I saw it as my chance to break free."

"I've Got The Power" was replaced by "I Want To Break Free" in my head. *God knows, God knows I want to break free . . .*

Wow. I really needed to update my soundtrack, perhaps drag it into the current century.

"I take my hat off to you," Marissa said, shaking her head, her blonde hair bouncing. "You've got balls."

I let out a short, sharp laugh. "Thanks!"

"No, really, you do. Doesn't she, Cassie?"

Cassie nodded, her lips pressed together. "Totally. Big, furry ones."

We all laughed at the bizarre image of my big furry balls. I told them how amazing I had felt handing my notice in this morning, how I had this wonderful excitement buzzing around my body, which had now given way to a wonderful sense of calm, and that all was right in my world. "I mean, it could just be the cake talking, but this feels so good, so *right*. You know?"

"Preach it!" Marissa said with a grin.

"Ooh, cake." Cassie's eyes lit up. "Your usual, Marissa?" Marissa nodded. Cassie stood up. "Back in a second." She walked through the near-empty café to the counter.

Marissa leaned in closer to me, watching Cassie out of the corner of her eye. "This decision of yours doesn't have anything to do with Cassie and Will, does it?"

I shook my head vehemently. "No. Absolutely not." I sounded three hundred per cent more convincing than I felt. Although I hadn't connected the dots in my head, I had an unsettled feeling in my belly. In quitting my job, I knew I was throwing caution to the wind in a much more reckless way than I would *ever* have done under normal circumstances. Will choosing Cassie over me had messed with my head, making me reckless and cautious, both at the same time. Reckless with my job, cautious with my love life.

Yup, I had officially become a hot mess.

"Good. I thought I needed to check." Marissa grinned at me. "So, now you can dedicate more time to finding your Last First Date."

The unsettled feeling in my belly intensified as my wonderful sense of calm evaporated into thin air. "About that—" I began, hesitatingly.

"I know what you're going to say," Marissa interrupted. "You're not going to go on your Last First Date. But you are, and we won't take no for an answer."

"Here you go." Cassie arrived back at the table with three slices of cake, one for each of us, our favorites, of course. "I'll go get the coffees. Bailey seems to be having some trouble with one of her staff."

I looked over at the counter where Bailey and Kayla appeared to be glaring at one another. It looked a like Mexican stand off—over gluten.

With Cassie temporarily absent, Marissa said, "We'll talk about this later, okay?"

I let out a sigh and nodded. My response would be the same, though. No Last First Date for me.

CHAPTER 5

*L*UCKILY, I DIDN'T NEED to have that particular conversation again right now. Our coffee and cake devoured —if I kept this up, I was going to have a serious weight issue and possibly even join Dad in the diabetes club—Cassie got called away and Marissa needed to get back to the office for a team meeting. As I watched them leave, my former euphoria at having walked out of my job forever returned. I leaned back in my comfy chair and looked through the window at the passersby: the businesspeople, rushing from A to B, all serious with their phones plastered to their ears; the students, walking in groups, chatting amongst themselves as they enjoyed the late summer's sun. I let out a contented sigh.

Man or no man, job or no job, life was pretty darn good for Paige Prudence Miller today.

My contemplation was interrupted by a loud crash, emanating from somewhere in the kitchen out back. Startled, I looked up to see Kayla throw her apron over her shoulder in Bailey's stunned face, stomp past the counter, rudely push her way through several café patrons, and bang through the doors. Through the window, I could see her stop and look up the street, then down in the other direction, seemingly deciding where to go. I watched as she turned on her heel and spun around, looking directly at me through the window with a red, angry face. I shrunk back into my seat and quickly looked away. I hated confrontation. The power to turn invisible would have come in very handy right about now. Out of the corner of my eye, I could see her stomping back into the café.

I stood up, concerned about what she was planning to do. I glanced over at Bailey and could tell in an instant she was worried as well. Kayla pushed through the patrons once more, past Bailey and back into the kitchen. As quickly as I could, I darted across the café and behind the counter. Bailey could be in danger; I had to get there fast.

A second later, Kayla reappeared at the kitchen entrance, her satchel slung over her shoulder. I noticed Bailey press herself up against the counter in what appeared to be an attempt to put as much space between herself and her employee as she could.

Kayla glared at her, seething. "I forgot this."

"Okay," Bailey replied uncertainly, trying to smile.

"Thanks for nothing, *bitch*," Kayla spat at Bailey to a collective gasp from both me and the café patrons, who were all watching the scene unfold with wide eyes.

To my relief, Kayla stormed off, out from behind the counter and through the door, leaving Bailey and myself watching her go, agog, the café silent around us.

I turned to Bailey and put my hand on her arm. She flinched at my touch. "Sorry, I didn't mean to startle you. I just wanted to make sure you're okay."

She blinked at me, as though in a daze, not speaking. People in the café appeared to spring back to life, talking amongst themselves. Kayla had certainly given them all something to talk about this morning, that was for sure.

I raised my eyebrows enquiringly at her. "Bailey?"

She appeared to snap out of her Kayla-induced reverie. "Yes, Paige. Yes. I'm fine. That was . . . unexpected."

"Um, yeah. What was it all about?"

Bailey let out a puff of air. "You know what? I have no idea. I mean, she had some weird notion the gluten in the baked goods could seep through her skin and give her celiac disease, but I didn't think she was serious." She shook her head in disbelief. "She seemed perfectly sane when I employed her a week or so ago."

I scoffed. "Well, she's pretty far from sane today."

"That is the truth."

"And I'm no expert, but I don't think you can catch celiac from touching a cake."

Bailey's eyes flashed as a smile teased the edges of her mouth. "No, I don't think you can."

I let out a chuckle. Maybe Kayla was just having a bad day—or perhaps she really did have a touch of the crazies.

Bailey looked at the growing line of customers, waiting to place their orders with her. She pasted on a smile and greeted the first customer. "Hello, sir. I apologize for the . . . whatever that was. What can I get you?"

The man smiled back at her and placed his order, making a remark about drama queen waitresses. I felt like an idiot, standing behind the counter, watching Bailey work quickly and efficiently. She was serving the long line of customers with a bright smile on her face, looking as though Kayla hadn't just abandoned her in an angry puff of smoke.

"Can I help?" I asked her as she stepped next to me, placing a blueberry muffin on a plate.

"Could you? That would be so brilliant. I wasn't expecting to be here on my own right now, and I'm short staffed as it is today."

"Just tell me what to do."

Bailey leaned down and pulled one of her trademark red polka dot aprons with the frill trim from under the till and handed it to me. "Got to look the part, chickadee."

I slipped it over my head and tied the apron around my waist, liking the way it made me feel. I'd always admired Bailey's style. She was a vintage dresser like me, but whereas I liked to wear clothes from all sorts of eras—the fifties, seventies, and eighties, mainly—she was a fifties devotee, through and through. The Cozy Cottage red polka dot apron sat beautifully on her cinched in waist, emphasizing her screen siren physique.

For the rest of the morning, we worked alongside one another almost nonstop, serving up cakes and slices, muffins and scones. Having no idea how to operate the behemoth coffee machine the café boasted, I left Bailey to that end of the job and fumbled my way through charging customers for their purchases. It was a steeper learning curve than climbing Everest, but I felt useful and it was so much fun. And it was the antithesis of sitting in an office with artificial light, staring at a screen all day.

During a much-needed lull, after the main lunch crowd had been served their paninis, stuffed croissants, and more and more cups of coffee, Bailey put her hand on my shoulder. "Paige, you are a Godsend. I'm so grateful you stepped in like that. Thank you."

I shrugged. "I liked it. And let's face it, I didn't exactly have anywhere else I needed to be today."

She let out an easy laugh, smoothing her hands down her apron. "No, but I bet you didn't think you'd be working in a coffee shop when you got up this morning. Now, you have to let me pay you." She pinged the till open and pulled out some notes.

I placed my hand over hers. "You don't need to do that. I was happy to do it. I had a lot of fun."

"You don't have a job anymore, so it's the least I can do." She counted out some notes, took my hand, and turned it palm up, closing my fingers over the money. "No arguments."

She was right. No job did equal no money. Sure, I had some savings thanks to the fact I hadn't had to pay rent since moving back in with Dad, but I knew that pretty soon, not having that AGD income pouring into my account was going to hurt.

"Now, while it's quiet, I need to make some calls to get someone to cover Kayla's shifts. She was scheduled for the rest of the week." Bailey stepped into the kitchen and pulled out her phone.

I slipped my apron off and folded it up. As I absentmindedly smoothed the fabric, a light bulb pinged above my head, like it did in the cartoons. I stood at the entrance to the kitchen. "Hey, Bailey? I could do it."

She looked up at me. "You could?"

The euphoria I'd felt after I had quit spread across my chest once more. "Yeah. I could. I'd like to. What do you say?"

She pressed a button on her phone and looked up at me, her smile spreading from ear to ear. "I say, yes."

* * *

I ARRIVED HOME TO DAD, utterly exhausted from working in the Cozy Cottage Café all day, with sore feet and the need to get horizontal as fast as humanly possible. My body was so used to sitting in front of a screen all day, being on my feet behind the counter serving customers and delivering orders had totally wiped me out.

"Hello, honey," Dad said when I stumbled into the kitchen, stifling a yawn. "You're home early."

I looked up at the clock above the doorway: five fifteen. At AGD, I would still be sitting at my desk, willing the minute hand to speed its slow progression to hit five thirty so I could go home. "Yeah, I had a .. . thing. A meeting, that's what it was, over this side of town. I decided to come home straight from there, rather than go back into the office." I shifted from sore foot to sore foot, the lie sitting uncomfortably.

Truth be told, I wasn't ready to tell Dad about my resignation. I knew he wouldn't take it well. He'd worry about me and my career and what I was doing with my life. A man who had worked his whole life to reach the dizzying heights of Supermarket Checkout Cashier Shift Manager wouldn't understand someone like me deciding to walk away from a good corporate job, especially without having another one to go to. Add to that the fact I was, at least for the time being, working at a café on almost minimum wage, he may be in risk of an aneurysm.

"Well, it's nice to have you home." He accepted my lie without question and kissed me on the cheek.

I swallowed my guilt and forced a bright tone. "What's for dinner?"

"I'm making my world-famous shepherd's pie. Your favorite." He bobbed my nose with his finger.

"Delicious." It was true, shepherd's pie had been my favorite meal when I was eight, but that was twenty-odd years ago now. I liked to think of myself as a little more sophisticated in the culinary stakes these days. "I'll go get changed and come help out."

"Good idea. You don't want to mess up your good work clothes. Got to look the part for the big bosses, right, lamb chop?" He winked and smiled at me, returning his attention to chopping an onion.

"That's right." I half laughed as I trudged up the stairs to my bedroom, each step rubbing more and more painfully against the blisters on my poor feet. Once inside my room, I kicked off my shoes with an audible wince and flopped down onto my bed. I let out a long sigh as I closed my eyes, loving the feel of my soft bed beneath me.

What a day. I'd gone from being pushed into a role I didn't want in another team to quitting my job to working in a café, all within twelve short hours. I smiled to myself as I thought of the look on Portia's face. For an actual facial expression to push through that amount of Botox and fillers is a testament to just how deeply my resignation shocked her. My smile broadened as I got more comfortable on my bed.

And now I was no longer an Email Marketing Assistant.

My belly twisted. Oh, my god. I was no longer an Email Marketing Assistant! Panic gripped me, and I sat bolt upright on my bed. What had I done? I'd thrown away a perfectly good job for . . . for . . . what? Sure, I hated it and it had been a fantastic moment when I'd resigned, but it was just that: a moment. Now I had the rest of my life to regret it.

I pushed myself off my bed and stood, looking at myself in my full-length mirror. I looked a fright. My hair was a mess and my mascara was smudged beneath my eyes. I'd been too busy in the café to give a second thought to how I looked. Usually, in the office, I'd see myself in the mirror whenever I went to the bathroom—which was often, thanks to the huge amount of coffee I drank every day to stave off the boredom.

I took a deep breath, giving myself a mental talking to. I'd made my bed. Whether I liked it or not, I was no longer an Email Marketing Assistant at AGD Telecommunications.

There was no going back.

CHAPTER 6

*M*Y ALARM CLOCK DRAGGED me out of sleep the following morning with a start, my heart beating hard against my ribcage. I'd been in the middle of a dream in which Portia, dressed as the Wicked Witch of the West—no points for originality there—was cackling at me as I sat on a child's seat, my bedroom walls crumbling around me while a guinea pig wearing a baseball cap munched on a stick of celery. Seriously, I couldn't make this stuff up.

I glanced at the digital clock on my nightstand. It was early, way too early. I rolled over and buried my head in my pillow. Although I'm a morning person, I'd got into the habit of hitting the snooze button one too many times, delaying the inevitable need to drag myself into the office.

I wasn't always like that. I used to leap out of bed, often before my alarm, ready to face the day and the joys it may bring. But that was when I was younger, my job was fresh, and though never exactly exciting, it was at least interesting. And I felt sure it would take me places; it was a stepping stone on my way to the big rock of my career. I don't know where I got the idea from, but I always felt I was destined for big things, and I carried that belief inside while I analyzed marketing campaign results and suffered through Portia's moods.

And now? Now, I didn't even have a job to lie in bed avoiding.

I rolled over onto my back and let out a sigh. I needed to get up. I knew I was unlikely to fall back to sleep again—the bad dream had put an end to that—and I also knew I had made a commitment to Bailey to get to the café bright and early this morning to help with the baking. I had no intention of letting her down, even if the reality of my resignation yesterday was sitting heavily in the pit of my stomach.

I got myself out of my bed and had a shower to wake up. Wiping the steam from the bathroom mirror, I looked at my tired and puffy face.

You've really gone and done it this time, Paige.

Doing my best to ignore the pang of guilt at lying, I left a note for Dad on the kitchen counter by the kettle, making up a story about having to get into the office early to work on a deadline, and drove through the quiet streets to the Cozy Cottage Café.

Bailey was there to greet me with her ready smile and a cup of coffee, which I accepted gratefully.

"Right, where do we start?" I asked.

"We've got the breakfast crowd to deal with first, so if you can get the ciabattas in the oven, I'll prep the coffee machine. Then, we'll need to bake some cakes and muffins and get the soup of the day underway."

I grinned at her. "Now you're talking. That must mean I get to see those cake recipes you've kept a trade secret all this time."

Bailey chuckled as she handed me an apron, tying her own behind her back. "I guess today is your lucky day. What do you want to listen to? I usually start off with something cruisy like Adele first up, then move onto something more upbeat once I'm fully awake."

"Adele sounds great to me."

The time flew by as we worked side by side in the kitchen, whipping up all those delicious baked goods, stuffing croissants, filling paninis. We sang along to the music and chatted about the café and life in general. When Bailey said it was seven and time to open up, I was genuinely surprised—it felt like I'd only been here for ten minutes, not two hours.

As Bailey unbolted the front doors and set the "open" sign out on the street, there was a knock on the back door to the kitchen. I wiped my hands on a tea towel and opened it up.

"Good morning. You're new." A man, probably a few years older than me, was smiling over a large box he was holding in his hands. He was tall, at least six foot one or two, with messy brown hair and an open face. Some might say he was good-looking, but he definitely wasn't my type.

Which was a good thing, now that I had decided to become a celibate spinster with cats and a rose-munching goat.

I smiled at him. "Yes, I'm Paige. I'm helping Bailey out for the week. Are you delivering something?" It seemed like a fair enough question to ask.

"No, I just like to carry a box around with me wherever I go." His eyes sparkled from behind his glasses.

"Very funny." I stood back to let Box Guy walk through the door, which he did, heading straight over to the storage area, clearly familiar with the layout of the place. He placed the box on the counter and turned around. My eyes immediately dropped to his T-shirt, which had "Words cannot espresso what you bean to me" emblazoned across his chest, accompanied by a picture of a smiling coffee cup.

I tittered. It was a cute T-shirt, one I might quite like to wear myself, despite the fact it was a little on the nerdy side.

Box Guy raised his eyebrows in question at me. "Something funny?"

"Just your T-shirt. I like it."

"I'm glad you approve." He pulled a folded piece of paper out of the back pocket of his jeans, took a pencil from behind his ear, and handed them to me.

He must have noticed me looking at them uncertainly. "You need to sign here." He pointed to a box at the bottom of the page. I glanced at the header. It read *Ned's*, presumably the name of the coffee roaster he worked for, although why anyone would call their business "Ned's" was beyond me. It hardly brought hot, aromatic coffee to mind.

"Okay. I'd better get Bailey. I'm not exactly authorized to sign this."

"Oh, hey, Josh. I didn't hear you come in," Bailey said as she entered the kitchen. "You've met Paige?"

He nodded, smiling at me as he took the paper and pencil from me and handed them to Bailey. "Your usual order, but I've thrown in a sample of a new blend we're doing. It's called 'Midnight,' and I think your espresso drinkers will love it."

Bailey scrawled her signature on the paper and handed it back to Josh. "Thanks. I'll give it a try and let you know."

"No worries." He walked past me toward the door, and I caught a whiff of his aroma: a mixture of freshly roasted coffee and a cologne I recognized but couldn't name. "Nice to meet you, New Girl. See you next time."

"Sure. See you."

"Right," Bailey said with a clap of her hands. "My first regulars turn up about now, so can you give the kitchen a bit of a cleanup while I man the counter?"

I scanned the counters. There were enough dishes to keep me tucked away in here for a good hour, maybe more. I smelled the baking cakes and thought of what I would be doing right now if I hadn't walked out of my job yesterday. I'd be lying in my bed, procrastinating about getting up, hitting the snooze button for probably the third or fourth time, dreading having to haul myself out of bed to go to work. Washing a stack of dishes for Bailey was a dream by comparison. I grinned at her. "I'm on it."

The morning whizzed by in a blur of customers, food prep, and dishes. Although my feet were sore from the get-go, thanks to yesterday's ill-advised Mary Jane heels, I pushed through the discomfort, loving every moment of working in the café. Thankfully, after the breakfast crowd and morning coffee brigade were gone but for a few hangers on, we got some quiet time to put our feet up at one of the tables for a few minutes—and enjoy a cup of coffee and a slice of Bailey's delicious cake.

"This tastes even better than usual because I'm so darned hungry!" I exclaimed after I'd cleaned my plate of an extra-large slice of carrot cake with cream cheese frosting.

"You definitely get to work up an appetite in this job, that's for sure. Not that it ever helps me work off these extra pounds." Bailey leaned back in her chair and patted her thighs. "In fact, sometimes I figure I won't even bother with eating the cake, I'll just slap it right on there."

I looked at her across the table and frowned. "You're beautiful, Bailey. You don't need to lose any weight."

She blushed. "Maybe. Hey, I've got some paperwork to get through, and then we need to talk about finding you your Last First Date."

"Ah, no, we don't," I said, shaking my head. Had she forgotten my decision? It was infinitely better to die an old-maid-slash-reclaimed-virgin than go through *that* heartache again.

"Yeah, we do. Marissa and I had a meeting and we've decided—"

"You had a *meeting*?" I asked, incredulous, my eyes wide.

"We're going to do this properly, Paige."

I bit the inside of my lip. "Look, I told you at the beach. I don't want to find a man. I'm over the whole Last First Date thing."

Bailey looked at me, a smile on her face. "Is that so?"

"Yes!" Why was she persisting with this? My mind was made up; I had given up on love.

"Hold that thought," Bailey said as she jumped out of her chair.

I'd been too lost in exasperation to notice there were a couple of customers standing at the counter, perusing the cabinet food. I stood up, collected our plates and coffee cups—with two hands and not Bailey's skillful one yet—and headed to the kitchen.

Once behind the counter, I looked across at the customers to give them a welcoming Cozy Cottage Café smile. My eyes met a man's at the counter, and I swear the breath was sucked right out of me.

Oh. My. God. This guy was *beautiful*. Tall, broad, his olive skin set off by his crisp, white, open-necked shirt, cropped black hair, and an I'm-sent-down-by-the-Greek-gods face. Angels sang, harps were strummed, and everything around me fell into nothingness as I stared into his dark eyes. He smiled back at me, holding my gaze for a beat, two. I could hear my heart thudding in my ears, and I had to stifle a nervous, girly giggle.

Too late, I felt the crockery in my hands begin to wobble. I took a step, tried to right them, but both my hands were full. The dishes came crashing to the floor, smashing into one hundred pieces, the dregs of our coffee splattering against my legs and the floor.

Uh-oh!

I quickly squatted down and began collecting up the shattered crockery, my face burning. This was mortifying!

"Paige! What happened?" Bailey looked at me down on the ground, startled.

"Sorry. I . . . I don't know." Which was, of course, not entirely true. I knew exactly what had happened. I'd been too busy staring at Adonis Guy and not concentrating on carrying the dishes to the sink. I shook my head, angry with myself.

I'd let womankind down miserably; my lack of multitasking ability was clearly equal to a man's.

A dark head poked over the edge of the counter. "Are you all right down there?"

I stopped what I was doing and looked up into those mesmerizing eyes once more. My mouth went dry. "I . . . yes, thank you." I stood bolt upright as the heat in my cheeks intensified.

Adonis Guy pushed himself up off the counter and shot me a gorgeous grin. "What did those dishes ever do to you?" He turned to his friend. "Is this the reason you like this place? The hot waitresses throwing dishes around?"

Adonis Guy just called me *hot*?

Bailey laughed. "Usually we just try to dazzle you through our excellent coffee and food. So that was two lattes. Anything to eat?"

Adonis Guy looked back at me. I hadn't moved an inch. "What do you recommend?"

"Oh, ah, me?" My blush deepened. "The, ah, carrot cake with the cream cheese frosting is out-of-this-world good."

"That sounds delicious. Sold." He turned to Bailey. "I'll have a slice of that, thanks." Adonis Guy returned his gaze to me.

His much less godlike friend shook his head good-naturedly, watching Adonis Guy quite obviously flirting with me. "I'll grab one of those spinach and feta muffins."

Bailey rang up their order. "I'll get this, Marcus. I owe you one," Non-Adonis Guy said.

I squatted down to collect the remaining broken dishes in my hands. Try as I might, I couldn't get my heart rate to return to normal, and you could have roasted s'mores on my cheeks, they were so hot.

Marcus. His name was Marcus.

"Thank you. We'll bring those over for you," I heard Bailey say from my position on the floor.

I peeked over the top of the counter. Marcus and his friend had walked over to the window and were now sitting down at Marissa's, Cassie's, and my usual table. Of all the tables in the café, he chose my favorite. Was it a sign?

No, it's not. I'd given up on love. I needed to remember that, difficult as it may have been in the presence of such manly perfection.

While Bailey expertly worked the coffee machine, I put the fragments of the dishes onto some newspaper, wrapped them up, and placed them in the trash. Once I'd swept up the shards, I washed my hands and paused, deep in thought. I may have given up on love, but I was still a woman. And women liked to look good, right?

I pulled my lipstick out of my bag and slipped the lid off. I held it up to my lips, peering in my small compact mirror, and stopped dead. *What am I doing?* One hot guy shows an interest in me and I'm throwing that all away? Talk about being flakier than one of Bailey's cheese filo puffs.

I snapped my compact shut and wound my lipstick down, unapplied, returning it to my makeup bag. I couldn't let the first cute guy I saw dissuade me from my new path. I'd made up my mind; I was a man-free zone.

My jaw clenched, I returned to the counter. "I'm really sorry about that, Bailey. I don't know how it happened. You can dock my pay."

The steamer on the coffee machine made a loud screech as she fluffed the milk for the coffee in a jug. "Don't worry about it, Paige. Accidents happen. Just don't let it happen too often, okay?"

"Of course." I pulled out a couple of plates and put a slice of the cake and a muffin on each. I glanced over at Marcus. He and his friend appeared to be deep in conversation.

Bailey nodded at the plates. "Can you please take those over? I'll bring the coffees when they're done."

Part of me wanted to leap at the opportunity of talking with Marcus again. Another part of me wanted to squirm out of it, come up with some sort of an excuse to avoid the temptation. I told myself I needed to be strong. It was inevitable I was going to meet cute men. I simply needed to learn to deal with them. My inevitable spinsterhood demanded it.

After all, my track record with men had been a miserable failure.

I smoothed my shoulder-length hair behind my ears, took a deep breath, and walked out from behind the counter over to the men's table. "Here you go, gentlemen," I said brightly as I placed their respective treats in front of them on the table.

"All recovered from your plate smashing ordeal?" Marcus asked with a cheeky half smile on his face, looking up at me from his seat.

"Oh, yes. It's all fine, thank you." I tucked my hair behind my ears. "Right. I'll leave you to it." I turned on my heel without a second glance and walked on wobbly legs back to the counter.

Done. Easy. Well, okay, not *easy* exactly, but done all the same.

As Bailey took advantage of the lull and got on with some paper-work, she left me to clean up the counter and wipe down tables before my shift ended. There was only Marcus and his friend in the café, and I was thankful they were so deep in conversation they ignored me, so I had free range to make the place spick and span, ready for us to do it all again tomorrow.

I was putting some things under the counter when someone cleared their throat next to me. I bobbed up, ready to serve like the good Cozy Cottage waitress of almost two days I was. My tummy did a flip when I saw who it was.

"Just checking you're not abusing any more defenseless crockery down there," Marcus said with a fake brow furrow.

My blush returned faster than you could say hot-guy-flirting-with-me. I let out a laugh. "No, no."

"That's good to hear. I'm from the Society for the Protection of Dishes, and we take these matters very seriously, you know." His face broke into a grin.

Wow, this guy looked like Channing Tatum when he smiled. This was *so* not a good thing right now.

I let out a light laugh, putting my hand on my heart. "I swear to give the dishes the respect they deserve in future."

"I'm glad to hear it." He reached into his pocket and pulled out his wallet.

"Oh, I think you already paid," I said.

By way of response, he offered me his business card. Dumbly, I took it in my hand, looking down at the words. *Marcus Hahn, Attorney-at-Law.*

"I would urge you to get in touch if you have any dishes-related concerns."

"Oh, I . . . thank you . . . Marcus." I blushed as I said his name.

He flashed me his Channing Tatum grin once more and I swear my legs ceased to function for a moment there. I watched as he sauntered out of the café, turning to shoot me one last smile before he disappeared out onto the street.

Resisting this guy was going to be trickier than I thought.

CHAPTER 7

*T*HE FOLLOWING DAY WENT much the same as the previous one had at the café: on my feet most of the day, baking, cleaning, washing dishes, serving customers, busy, busy, busy. Only today there had been no broken dishes and no handsome, flirty men distracting me from my new job. Which was a good thing, a very good thing. Or at least, that was what my brain was telling me.

I hadn't known quite what to do with Marcus's card, so I'd slipped it into my purse where it now sat, burning a hole in the side. Yes, he was cute and had made it clear he was interested in me, but there was no way I could go there, not since I'd given up on love.

What's more, I liked him, which was a sure sign as anything he was wrong, wrong, wrong for me.

I'd shrugged my jacket on at the end of my shift and walked out into the empty café to say goodbye to Bailey. My feet were screaming at me, and I was almost cross-eyed with tiredness, having gotten up before any sane person should be out of bed two days running. Bailey was sitting at one of the tables, poring over her laptop.

"Hey, I'm going to head off," I said.

"What?" She looked up at me, bleary-eyed. "Oh, sorry. I'm trying to work out something on the webpage. It's doing my head in."

"Here, let me take a look. I know a bit about html." I pulled up a chair next to her, dropping my purse on the floor. "What are you trying to do?"

"I heard about this café that gets new customers through coupons. I'm trying to work out how to put that onto the website. It's not working."

"What are the coupons for? Free coffee?"

She nodded. "Yup. Just for a limited time, though, to attract new customers. I'm not running a charity here!" She smiled.

"Okay." I put my hands on her laptop. "Do you mind?"

She leaned back in her seat. "Be my guest. It's driving me insane."

I sized up the website. The homepage had the Cozy Cottage's name in the handwriting style I knew so well, an image of a cup of coffee, and one of the outside of the café. So far so predictable. I clicked on the menu tab and up popped the location of the café and its opening hours. I looked for other tabs, but there were none.

"Is this it? No other pages?"

Bailey nodded. "A friend did it for me last year. What do you think?"

I tried to be positive. "It's a good . . . start." I was no expert on web design, but I knew a thing or two about marketing. This website told people the Cozy Cottage was a place where you could get coffee. That was it. Nothing about the food, the character, the charm of the place. It could have been one of those Joe-average chains, for all you could tell.

"Okay," she replied uncertainly. "What are you saying?"

I turned to face her. "Look, you just asked me to help you upload a coupon. I can do that for you, no problem."

"You were going to say something else, weren't you?" She scrunched up her face. "Is it really bad, is that what you think?"

I could have sugarcoated it, I could have told her that her friend had done an amazing job, stood up, and went home. But I cared about Bailey and I cared about the Cozy Cottage—not just because I used to come here to drink coffee and eat cake most days of my working life, but because it was an incredibly special place.

I chose honesty. "It's not great. This place is unique. It's not like any other inner-city café. There's no glitz and glamour, just good food, great coffee, in a place that feels relaxed and welcoming." I turned the laptop around so she could see the website. "This says none of that." I held my breath. What was she going to say?

Bailey bit her lip as she looked at the screen. "It doesn't, does it?" She let out a sigh. "I can't go back to her and ask her to do it again. She did it as a favor for me."

"Well, if you'd like, I could have a look at it for you. Try and inject some of the café's personality into it? As well as upload the coupon, of course," I suggested cautiously.

"Would you?" she gushed and I smiled. "Oh, Paige, that would be fantastic."

"It's the least I could do after you gave me a job this week. Oh, and those broken dishes."

She laughed. "I think an improved website might be worth a little more than a few broken plates."

* * *

THAT EVENING, I sat at the kitchen table, working away on my ideas. I was totally inspired. There were so many things Bailey could be doing to attract more customers. I researched marketing plans for cafés and saw the coupon idea Bailey had talked about. I added it to my growing list of marketing ideas as I perused her competitions' web and social media pages.

"Are you coming to join me?" Dad called from his usual recliner in front of the TV. "*MasterChef* is nearly on."

"You watch it, Dad. I've got work to do."

"They work you too hard, you know."

A spasm of guilt clenched my chest. "Nothing to worry about, Dad. Just that deadline I told you about."

I didn't know how to tell Dad I'd left AGD and that I was now working as a temporary waitress at my friend's café. So, I simply hadn't. I needed to work out what my next step was before I did that, a *fait accompli*, as the French would say. That way he wouldn't worry so much about me—and I wouldn't feel like I was disappointing him so much.

I planned on researching recruiters and looking for another job in marketing, but to be honest, I was loving the mental break from it all. I knew working as a waitress at the Cozy Cottage was only a short-term solution, but I was enjoying it more than I would ever have thought. I had even learned Bailey's well-guarded recipes for all those delicious treats, although she'd threatened to have me killed if I shared them with anyone else.

Needing a break, I reached into the back cupboard and fished out my secret tub of chocolate chip muffins. I looked at it and blinked. I was sure there were at least two left. Now it was empty but for some stray crumbs.

I walked into the living room, holding the tub. Dad was so engrossed in his show he didn't notice me until I stood right in front of him, waving the empty tub around, my eyebrows raised in question. "Dad, either we have a mouse who can open Tupperware or you ate the muffins."

He gave himself away immediately. "Oh, right."

"Did you eat these, Dad?"

He pressed his lips together, looking up at me. Eventually, he nodded.

"Dad!" I cried in exasperation. "You're not meant to have them. Remember what the doctor said? Limit your sugar, not devour your daughter's secret stash of muffins."

He hung his head. "Sorry, honey. They're just so delicious, and you're such a good baker."

I knew he was hoping flattery would work.

I crouched down next to him, using the remote to pause the cooking show. "Dad, you've got to take this seriously. It's your health at stake here."

He looked up into my eyes. "I know. I'm sorry."

I shook my head at him. "That does it. I'm not baking here

anymore." I stopped myself from adding "I'll do it all at the café" in the nick of time. "It's too tempting for you, and you obviously know my secret hiding places, too."

"All right. Is the lecture over?" he asked, taking the remote from me.

I gave an exasperated huff. "It's not a lecture, Dad. I love you. I want you here, not in some hospital bed, or worse."

He patted me on the shoulder. "I know. I love you, too. It's just you and me, huh, kid?"

I let out a sigh, thinking about my decision to give up on love. "Yup. Just you and me, Dad. Just you and me."

BAILEY HAD other staff scheduled in the café for the next two days, so I told Dad I was working on a special project from home and I set to it, designing the website and social media sites and devising a marketing plan I hoped Bailey would love. I knew I was going outside of the brief, but I figured I had the opportunity to really help my good friend out here. Plus, I was loving the work.

My vision for the café's online presence required a few photos, so I reached into the depths of my closet and hauled out the old Canon I'd bought secondhand back when I'd fancied myself as a bit of an Annie Leibovitz. I knew exactly what I wanted, and one of them was a photo of a good-looking couple enjoying a cup of coffee at one of the tables.

Some may have thought I had some kind of masochistic streak when I decided to ask Cassie and Will if they could model for me. After all, they fitted the bill perfectly and already loved the Cozy Cottage. They were more than happy to oblige, especially when I told them it was to help Bailey out.

I reached the Cozy Cottage late morning, between the morning coffee and lunch crowds, timed so the place wouldn't be too full.

"You do know it's your day off today, don't you?" Bailey said with a wry grin. She was looking particularly beautiful today with her dark hair piled up on top of her head and a pretty pale pink summer dress under her polka dot apron.

I pulled the lens cap off my camera. "Give me one of those fabulous smiles of yours."

Bailey did as I requested and I snapped a bunch of photos of her looking like an Italian movie star from the fifties behind the counter, flashing her gorgeous grin.

When I lowered my camera, she asked, "I'm all for being the center of attention, but what's with the photos?"

"They're for the website, Facebook, Instagram, that sort of thing. Here." I pulled out my rough plan for the website landing page and slipped it across the counter to her. Although I'd only worked in the café for a couple of days, it already felt odd being on this side of the counter for a change.

She looked it over. "It seems great, but I'm not sure I want photos of me all over it."

"Are you crazy? You're a huge part of the success of this place, Bailey. I think you're a total asset and we should put you front and center."

She wrinkled her forehead and cocked her head to the side. "It's not about me, it's about the Cozy Cottage."

"I know, but you're a massive part of that. In fact, without you, this place would just be any other café."

She didn't look convinced.

I scooped my plan back up from the counter. "Trust me, okay? I think you'll love it."

Her face broke into her trademark smile once more. "Sure. I'm looking forward to it, only, make me just a small part of it, okay?"

I shook my head. We lived in a culture of endless selfies and self-promotion, and Bailey didn't want images of her beautiful face to dominate her new website. "Deal."

"Oh, look it's Cassie . . . and Will," she said, her eyes wide. "Cassie and Will . . . here. Together." She looked back at me as concern clouded her face.

I let out a laugh. "It's all right, Bailey. I'm meeting them here."

She blinked at me. "You are?"

"They're modeling for me. I promised to buy them some coffee and cake in return." I turned to greet them—and ignored the twist in my belly at the sight of them together.

"Hey, Paige," Cassie said, giving me a hug. "It's so weird not to have you at the office anymore. I miss you."

"I miss you, too. Not the job, though." I smiled at Will. Giving him a hug felt a step too far just yet. "Hey, Will."

"Hey, Millsey. Looking good."

I glanced down at my oversized white linen shirt tucked into a pair of skinny, yellow sixties-inspired cropped pants and slip-on silver flats. "Err, thanks" was all I could manage.

"Paige tells me you're modeling for the new website today," Bailey said.

"Sure are. We're ready for our close-up, Mr. DeMille," Cassie said, referencing that famous line from *Sunset Boulevard*. I knew: we'd watched it together. She grinned at me. I noticed Will gave her hand a little squeeze. I chewed the inside of my lip.

"Is it two lattes?" I asked, pasting on a bright smile.

"Yes, please," Will said.

"And some cake. It wouldn't be a visit to the Cozy Cottage without cake," Cassie added solemnly.

Bailey laughed. "True. Your usual, Cassie?" She nodded. "And what about for you, Will?"

"Same for me, thanks, Bailey."

While Bailey filled their order, I got the happy couple to pose at different spots around the café. I wanted them to look happy, relaxed, and in love. I got all three in spades and it was almost killing me.

Yup, I had definitely entered masochistic territory here. At this rate, I'd may as well have just gone out and found myself a Christian Grey-type billionaire and been done with it—although, I wasn't sure all that torture room business was quite up my street.

After about twenty minutes, I'd had them sitting outside with their sunglasses on, sitting in the window, sipping their respective coffees, and at a table with Bailey and the counter in the background as they shared a slice of flourless raspberry and chocolate cake. In the end, the pain I'd put myself through was worth it; the photos looked amazing.

"Hey, thanks, you two. That was awesome."

"Anything for you and Bailey," Cassie said with a grin.

Once the lovebirds had gone off to feather their nests or eat worms together or whatever the metaphor was, I wandered around the café, taking some more shots. I spotted Helena, walking through the door. I hadn't seen her since the day I left my job at AGD, and I was genuinely pleased to see her.

"Hey, Paige," she said. She greeted me with a warm hug as I held my camera out to the side to protect it. "I heard you were working here."

I grinned at her. "I get to hang out here all day." I glanced around the café at the tables of happy customers, enjoying Bailey's and my food, sipping their coffee. Would I choose the Cozy Cottage over staring at my computer screen in my old cubicle at AGD? Every freakin' day of the year.

She rolled her eyes and let out a puff of air. "God, that must be so good. You're so lucky, you know that? We're all still talking about that Bride move you pulled on her highness. Genius."

I laughed. I'd forgotten how much Helena hated Portia. Funny, it'd only been a few days and already it felt like some horrible, distant memory.

"You know what she's gone and done now? Got engaged." She shook her head. "That poor schmuck. He doesn't know what he's got himself into."

I raised my eyebrows. "Portia's engaged? Not to Juan Felipe, is it?"

"Ha! She wishes. He's too much of a hotshot playboy for the likes of her. No, it's some other guy. My brain goes into automatic shutdown mode when she's on one of her spiels about how fabulous she is. She drones on about him like he's Prince William, but I bet he's just some social-climbing ass."

"I bet." In the past, I could have complained about Portia with

Helena until the cows came home, but now I really couldn't have cared less. She could actually *be* marrying Prince William, for all I cared, although I suspected his current wife may have had a thing or two to say about that.

"Hey, I've only got a few minutes. Can we catch up soon?" Helena asked.

"Yes, that'd be fun. Take care." I gave her a hug and returned my attention to my camera as she walked to the counter to place her order. I was scrolling through my latest crop, happy with the way they had turned out, when I felt someone standing beside me. I looked up from my screen and saw the guy who delivered the coffee beans on my first day.

"Hi, Paige."

I looked up into his eyes and smiled. "Hey, there . . . you!" I said a little too brightly. *What is this guy's name again? Geoff? John?* I searched my brain, came up with nothing.

If he noticed, he didn't let on. "What've you got there?" he asked, peering at my screen.

I quickly flicked the camera off and let it hang back down by my midriff. I wanted the new Cozy Cottage "brand" to remain for Bailey's and my eyes only until it was ready. "Just a project I'm working on."

He raised his eyebrows and smiled. "Sounds mysterious." I noticed a sparkle in his hazel eyes.

I let out a self-conscious laugh. "Not really. It's for the café website and stuff. I thought it needed some work."

"Great idea. And between you and me, I have to agree. No offense to Bailey, of course. Last time I was on there, it seemed a little"—his eyes shot up to the ceiling, trying to find the right word—"dull. Not representative of this place, which is not dull in the least. In fact, it's just about as perfect as a café can be, in my humble opinion."

I couldn't help but smile at him. He was right; the Cozy Cottage *was* special. It had such a welcoming feel, it would be hard not to feel at home the moment you walked through the doors.

"Exactly. Anyway, what are you doing here?" I glanced down at the image on his T-shirt of a smiling coffee bean and read it aloud. "'Coffee is a state of bean.'" I shook my head and smiled. "Sweet."

"Yeah, that's the reaction us single guys are aiming for with women: 'sweet.'"

I chuckled. "Maybe you should consider trying a different type of shirt, then?"

"And give up my trademark 'sweetness'? Are you *insane?*" He laughed. "In answer to your question, I'm here for the soup. Bailey makes a mean Mexican chicken tortilla." He leaned in toward me and raised his eyebrows. "Even us coffee delivery guys need to eat lunch, you know."

Before I had the chance to respond, Bailey greeted him with, "Hey, Josh. Great to see you."

Josh. I needed to remember that.

He grinned. "Hey, Bailey." He put his hand on my arm. "See you later, Paige the mysterious photographer." He turned back to Bailey, and said, "How's that new blend working out for you? I've had a lot of positive feedback from customers so far."

They peeled away from me, deep in their coffee talk.

"Who was *that?*" Helena asked, materializing at my side.

"Who? Oh, that's Bailey. She runs the place. She's my boss." I grinned at the thought.

"No, silly. I meant the hot guy. He's yummy." She nodded at the coffee delivery guy—*Josh*—still deep in conversation with Bailey. "He looks familiar."

"He does?" I looked at Josh. "Yummy" wasn't quite the word I'd use to describe him. Probably more "forgettable," if I was totally honest.

She stared off into space. "Yeah, he does." She shook her head. "Anyway, I'd better get back. Her royal bitchiness will be looking for me. I'll need this to give me strength." She held her takeout cup up. "Great to see you."

"See you, Helena." I watched her walk through the door out onto the street. Only one Tarantino reference today. I smiled to myself; she must be in a good mood. I noticed the café was starting to fill up with the lunch crew. I wanted to finish up taking the shots I needed so I could get home to do some more work on the website.

I was standing in the corner, capturing as much of the café as I could in one final shot, when through my lens, I noticed a man walk in the entrance. My heart skipped a beat. It was Marcus. I lowered my camera and watched him. He was on his own this time and appeared to be searching for something—or someone.

Could it have been me?

My mouth went dry at the thought. He had definitely been flirting with me that day in the café, and he had given me his business card, clearly with the intention of me calling him. I thought of it, still burning a hole in the side of my purse. Maybe, since he hadn't heard from me, he'd decided to track me down again?

I watched as he continued to scan the room until his eyes settled on me. I couldn't help but look back at him, my tummy flip-flopping as our eyes locked. His handsome face broke into a grin, and he began to walk toward me, past the growing line of lunch customers and through the tables.

I swallowed. Hard. *I've given up on love, I've given up on love.* I was literally cornered by this guy, with nowhere to hide. But then, part of me wanted to see him, to stay right where I was. In the end, I had no choice, and he was by my side in seconds.

"Hi, Paige."

"Hi, ah, Marcus." My cheeks began to burn, butterflies batting their wings in my belly.

His expression became suddenly serious. "I had thought I might have heard from you by now."

"Oh . . . I . . ." I didn't know quite what to say. He was being very direct.

"We take dish abuse very seriously at the Society for Dishes, you know."

"Society for *the Protection of* Dishes," I corrected him, not quite understanding why I was doing so. Why did it matter?

He grinned his gorgeous smile. "I'm glad to hear you were paying attention."

I let out a nervous laugh.

He glanced down at my camera. "You a photographer, too?"

"I'm just taking some shots for the café's website."

"Wow. Beautiful *and* talented."

I bit my lip, trying not to blush. Failing, of course. This guy was funny, obviously interested in me, and persistent. He could prove incredibly hard to resist. "Ah, thank you."

"So, do you think I might be able to get your number? Since you've obviously lost my card."

My tummy flipped and flopped and flipped again. As I looked into his brown eyes, teasing me gently, for the life of me, I couldn't remember why I ever decided to give up on love. Something to do with the One Last First Date pact and not choosing the right sorts of men. It was all a distant, fuzzy memory right now.

"I . . ." God, he was tempting. But I needed to stick to my guns. "Here's the thing. I've sort of made up my mind not to date."

He raised his eyebrows in question. "You have?"

"Mm-hm." I nodded, pressing my lips together.

He shook his head. "Why would you go doing something stupid like that?"

Why indeed?

"Well, I'm not very good at choosing the right guys, you see." The heat in my cheeks turned almost nuclear.

"Is that so?" He tapped two of his fingers against his chin. "Well, if I ask you out, *I'm* choosing *you*, not the other way around. Right?"

My heartbeat raced. Part of me screamed, *he makes a very good point!* And the other part? Well, in that moment, I couldn't have heard it if it had jumped up, slapped me across the face, and yelled in my ear.

A smile crept across my face. "Okay."

He smiled back at me. "So, what's your number, Paige?"

Before I had the chance to change my mind, I gave it to him and watched as he added it to his contacts list, admiring his long, tan fingers as he typed.

He slotted his phone into the back pocket of his pants and looked into my eyes once more. "I hope to see you soon."

My mouth went dry. "Yes, I'd like that."

As he turned and walked away, I took several large gulps of air, trying to steady my heart, which seemed to think it was in an attempt to break the land-speed record. Marcus joined the line of customers waiting to order their lunch and smiled at me across the room. I smiled back, swallowing down a rising sense of unease.

What have I done?

CHAPTER 8

I SLUMPED AGAINST THE café kitchen wall, my mind full of Marcus and the pickle I'd just landed myself in. Not only had I broken my vow to stay away from men by giving him my number, but *I* had chosen *him*—despite the cute argument he'd put forward to say I hadn't. As far as Marissa and Bailey were concerned, I was waiting for them to come up with my Last First Date, a vetted man of their choosing who ticked all the right boxes. Not going around flirting with cute guys and giving out my number.

I was too deep in thought to notice I wasn't alone.

"Are you all right?"

I looked up and straight at Josh, the coffee delivery guy, who had a concerned look on his face. He was holding a large bag of coffee beans. "Yes, I'm fine, thanks." I forced a smile to show him just how fine I was. "What are you doing back here?"

"Just grabbing these for Bailey." He gestured to the bag. "She's snowed under out there."

"Coming through!" Fiona, one of Bailey's part-time staff, came bustling through with a tray filled with croissants and paninis. To keep costs down, Bailey only served cabinet food, other than soup, which we scooped out of large pots on the stove and served with toasted ciabatta. Fiona was responsible for the heating, toasting, and plating of the lunch orders today. And she had her work cut out for her, by the looks of the long lunch line out there.

"Sorry, Fi. I'll get out of your way." I clipped my lens cap back on my camera, grabbed my purse, and headed toward the back door.

"See you later," Josh called as I pushed the door open and breathed in the fresh outside air.

Distracted, I turned back and shot him a quick smile. "Sure, yes. See you."

The rest of the day was spent choosing the best photos and compiling them into the landing page, menu pages, and events pages I had created—and thinking about Marcus. I must have looked at my phone, sitting next to me on the kitchen table, at least a thousand times, wondering what I was going to say to him when he called.

Yes, I wanted to see him again. Yes, I wanted to go out on a date with him. And, yes, I wanted to kiss him until my lips were raw. *God, yes.* Those eyes, that mouth, those broad shoulders. I let out a long sigh. I didn't know him, but he was the kind of guy I always saw myself ending up with: confident, fun, sure of who he was and his place in the world.

I leaned back in my wooden seat and ran my fingers through my hair. My decision to give up on love suddenly felt childish, rash, a knee-jerk reaction to not being chosen by Will. That night on the beach when we reset the pact, I was at an all-time low. Now that time had passed and I was moving on, the idea of finding The One, someone to spend my life with, felt good, it felt right.

I let out a sigh, gazing out Dad's kitchen window at the trimmed hedge by the lawn. It was time; I was ready. I wanted to find my Last First Date. I wanted to be in love.

And anyway, how could a girl be expected to stay away from men with the likes of Marcus Hahn around? I mean, I was only human, after all.

No. Being a spinster with all those cats did not appeal—nothing against cats, of course. I wanted to give it a shot. And if I was going to do this, if I was going to go in search of love once more, I needed to do it right. Because attraction—as amazing as that was—wasn't enough for me anymore. I needed to know more about Marcus before I made the leap. A lot more.

A smile crept across my face. Whether he had any inkling or not, I intended Marcus Hahn to be my Last First Date. Now, all I had to do was engineer it so Bailey and Marissa thought so too.

* * *

I SPENT the next day working on the Cozy Cottage brand and marketing plan, and by the time Dad got home that evening, I was more than a little bit proud of what I'd achieved. I had a full webpage, all laid out and ready to go live with Bailey's say-so, I had created Cozy Cottage Facebook, Instagram, and Twitter pages, and I had come up with a list of promotional ideas, laid out clearly in a twelve-month plan. I hoped Bailey would love it as much as I did.

I snapped my laptop shut as Dad walked into the kitchen, lugging bags of groceries in his hands. I jumped out of my chair. "Here, Dad, let me help you with those." I took the bags out of his arms and set them down on the kitchen counter.

"Thanks, honey. Have you been working here all this time?"

Dad had left for work this morning as I was sitting at the kitchen table, my head filled with ideas.

"No, I went out to get a couple of photos of the café I'd forgotten to take yesterday, too," I said as I began to unpack the groceries and put them away. "Oh, good. You got some more broccoli. I know you're not a huge fan but I thought I'd do some broccoli soup tonight, get some of that green goodness into you."

"If you have to," Dad replied with a grin and a roll of the eyes. Vegetables were not exactly at the top of Dad's food list. He handed me some carrots and I placed them in the vegetable drawer at the bottom of the refrigerator. "Why did you have to take photos of a café?"

I stopped dead. That was a rookie's mistake. I had to think fast. I buried my head in the vegetable drawer so he wouldn't be able to see I was lying. "It's just for a mock-up for a website. An example, I guess," I bluffed. I held my breath, hoping he'd buy it and move on.

"Well, I'm sure you did a wonderful job," he replied.

My belly twisted at how easily he accepted the lie. It was best to change the subject. "How was your day? Did you manage to go for a walk?"

"Yes, yes. I went for a walk during my lunchbreak with Trevor. He's carrying a bit extra around the middle, too, so we're trying to encourage each other."

"That's awesome, Dad," I said, and gave him a kiss on the cheek.

"I've been listening to you and I am taking my health seriously."

I beamed at him. Since his diagnosis of Type II Diabetes, I've been on Dad to always remember to take his medication, get daily exercise, and try to avoid sugar. He's pretty good on the medication, but the other two have been a work in progress, with me having to parent my parent all too often. Hearing he was finally taking things seriously and managing himself lifted a huge weight from my shoulders.

I made the soup and we ate it together at the kitchen table, although I wouldn't say Dad exactly enjoyed the experience. "Now, where's the real food?" he asked once I'd cleared the plates away.

I laughed. "You're hilarious, Dad."

"No, I'm serious. What else are we having?"

I swiveled around and looked at him. "Are you still hungry?"

"No, but a man cannot live on broccoli alone, you know." His warm Dad-smile crinkled the skin around his eyes.

I shook my head. "There's some shredded chicken in the refrigerator. Want me to make you a chicken salad?"

I noticed his smile drop. He was probably holding out for a burger and fries, but somehow, they had been left off the doctor's list. "Thanks, lamb chop. I'll just nip upstairs while you do that." He pushed himself up from the table and left the room as I busied myself with making the salad.

A few moments of chopping and vinaigrette-making later, I called out to Dad. No response. I went upstairs. No sign of him. I got to the bottom of the stairs and heard a strange rustling sound coming from the garage. I put my hand on the doorknob and pressed my ear up against the door. What was that? A mouse? Something larger? My heart began to race. What if it was an intruder? The rustling continued, and I swore I heard a human sigh.

Just to be on the safe side, I grabbed an umbrella from beside the front door. It might not be a terribly threatening weapon of choice, but it was the best I could do on short notice. Gripping the umbrella in my left hand, I swung the door open and flicked on the garage light.

I wasn't faced with a mouse or a rat or even an intruder. Just Dad, slumped in one of our deck chairs. I took in the empty cookie and chocolate wrappers dropped carelessly on the floor.

"Dad?" I questioned in shock.

He looked up at me, his mouth opened midway to take a fresh bite of the bar in his hand.

"What are you doing?" I glared at him.

He lowered the bar and smiled weakly at me. "I was hungry."

I put my hands on my hips and raised my eyebrows at him. He had the decency to look guilt-stricken as he pushed the remainder of the bar back into its wrapper.

I walked over to him, leaned down, and picked up a box that was sitting by his feet. I peered inside and gasped as I saw rows of what I knew were his favorite bars, lined up neatly, almost a third of them gone.

"Did you get this from work?"

"Yes," he replied, still looking shame-faced. "I paid for them."

I guffawed. As if paying for the bars made this okay. "How long have you been hiding away, eating this . . . junk?" I may spend my days now baking sugar-laced cakes and treats—and eating a few of them, too, I admit—but at least they were actual *food*. These bars were full of unpronounceable crap and a bunch of numbers, barely food at all.

"Just a short while."

I scowled at him, tapping my foot.

"Okay, maybe more than a short while."

I shook my head, letting out a heavy sigh. I studied my dad's face. "Why are you doing this, Dad?"

"I always liked a treat after dinner, you know that."

I squatted down next to him and put my hand on his. "Do I need to tell you again why you shouldn't be doing this?"

He hung his head. "No."

I chewed the inside of my lip, willing the tears prickling my eyes to disappear. "I'm going to have to get rid of this stuff, you know that, right?" He nodded. "Do you think . . . Could you try a little harder? Please?" My voice cracked as I lost the battle to hold back the tears.

Dad looked up at me in alarm. He gripped my hand. "Oh, honey. I will. I'm sorry." His eyes were glistening as he smiled at me.

I nodded at him, not trusting myself to speak again.

"Come here." He pulled me in for a hug. He smelled of chocolate, an aroma I had associated with him since I was a little girl and we'd share a bar, sitting on the front steps.

When I regained my composure, I said, "You can't keep doing this, Dad."

He nodded, his face grim. "It's been so hard. But I'll try. Honestly, I will."

I studied his face. I nodded. "All right. I guess I'll have to trust you."

"Look, there's a group Janice from work told me about. She joined it when she was diagnosed a couple of years back. Sort of a support group, but it sounds like they have some fun, too. Maybe I'll go to that?"

I smiled at him, despite the rock in my belly. "Sounds good." I pushed myself up and extended my hand to help Dad out of his seat. He grabbed it, and I hauled him up—not an easy feat with a man of his size.

I collected the discarded wrappers and put them in the box. I opened the garage door, and, without a word, Dad and I walked outside to the large trashcan. He lifted the lid and I dropped the box inside. It landed with a loud *thud* at the bottom.

"I guess you won't be wanting that salad now."

He laughed as he took my arm in his and we walked back inside the house. "I'd love that salad."

I swallowed down an uncomfortable feeling. I knew all about Dad's secret now, but he still had absolutely no clue about mine.

* * *

AFTER BAILEY and I had closed for the day later that week, we sat down together for me to show her the work I'd done on the website. I was proud of it and excited to show it to her. I'd compiled the best photos I'd taken into a tiled home page, with the Cozy Cottage name and a gorgeous, smiling shot of Bailey front and center. I'd chosen the font carefully, trying to capture the homey feel of the place without being cutesy, and had shots of the food, the coffee, and Will and Cassie, smiling and enjoying their food together.

I sat on the edge of my seat. I watched Bailey's reaction closely as she looked at the homepage for the first time. Slowly, a twitch of a smile grew, spreading across her face, lighting it up.

"Oh, Paige. This is *gorgeous*," she declared, her eyes wide.

I beamed at her. "You like it, then?"

"Like it? Are you kidding me? I don't know how you've done it, but you've captured the essence of the café and made it look really chic and elegant and cozy, all at the same time." She looked in wonder from the screen to me. "You have a real talent for this."

"Do you think so? Thanks. I loved doing it. Let me show you how it works. See the menu tab there?" I pointed to one of the tiles. "Click on that and it'll take you to the menu choices for lunch and snacks. If you ever decide to do dinner, you could offer that here, plus I made seasonal variations, since you change the menu during the year."

She studied the screen. "It looks fantastic. Oh, look at Cassie there. She looks like a model!"

I peered at the picture. It was one of Cassie laughing with Will as they sat outside under one of the café's umbrellas. They looked so happy, so connected. Looking at that image right now, how did I not know how they felt about each other? I swallowed down a lump. "Yeah, she sure does."

I took Bailey through the rest of the site and showed her what I'd done on Instagram, Facebook, and Twitter, carrying the same branding across all the platforms. "And here is my design for the coffee coupon you wanted." I showed her a graphic I'd mocked up with the words "Cozy Cottage Café Coupon" and an illustration of a cup of coffee with steam coming out the top. "I haven't uploaded it yet, but as soon as you say to pull the trigger on the promotion, it's ready to go."

Bailey shook her head. "Paige, I've said it before: you are a Godsend. This is amazing. Thank you." She collected me into a hug, and I breathed in her perfume. "You have to let me pay you for this."

I waved her offer away with my hand. "No, don't be silly. I'm happy to help you out. I've got loads of ideas for future promotional stuff, too." I pulled up my marketing plan for the café.

"Wow, you really have got a lot in there," Bailey said as her eyes scanned the page. "Free Wi-Fi and a work zone?"

"Yes. A lot of cafés are doing it. You provide power outlets at tables so people can plug their devices in and work on the free Wi-Fi. If you get one of those unlimited plans AGD offers, you would know exactly what your costs would be each month to run it. The café is in the perfect location for this, and you've got the space."

Bailey looked around the room. "Yes, I guess I do. As long as they buy things while they're here."

"Oh, they will, believe me. With your food, I don't think you'll have any trouble with that. Having this sort of thing on offer will attract customers throughout the day, filling in those quiet times I've noticed you have. Once they're here, they'll eat, trust me."

Bailey nodded, sucking on her lip. "I think you may be onto something with that."

"And it wouldn't be too costly to set up. Just moving some furniture around, setting up the Wi-Fi, and putting in some more power outlets. It's worth a shot, right?"

She grinned at me. "I like this idea. What else have you got?" She read the next couple of ideas on the screen. "Local artists and musicians?"

"Yes! I thought we could offer some space for local artists to exhibit their work, even have exhibition openings, that sort of thing. You could set musicians up over there"—I pointed at an area at the back of the café—"and charge a small fee for admission, say five dollars. Solo artists or duos would be best for the space. With enough in attendance, ticket sales could cover the musician's fee, and then you make money from food and drinks. It would mean opening in the evenings, but I've got some thoughts about that, too."

She raised her eyebrows, quite possibly in alarm. "You do?"

I stood up, aware this idea may seem a step too far for her. "Come with me."

Bailey followed me out into the kitchen. "See that area there?" I gestured at a disused section at the back left of the kitchen where Bailey had empty boxes and other miscellaneous items stacked. "If we opened in the evenings, we could convert this space to use for things like plating and we could offer light meals, kind of like we already do for lunch."

"You want us to serve dinner?"

"Yes! I think it's a massive untapped market for this place. We could put some candles on the tables and . . ." I trailed off when I noticed the look on her face. "What is it?"

"I don't know. Dinner? Musicians? The free Wi-Fi and work space thing is great, but this? It's a lot to take in."

"But don't you see how amazing it could be?" I wasn't going to let her reaction diminish my enthusiasm. "You don't need to do it all at once. You could take baby steps. Coupons first, then maybe introduce one night a week with some entertainment. That sort of thing."

I watched as she chewed on her lip once more, deep in thought. After a moment, during which I wondered whether I'd completely overstepped the mark, she said, "Shall we sit down?"

"Sure." Intrigued, I followed her out into the café, back to the table we were sitting at earlier.

She placed her clasped hands on the table. "Look, the thing is I own this place with a partner."

"Yes." This wasn't news; she had mentioned it before.

"And we've talked about doing a few of these types of things in the past. In fact, I even had an artist lined up to do an exhibit at one stage, but, well, she likes things the way they are."

"Does she get involved in the running of the café?" I hadn't seen anyone who looked like she might be Bailey's business partner in my time as either a frequent customer or member of staff. She was a woman of mystery, with a set of handcuffs tying Bailey's hands.

"No. That's why I've been doing all the books and things I haven't spent much time on before. She's . . . taking a step back."

"Okay. Well, I just wanted to show you some ideas. It's up to you what you do with them. I'm just the hired help, after all." I shrugged and smiled at her.

She placed her hand on mine, and for a moment, I thought I detected tears welling in her eyes. "Paige, you are so much more than that. And these ideas? They're great and I would love to do them. Let's just hold off for now, okay?"

"Sure." I wanted to ask her more. I wanted to know who this partner was who wouldn't let her do anything with the café. I wanted to help her, to be there for her, but I didn't know where to start.

Bailey jumped up from the table, bringing me back to earth. "Look who's here!" she exclaimed, her tone bright.

I looked up at the door and saw Marissa waving at us. She was dressed head-to-toe in exercise clothes, looking slim, energetic, and healthy, her blonde hair pulled back in a high ponytail. She looked like Workout Barbie on her way to a class—I know, my Workout Barbie went to many such a class when I was a kid.

Bailey unhooked the front door and Marissa came sailing into the room in a puff of energy. "You haven't started without me, have you?" She dropped her keys on the table and pulled a chair out to sit on.

"You look sporty," I commented, pointing out the obvious. Marissa was usually dressed in slick and stylish corporate attire, her hair perfectly styled, her heels high and sexy—not like an advertisement for a gym.

"I'm about to go on a run with Cassie. It's a One Last First Date thing. I've got to look my best, right?"

My eyes skimmed over her perfect physique, encased in tight

Lycra. I squirmed in my seat, feeling the waistband of my skirt digging into my belly, my newly acquired muffin top poking out uncomfortably above. Somehow, a while ago, I'd got out of the habit of exercising. I used to enjoy a run or a swim, loving being outdoors and the way exercise made me feel—more afterward than during, of course. But then I simply dropped it and started spending more and more time on my own, hiding under my duvet, putting off facing the world. It could have been because of the drudgery of my job, or because Will had chosen Cassie.

Or it could have been all of it.

"Hey, you should come with us! We're training for the next Color Run. It's so much fun," Marissa declared, her eyes shining with excitement.

"Um, no," I replied instantly, not even having the vaguest idea what a Color Run was and not wanting to know, either. Something to do with laundry? Running your clothes to the laundromat? I had no clue. "But thanks," I added so as not to offend her.

"Aw, come on! It'll be so great. Have you ever done a Color Run before?" Marissa asked, not letting this thing go.

"Isn't that where people throw colored powder at you as you run past and you end up covered in the stuff?" Bailey asked.

I scoffed. That sounded like my own special kind of hell.

"That's the one. It's only a few miles, so hardly taxing, but I figured it was a good start. And it's amazing fun. I did one in Sydney a couple of years ago. It's not far away, which is why we're in training." Marissa turned back to me. "Come on, Paige. Say you'll do it with us. Please."

I looked at Marissa. Her eyes were so liquid brown and pleading, she could give a puppy a run for its money right now. I let out a sigh. I *did* need to get out of my funk and try to lose this muffin top, and "a few miles" didn't sound too horrendous. I shrugged. "Why not?"

"Awesome! You can be in our team." Marissa beamed at me. "We can all look fabulous for our One Last First Dates."

"Marissa, I didn't think you were particularly into the pact," Bailey commented, raising her eyebrows.

She shrugged. "I figured, why not? It's worth a shot. I know I've maybe been a bit cynical about it in the past"—she shot us a look when both Bailey and I scoffed at her blatant understatement—"but look at Cassie. She's so happy now. I want what she has." She glanced at me, scrunching up her face. "Sorry."

I shook my head. I wanted what Cassie had too, only a little more specifically than Marissa. "Don't be. I'm fine." And if I wasn't one hundred percent fine right now, I knew I would be. And it was a nice feeling.

"That's really good to hear." Marissa smiled at me before turning her attention to Bailey. "You haven't started without me with the thing, have you?"

Bailey shook her head. "We were doing some café stuff. We haven't started."

I narrowed my eyes at their smiling faces. "What's going on?"

"Well, Marissa and I have made progress." Bailey said, her smile broadening into a grin.

"With what?"

Marissa had also started grinning at me now. It was unnerving.

"Your Last First Date," Marissa replied, sitting back in her seat and crossing her arms, looking thoroughly satisfied with herself.

"You have?" If I had been drinking coffee, I would have spat it out all over the table.

"Mm-hm." Marissa looked like she was about to pop. She leaned forward. "Look, I know you said you wanted to give up on this whole thing, but we think you just haven't met the right guy yet. So, we decided that—"

"It's okay. I want to," I interrupted, thinking of Adonis Guy Marcus.

"You do?" Bailey asked.

I nodded, trying to suppress a grin as I imagined our Last First Date together. I knew it would be perfect, just like him.

"Oh, Paige, you are not going to regret this," Bailey said, shaking her head.

"Should I tell her, or do you want to?" Marissa asked Bailey.

There was a "you say it" no "you say it" conversation that went on for some time. Too long, truth be told. Eventually, in exasperation, I said, "Will one of you please just say it?"

"We've found someone for you!" Marissa declared.

My belly performed an elaborate twist. "You have?" I squeaked.

"Yes, and so far, we think he's absolutely the guy for you." Marissa beamed. "This living vicariously thing is really great. But"—Marissa put her index finger in the air—"we still need to do all the vetting and so forth before we let you know who he is." Marissa turned to Bailey. "Oh, you know who we should bring in on this? Cassie. She vetted Parker to within an inch of his life before she went on her One Last First Date. I bet she'd have some good tips for us."

"Yes, I think that's a good idea," Bailey agreed.

"Hang on," I said, interrupting their discussion about some mystery man who could possibly be my future husband. "Are you saying you've met someone for me?"

"Yes!" they both said. "Have you not been paying attention?" Marissa asked, her eyes wide.

I shot her a look.

"And although we can't tell you who it is yet, he was here a couple of days ago," Bailey said, mysteriously.

My eyes got huge. "He was?" I breathed. *Marcus.* He was here a couple of days ago. *It has to be him!* I tried my best to suppress a smile. Failed. Marcus. It was Marcus!

"You're pumped, I can tell," Marissa said. "Oh, Paige. This is going to be so great. You are not going to regret giving up becoming a sad old spinster," she gushed.

"You'll have to hold tight until we find out everything we need to know, though," Bailey warned.

"Sure. No problem." I grinned at them both. "Can I ask a couple of questions?"

Marissa and Bailey glanced at one another. "As long as they're not too specific," Bailey replied.

"All right." I bit my lip, thinking of nonspecific questions that could point to Marcus. "Is he tall?"

They nodded. A good start: Marcus was tall.

"Does he have olive skin and look like he was sent down from the heavens?"

"What?" Marissa said with a chortle. "Too specific. We can't answer that one." Bailey agreed.

"All right." I wracked my brain for something else. "Did he come in here at lunch two days ago?"

Bailey's eyes shot up to the ceiling as she thought. "Yes, yes I think he did."

It was Marcus! My belly did a flip-flop, and I was glad I was sitting down—otherwise I might have actually swooned.

"Can I ask anything else about him?" I asked once I'd recovered.

"No! You already know too much. You'll need to be patient and trust us," Bailey said.

I could be patient. Well, for a short while, anyway. I grinned, excitement pinging around my body. I was going to go on a date with cute and sexy Marcus. A Last First Date. Things could not be better.

CHAPTER 9

I FLOATED AROUND ON Cloud Nine for the next few days, hoping—okay, praying with all my might—everything Marissa and Bailey had found out about this guy they wanted to keep secret from me was good. Only, I knew it was Marcus, so it had to be, of course. He was cute, totally my type, and had already told me he was going to ask me out. Not that I'd mentioned that to them, of course. I wanted them to feel like they were in control of this. If I told them about us, I'd take the fun out of it all for them.

I was sitting with Dad in the living room after dinner, watching another reality cooking show. Some poor schmucks had burned their desserts and were on the end of some nasty comments from the judges, one of them sobbing her heart out.

My mind began to wander to my current job situation—or, rather, lack thereof. Although I loved working at the café, it wasn't exactly my career. I reached by the side of the chair and lifted my laptop up onto my lap. I needed to find another marketing job, only one that didn't bore the pants off me like my last one did. I pulled up the available positions listed with one of the recruiters I'd registered with and scrolled through the roles. Email Marketing Assistant? *Bleh.* Email Marketing Manager? *Bleh bleh.* Marketing Analyst? I snapped my laptop shut. Although I knew I'd need to start applying for some jobs soon, I couldn't get my fingers to click on the job descriptions. It all felt so . . . well, *bleh*.

What was I going to do? I needed to find another job soon. Just, I had no idea what I actually wanted to do with my life anymore.

As if by some cosmic coincidence, my current "boss"—although she was about as far from Portia's overmanaging, overcontrolling, over-everything-ness as any one person could be—Bailey's name flashed on my screen.

"Paige, I need your help." She sounded stressed. "Do you think you could do some more shifts at the café? I'm in a bit of a staff pickle."

The thought of spending more time at the Cozy Cottage was a pleasant one. I enjoyed the food prep, working with Bailey, and feeling part of something worthwhile. It was busy, never a dull moment for someone who'd spent the last few months in a veritable haze of boredom. Plus, there was the chance to see Marcus again while Bailey and Marissa vetted him for our big date.

"Of course. When do you need me?"

"You are a life saver, Paige. I cannot tell you."

We agreed I would come in to work several days over the coming week while Bailey kept looking for a more permanent replacement. She told me getting quality staff who stuck around was the hardest thing about running a café. I was happy to help out while I tried to work out what to do with my life.

I slid my laptop back down against the chair and returned my attention to the TV. The sobbing cook now looked inconsolable, as her partner stared grimly at the camera, predicting certain doom.

"They're for the chop," Dad pronounced.

My phone rang again, and I flipped it over to look at the screen. My heart leapt into my mouth. It was Marcus. In a moment of positive visualization, I had saved his contact name as "My Last First Date." When it flashed on my screen, I jumped up, clean out of my seat, and rushed from the room. Dad probably thought my pants had caught fire or something.

I raced up the stairs, taking them two at a time, and into my bedroom, where I tried to steady myself before pressing "answer."

"Hello?" I breathed, still catching my breath.

"Hi, is that Paige?" Marcus asked at the other end.

"Yes, it is." I was pretending I had no idea who he was and I got calls from hot men all the time. Which, sadly, was about as far from the truth as I could get.

"It's Marcus here, from the café."

"Hi there, Marcus from the café." I tried to find the right balance between being happy to hear from him and desperation. It was a surprisingly fine line.

"How are those dishes? Any abuse you need to report to me?" he teased.

"Yes, I have to admit there have been some goings on. Nothing too sinister, but I did notice someone let their dog lick a plate clean yesterday. Does that constitute abuse?"

"No, that constitutes gross."

I let out a laugh. With all my pent-up adrenaline, it came out in a gush and I launched straight into a coughing fit, having to put my hand over the receiver. Once I'd finally recovered my equilibrium, I spluttered, "Sorry about that. My gin and tonic must have gone down the wrong way."

"A G&T, huh? Classy."

"That's just the way I roll." Actually, I'd been drinking a post-pot roast cup of tea with Dad in front of *MasterChef*, but Marcus didn't need to know that.

We flirted and messed about, and I have to say, I loved every moment of it. If my cell phone had one of those long, curly cables, like you see in old movies, I'd have been winding it around my finger as I giggled and flirted my ass off with him. I'd been hurt when Will had chosen Cassie over me, but meeting someone new, with all the possibility of him, had mended my broken heart well and truly.

Why had I ever decided to give up on love?

"Hey, so I was wondering, I get off dish inspection some evenings. Want to go out?"

I punched the air, pressing my lips together so I didn't squeal. I wanted to scream "Yes, yes, a thousand gazillion times yes!" but I couldn't. My hands were tied. Until Marissa and Bailey had finished their vetting and set us up together, I couldn't go out on a date with Marcus. Until then, I had to put him off without completely putting him off, if you know what I mean.

I closed my eyes and beamed. "I would love that." I held my breath.

"Awesome. How's Friday night for you?"

"This Friday? Let me think. Oh, yeah, I have a thing. Sorry."

"Sure." Did I detect a note of disappointment in his voice?

"But I would really love to go out with you another time," I gushed.

"Yeah, me too."

I pictured him smiling into his phone, thinking about me. Maybe he was in a pair of shorts and a T-shirt, lounging on a recliner by his pool, the evening sun low in the sky, casting a warm glow over his beautiful olive skin. Maybe he was even shirtless on the recliner by the pool. *Mm, shirtless Marcus.* I sighed. I had no idea whether he even had a recliner, let alone a pool, but it was my fantasy and I was running with it.

"When can I see you, then?"

"Can I get back to you? I've got some things going on right now." Like having you vetted by my super-sleuth spy-friends. "Is that okay?"

"Sure. I'll hold you to it. Perhaps I'll see you at that café of yours again."

I hung up and lay back on my bed. I couldn't have wiped the grin off my face if I'd been offered a million bucks. Someday soon, I was going to go on my Last First Date with the swoon-worthy Marcus Hahn. I could barely believe my luck.

* * *

I WAS PULLING a tray full of cheese, bacon, and chive muffins out of the large oven the following morning when Josh arrived, his usual box of beans held out in front of him.

"Morning, Paige," he said brightly as I opened the door to let him in.

"Hey, Josh. Gorgeous day." It was one of those crisp, clear early-fall days we get in Auckland, a time of the year when the humidity is mercifully low and the days begin to shorten as we hurtle toward winter.

He brushed past me and into the storage area where he deposited his box of beans. "Yeah. I was out for a run this morning on the beach. It was stunning out there."

"Oh. I didn't know you were a runner?" Actually, I didn't know anything about him at all, other than the fact he delivered the coffee beans and liked Bailey's Mexican chicken tortilla soup.

He walked back into the kitchen. "Mm. They smell good."

"They do, don't they? I'd sneak you one, but I might get in trouble with the boss."

He grinned at me, and I was struck by how unexpectedly cute he looked. Huh, I'd never noticed.

"With Bailey? Nah, she's a total pussycat." He reached down and picked a muffin up out of the tray, immediately dropping it. "Ow! That's hot."

I laughed. "Serves you right, trying to steal one." I glanced down at his T-shirt. I cocked an eyebrow as I read it. "'It's a brew-tiful day'? Seriously?"

He shrugged. "What's wrong with 'It's a brew-tiful day'? It is, we just agreed."

"Isn't it a little cheesy?"

"Paige, it's cheesier than a Frenchman's fridge, but I'm okay with it."

I chortled. "If you say so."

"Hey, what about you? Do you run?"

"I have been known to in the deep, distant past, yes. Plus, I've kind of agreed to do this run with a couple of my friends. Something to do with color?"

"Oh, The Color Run. That's awesome fun."

Running was hard enough without people throwing powdered

colors in your face, in my opinion. "Well, I've put on a bit of weight lately, so I need to try and run it off, but my friends train after work and I'm totally spent by then."

His eyes scanned my body. It felt . . . unusual.

"I don't see why. You look great to me." He smiled and something tingled in my chest. "But exercising is great for you, as we all know. Do you want to come on a run with me tomorrow? I head out early, but then I guess you start pretty early anyway."

I took in his tall, lean, runner's build. "I'm not sure I'm fit enough to keep up with you." Scratch that: I was *certain* I wasn't fit enough to keep up with him.

He leaned against the kitchen counter. "Ah, come on. I don't go that fast, and you need to train, right?" I nodded reluctantly. "I'll tell you what, if you hate it, you don't have to come out with me again."

As if my body was trying to send me a message, I became suddenly aware of how tight the band on my vintage bell-bottom jeans felt across my hips.

I shrugged. "Sure. It can't hurt." Plus, I wanted to look the best I could for my impending date with Marcus.

Josh pushed himself off from the counter and pulled his phone out from the back pocket of his jeans. "Cool. What's your number?"

I gave it to him, and he grinned at me before turning to leave. "I'll text you. Well, gotta go. These beans won't deliver themselves, you know. Even though, that would be funny to see little marching beans, walking in a line." He smiled at me. "What? Nothing?"

I shook my head, laughing lightly. It was a weak joke. Before he disappeared out the back door, I called, "Josh? Catch."

He turned, just in time, to catch the warm, airborne cheese, bacon, and chive muffin I'd launched at him. As quick as the Flash himself, he caught it, shooting me a grin as he disappeared out the door.

"Was that Josh?" Bailey breezed into the kitchen a second later.

"Yep. Delivering the beans."

"Dammit. I needed to talk to him."

"What about? I'm seeing him tomorrow. I could mention it, if you like."

She raised her eyebrows at me. "You're seeing him tomorrow, are you?"

I brushed her insinuation away with my hand. "It's nothing. He invited me on a run, that's all. I'm training for The Color Run, remember?"

She nodded and smiled at me. "Sounds fun. Now, if you can get those muffins out, we're almost ready to open up."

And so the day went with the breakfast crowd first up, with their bacon and egg paninis and smashed avocado and tomatoes on toast, followed by the pre-work takeout coffees, through to the morning coffee and cake gang.

And there were a lot of customers with coffee coupons. Each time someone handed one over to me, I felt a little surge of pride. With Bailey's permission—and pocketbook—I'd promoted the offer on Facebook, and by day two, the Cozy Cottage page had received over a thousand likes and even a handful of positive reviews—and only one of them was from me. People had been liking our website, and I'd been posting photos of the gorgeous cakes and muffins on Instagram.

In a quiet moment, I collected the growing pile of coupons and waved them in the air in front of Bailey in the kitchen. "Check these babies out."

"Wow." She took them from me, and I watched as she did a rough count. "That's a lot of free coffee. I think I'm happy about this."

"Sometimes you've got to give a little to get a lot. I bet you my week's wages at least half of the customers who brought those in will return soon. Plus, I've been up-selling them on the food. We may need to bake considerably more if this keeps up."

Bailey's face broke into a smile. "It's a brave new world, that's for sure. I'm going to run the numbers tonight, so we can gauge how we're doing."

"Do you need a hand with that?" I offered. I'd dealt with a fair few spreadsheets in my time.

"No, I'll be fine. Josh has set something up for me. If you get a panicked text late tonight, you'll know things didn't go well."

Josh again? He sure did like helping Bailey out. *Huh.* Perhaps he was in love with her? That could explain a lot.

I returned to the counter, working alongside Sophie, one of the café's baristas, collecting more coupons and handing out a lot of coffees and snacks. At about half past ten, Cassie and Marissa turned up for their usuals and I was only able to grab about three seconds with them, catching up on their news.

"Oh, but he's so cute!" Marissa declared as I placed her orange and almond syrup cake and latte in front of her.

"Who is?" I asked.

"Oh, just this guy who's joined the team," Cassie explained. "Marissa thinks he looks like that guy who played Superman, but I don't see it."

I put Cassie's raspberry chocolate cake and coffee in front of her, tucking the tray under my arm.

"Henry Cavill. And he does," Marissa said dreamily. She sighed. "I think I'm going to start the vetting process on him."

I sucked in air. We all knew what "the vetting process" meant: Marissa was planning to go on her One Last First Date with this Superman look-a-like. "You are?"

She nodded, looking serious and excited in equal measure. "I am."

I glanced at Cassie with wide eyes. She shot me a knowing look. You see, the thing was, Marissa was legendary in her fussiness over men. She would start out all gung ho and ready to see the best in a guy, and then he would do or say something or she'd notice something about him that she didn't like and *wham!* she would drop him without a moment's hesitation. The guy would be left stunned and bewildered, wondering what on earth had just happened.

I kind of felt sorry for the guys.

I glanced around the café. Noting Sophie was coping just fine with the few customers left at the counter, I pulled out a chair and sat down at their table. "Oh, my god," I said, looking from Marissa to Cassie.

Marissa nodded. "I know. So far, he's looking pretty good."

"So far?" Cassie asked.

"Mmm-hmm. I kind of already started vetting him."

My eyes bulged. "You're totally serious about this one."

"Yup."

"Well, that's so exciting." I could barely believe Marissa was planning on making this guy her One Last First Date. This was big. Huge!

I turned to Cassie. "What do you think of him?"

She shrugged. "He seems like a good guy. I mean, I employed him, so I know he's not a slippery character or anything."

"A 'slippery character'? What are we, in some kind of gangster movie from the fifties?" Marissa said with a laugh.

"Yeah, tell Pistol Pete and Scarface the guy's okay," I said with a sneer in my best Chicago accent, although I was pretty sure Francis Ford Coppola wouldn't be hiring me anytime soon.

"Can you tell me some things about him? I mean, you know a lot more than I do already," Marissa asked Cassie.

Cassie shook her head. "Sorry, but no. I have to keep the personal information he gave me as part of the interview process confidential."

"Why do you have to be so ethical?" Marissa complained. "I guess I'll have to do it the old-fashioned way."

"Stalk him?" I offered.

"Exactly," Marissa replied with a grin. "It's going to be fun."

I glanced over at the growing line of customers at the counter. Sophie looked like she needed my help. I stood up to leave. "Eat your cakes, ladies. They're extra good today, I promise. And I want to hear all about him, okay?"

Marissa nodded, biting her lip. "Okay."

I reached the counter and immediately started helping Sophie serve more customers. This was one of our busy times at the café, and Sophie, Bailey, and I were flat out.

I'd had my head down so much, I hadn't noticed Bailey chatting to a tall man in a navy suit by the café door. He had his back to me, but I could tell from their body language they were involved in a serious conversation.

I continued to serve a customer, who wanted a chocolate chip muffin and a pot of tea—tea I could manage, whereas coffee was still a whole other country to me—and when she left to sit at a table, I caught sight of the man as he turned to leave. He looked directly at me, and I could feel my cheeks instantly heat up. *Marcus.* My tummy flip-flopped at the sight of him. He grinned at me and I smiled back, hoping he would come over and flirt with me some more, despite the fact it was hectic in the café right now. But instead, he turned back to Bailey, said something to her, and disappeared out the door.

My chest deflated. Why didn't he come over to talk to me? I chewed the inside of my lip as I poured the hot water into the tea pot. And then I knew. Bailey must have started the vetting process! She was asking him questions, taking mental notes. Hope rose inside me.

When Bailey returned to the counter, I asked, "Did you have a good chat?"

She looked at me blankly.

"With that guy I saw you with. Marcus Something-or-other?" As if I didn't have his name emblazoned on my brain: Marcus Hahn. I willed the blush in my cheeks to dissipate.

"Oh, yes. It was really useful." She turned her attention to the food in the cabinet.

Useful? I smiled to myself. She must be making progress. I tried to make my voice as nonchalant as possible. "Oh, that's good." Inside, I went all Michael Flatley in *Riverdance.*

The café had begun to empty out, the relative quiet before the lunchtime storm, and Bailey, Sophie, and I were working to get everything ready. I was torn between asking about Bailey's conversation with Marcus and pretending I had no idea who she had lined up as my Last First Date.

"Can you please move the remainder of that cake along so we can make room for the paninis?" she asked as she headed to the kitchen.

"Sure." I did as she asked, and then followed her. "Bailey?" I asked, my voice light

"Mm?" She was studying a sheet of paper, ticking items off as she ran her finger down the margin.

I was suddenly nervous. "How's the . . . ah . . . research going?"

She put her finger in the air, her head still down. Eventually, after I stood there, waiting for some time, a nervous wreck, she raised her head and looked up at me. "Sorry, what?"

I played with the frill on my apron. "I was just wondering how things were going with you and Marissa, ah, finding me my Last First Date."

"It's going well." Her face broke into a smile. "In fact, he was here today."

"He was?" I tried my best to seem surprised and only mildly interested. I hoped it worked. Inside, Michael Flatley was at it again.

"Yes, but I'm not going to say anything further. Only that the more I learn about him, the more I'm convinced he's so the right guy for you. I think you're going to be very happy."

I beamed. Bailey was right; I was going to be very happy, very happy indeed.

CHAPTER 10

$\mathcal{T}$HE FOLLOWING MORNING, BEFORE the sun had woken up and had its first coffee of the day, I met Josh at The Domain, a beautiful green and leafy park in central Auckland. The air had a distinctive chill, which suited me just fine—it meant I could throw on a loose-fitting sweatshirt over my straining sports clothes. Oh, yes, it was more than time I got myself back on the exercise wagon. Either that or give up my cake habit, and there are some things in this life a woman just wasn't prepared to do, especially if she worked at the Cozy Cottage Café.

"Morning, sunshine." Josh greeted me with a grin, far too chipper for this early hour.

I took in his long, lean physique, his runner's legs, his formfitting T-shirt and shorts. He was the consummate runner and I had to admit, he looked good. Not in Marcus's league of course, but not too shabby for the coffee delivery guy and my self-appointed exercise buddy.

"What? No cringe-worthy coffee slogans this morning?" I asked, nodding at his Nike T-shirt.

"You can overdo a good thing, you know." He winked at me. "You ready for this?"

I shrugged. "No!" was the honest answer, although I wasn't about to tell that to Mr. Supreme Athlete Josh. "Sure. Why not?"

"We can take it slow." He flashed me a cheeky grin, and I wondered why.

"Yes, I'd like it if we—" I began, only to stop and stare in bafflement as he raced away from me, into The Domain. Cheeky grin explained, I yelled "You cheater!" at the top of my voice as I watched him, my mouth dropping open in disbelief, as he became smaller and smaller the farther away he got.

He wasn't turning back. Without another thought, I sprang into action, chasing after him, running with all my might to catch him up. At first it felt good, stretching my legs, moving at speed, hoping to gain on him. Then, the pain began to set in. My lungs began to burn, my heart pounded heavily in my chest, and my legs screamed all sorts of expletives at me, questioning why I was putting them through this torture when they could be curled up in bed instead.

Finally, after sprinting up a hill with what could only be bionic strength, he stopped and turned to watch me, bouncing from one foot to the other. "Come on, Paige! You can do it!" he encouraged.

I eyed the hill. It wasn't too big, but with my body yelling abuse at me, it felt insurmountable.

"Come on! Get your ass up here!" Josh yelled as a slim, fit woman glided past me and up the hill, making me feel even more like an out of shape muffin. *Ooh, muffins.* No, I had to concentrate. I couldn't let this guy get the better of me. I glared at him and summoned every last bit of strength. I forced myself to run as fast as I could up that hill. I must have looked like I had one of those vertical bungee cords strapped to me, because no matter how hard I ran, I still felt like I was moving no faster than a sloth with a hangover.

Finally, after a Herculean effort, I arrived at Josh's side. I shot him a death stare before I leaned down, my hands on my knees, gasping for breath, trying my best to resist the almost overwhelming urge to vomit. "What did . . . you . . . do . . . that for?" I panted, looking up at him accusingly.

"I just wanted to know what I'm dealing with here. And now I know."

I stood back up, wiped the sweat away from my eyes, and tried to catch my breath.

"You said you needed to train for The Color Run, and I would say you've got your work cut out."

Finally catching my breath, I replied, "I know . . . but there's something to be said for starting slow." My breathing finally began to return to normal. "Do you always run that fast?" I had decided there and then never to repeat this experience with him, despite my need to train for the run.

He nodded, smiling at me. "I guess. I don't have all that much time in the mornings, so I like to go short and sharp."

I scrunched up my face. "Short sounds good, but maybe not the sharp part."

He let out an easy laugh. He was enjoying my pain and humiliation. "Come on. It's downhill for a while, then we'll run on the flat through Newmarket for a bit. Okay? I promise to go easier on you from now on."

The downhill I could get on board with, but the running through streets I usually spent my time at shopping and brunching sounded less appealing.

Josh must have sensed my hesitation, adding, "I won't go as fast this time. Scout's honor." He saluted with two fingers and looked so funny, I let out a laugh.

"Sure. But only if we run together at a reasonable pace, okay?"

"Agreed."

We took off down the hill, side by side. Josh bounded along with his long, gazelle-like legs, looking effortless and talking away. I, on the other hand, could only manage grunts and two-word sentences I could get out in one breath. By the time we'd run past my favorite fashion stores, my nail bar, and the spa I had a facial at a couple of weeks ago, we reached our starting spot. I was filled with relief and completely drenched in sweat.

"Great job, Paige," Josh said as we came to a stop by a park bench. He held onto the back and began to stretch out his quad muscles.

I wanted to follow suit, but my legs were so wobbly I didn't trust myself not to fall to the ground in a large blob of exhaustion. Instead, I sat down heavily on the bench and let out a long puff of air, thankful the torture was finally over.

Josh finished up his stretches and joined me on the bench. "You're fitter than you think, you know."

I looked at him in surprise. "You almost killed me back there. I nearly puked all over your shoes." Part of me wished I had.

He chuckled. "Well, I'm very pleased you didn't. These shoes cost me a lot of money."

We both looked down at his shoes.

"Do you run every day?" I asked.

"Most days. I like to get a cycle or a sail in, too, usually on the weekends when work isn't so busy."

I thought of him darting around town with his boxes of beans. This city has a serious caffeine addiction, and there are a lot of cafés out there. Now that I knew the Ned's Coffee brand, I had begun to see it everywhere, even in the supermarket. Josh must be one busy delivery guy.

"Are you still working at the Cozy Cottage?"

I couldn't help but smile. "Yeah, I am. It's pretty cool. I'm doing some design work for Bailey right now, helping her out with the website and things."

"That's awesome!" He seemed genuinely impressed. "That's what you were doing with the camera the other day, right?" I nodded. "I'd love to see it. Hey, you should add some Ned's info on there, too. People like to see what sort of coffee a café serves. There are some total coffee snobs out there, you know?"

I raised my eyebrows at him. "Is this the pot calling the kettle black, by any chance?"

He chuckled. "Maybe. I'll get something to you." He pulled his phone out of his armband. "What's your email address?"

I gave it to him, and he promised to forward some information to me later in the day.

"So, tomorrow. Same bat time, same bat channel?"

Now that my heart was no longer threatening to burst out of my chest and my lungs no longer felt like someone had set them on fire, going on another run tomorrow didn't feel like such a dreadful idea. After the initial torture, running with Josh had been fun. Well, almost fun. Eating cake would still beat it, hands down.

I smiled at him. "I'd like that, on one condition."

"What's that?"

"You don't ever trick me into sprinting to catch up with you again."

He laughed. "I promise. But you did it, didn't you?"

He had a point. I had done it, and I felt good about myself because of it. Perhaps for the first time in quite a long time.

* * *

My body was screaming at me when I delivered coffee and cake to Cassie and Marissa at their usual table, grabbing the chance to chat with my two friends while there was an unexpected lull.

"I hear you're doing The Color Run with us. That is so cool," Cassie said.

"Well, I'm going to give it a shot," I replied, my thighs burning as I crouched to place the order on the table in a dip a sixties Playboy bunny would have been proud of. I'd been getting progressively stiffer as the morning had gone on, but it couldn't dent the sense of achievement I'd had doing the run.

Cassie smiled at me. "You'll do great." She glanced around the café. "Why don't you sit down with us for a bit? There's no one here right now."

I looked around the café. Bailey was doing an inventory check out back, Jacob, one of the baristas, was organizing things behind the counter, and there were no customers waiting to be served. "It'll be like old times," I said with a smile as I pulled out a chair and gingerly lowered myself down on it.

"Exactly. The three amigos," Cassie replied.

Marissa let out a laugh. "The 'three amigos'? Really?"

"Well, I could have said the three caffeine- and sugar-addicted

95

princesses, but amigos seemed better."

"I don't know. I like the idea of being a princess," Marissa said, a whimsical look on her face.

Cassie smiled at her, shaking her head. Turning to me, she said, "I'm really happy to see you're getting out there and doing something new."

"Yeah, me too," Marissa added, nodding.

I studied my friend's faces. "I get out and do things," I retorted defensively.

"Well, you used to," Marissa replied carefully. She darted a look at Cassie across the table.

Like some kind of orchestrated tag-team, Cassie picked up the gauntlet. "Marissa's right. You haven't been your usual self for a while. We've been worried about you."

If I'd known I was going to get the concerned-parents talk, I would have stayed safely tucked away behind the counter. "There's nothing to worry about. I'm fine."

My friends shared another look.

"We know you've had some things going on." Marissa glanced at Cassie and cleared her throat.

We all knew the elephant in the room was Cassie's boyfriend, Will. What my friends didn't know was I had moved on: to one Marcus Hahn. My tummy did a little flip at the thought.

I shrugged. "I'm okay now." When neither of them appeared to accept it, I added, "Really. I am. I know I was . . . knocked back with the whole thing, but I'm good now." I could feel my face heating up.

"It's more than just that, although it's really great to hear you're okay with . . . *that*, now. But you did walk out on your job with nothing else to go to," Cassie said.

I bit my lip, my tummy sinking at the sorry state of my career. "I've started looking for something else already."

"That's so great!" Cassie declared.

I thought of my total lack of interest in applying for any of the jobs I'd seen advertised. I knew I needed to get on with it and start applying, but I lacked the drive to do it. Every time I read about a job that could be right for my skills, I'd get a strange feeling in my chest, weighing me down. Then, I'd snap my laptop shut and think about something else.

I pasted on a smile. "Yeah, it is. And for now, working here is great."

Marissa pulled a face. "But it's not a real job, is it? It's just a stop-gap, while you look for something else."

She sounded so certain, I nodded along. I knew I didn't see being a waitress as my career exactly, but I did love being here: working with Bailey, preparing the food, serving the customers, feeling a part of something. I knew I'd have to pull myself together and get back to the real world at some stage, but right now I was more than happy with how I spent my days.

Not that I expected my two career-minded friends to understand.

"It's all in hand. I'm registered with recruiters and am actively looking. Watch this space!" I added with a smile.

They both appeared satisfied with my response and moved on to Marissa's potential One Last First Date, much to my relief.

"So, you're saying after stalking him, he's not the guy for you?" Cassie asked.

"Look, I found out he's not quite the guy I thought he was," Marissa said with a deep sigh. "So, it's back to the drawing board for me."

"Is this the Henry Cavill look-a-like?" I asked, and Marissa and Cassie nodded. "What was wrong with this one, then?" I couldn't help a wry smile spread across my face.

"Don't say. Let us guess," Cassie said, her hands in the "stop" sign. "His nose was too big?"

"No, I know what! He had a less than good-looking mother and you got worried your kids would be ugly," I offered with a cheeky grin.

"Oh, no. I've got it! He has those dark hairs that curl over his shirt cuffs. Which he does, incidentally." Cassie nodded at me.

"Thanks, guys. I'm not *that* picky, you know," Marissa huffed, crossing her arms.

Cassie and I shared a look and laughed. She *was* that picky, and then some.

"Sure, you're not," I said.

"Who said you were?" Cassie added, her eyebrows raised.

Marissa tucked her hair behind her ears. "He just wasn't right. And it has to be perfect, you know?"

My mind instantly darted to Marcus. He was perfect. Well, as close to perfect as a guy could get.

"Paige?"

I looked up to see Bailey gesturing me back to the counter where a couple of customers were peering in the cabinets, deciding which of Bailey's delicious treats to indulge in.

I pushed my chair out from the table and stood up. "Duty calls. I'll leave you to it."

"Let us know what happens on the job front, won't you?" Cassie said, smiling up at me.

"I sure will!" I said, possibly overdoing the enthusiasm.

Cassie shot me a quizzical look before I turned and walked back to the waiting customers, pushing the uncomfortable topic of my career out of my head. I'd deal with it later. And anyway, something just right for me was sure to pop up. What was that expression? "Good things come to those who wait." That was it; I simply needed to be patient, like I was being with Marcus.

After filling the customers' orders, Jacob left to run some errands for Bailey and I leaned up against the kitchen doorframe and waited while she did some work on her laptop. She looked up at me with a furrowed brow.

"How are you with numbers?" she asked.

I shrugged, pushing myself off the frame and walking over to her. "Not bad. What are you trying to do?" I peered at a complicated, multicolored spreadsheet on her screen.

"See this here?" She pointed at one of the columns. "It's meant to show my weekly food profit minus spend and staff pay, but it's not calculating anything. I feel like tearing my hair out!"

"Here, let me have a look." I moved the screen so I could see it more clearly and checked the cells. "It's the formula. It's calculated based on an empty cell here." I pointed to the screen. "Is there something that's meant to be in here?"

"That's weird. I don't think so."

"Okay. What I'll do is delete that part of the formula and we'll see how it looks." As I did so, the column changed in an instant, with numbers listed in long, neat rows.

"Wow, that's so great. Look, it all makes sense. Paige, you are a genius."

I shrugged, enjoying the feeling of being needed. "Hardly." I laughed. "Did you set this spreadsheet up?"

"No, Josh did."

I raised my eyebrows. "Josh, as in Josh the guy who delivers the coffee?"

"The one and only. He's good with this sort of thing."

I crinkled my forehead. "Why would a delivery guy be good at spreadsheeting?"

Bailey shot me a look I couldn't read. "Oh, Josh is—"

"Hey, you two," a voice said, interrupting Bailey mid-sentence. We looked up and saw Marissa leaning over the counter. "You've got customers out here."

Bailey leaped up from her seat. "Sorry. We were lost in numbers, weren't we, Paige?"

"I've got this. You do your work," I said to her. I took three short strides over toward the counter. "Thanks, Marissa."

"No problem. And Bailey? I've got some info for you on you-know-what." Marissa raised her eyebrows at me meaningfully.

My belly flip-flopped. I knew exactly what "you-know-what" was. I hoped they'd be through the vetting process soon and he would come out smelling of roses.

"I think you're going to love this guy, Paige," she added.

"Well, that is the general idea," Bailey said with a laugh.

My smile almost reached my ears, it was so wide. It was almost time, and I couldn't wait for them to finally send me on my Last First Date with Marcus.

CHAPTER 11

I DIDN'T HAVE TO wait until Bailey and Marissa gave me their Last First Date blessing to see Marcus again. I had said goodbye to Bailey at the end of my shift, leaving her sitting at one of the tables, working on her spreadsheets.

"What are you up to now?" she asked, looking up from her laptop at me.

I shrugged. "Heading home, I guess. It's my night to cook for Dad and me." An exciting evening of steamed fish and reality TV lay ahead.

Bailey's face creased into a grin. "Well, whatever you end up doing, I hope it's fun."

I shot her a quizzical look. "You too."

No sooner had I closed the café door behind myself than I spotted Marcus, leaning against the wall of the next building. He was studying his phone but looked up with the bang of the café door, his face breaking into a grin when he spotted me.

Excitement at the sight of him, standing there in his Channing Tatum yumminess, pinged around my body. "Hi, Marcus," I breathed, as he pushed himself off the wall and sauntered over to me.

"Good afternoon, gorgeous waitress who refuses to go out with me."

I smiled through my growing blush, pleased I was wearing my fifties-inspired dress with the nipped-in waist and a bucketload of *va-va-voom*. How could I explain we needed to wait just a little longer until we could be together?

"I . . ." I opened and closed my mouth like a fish. I couldn't think of a single word to say in response. He was right; I had refused to go out with him, but only because I had to. Should I say, "Oh, I have to wait for my friends to give you the seal of approval first"? It sounded so very elementary school to me, and I could only imagine how ridiculous it would sound to a grown man.

To my relief, he winked at me and reached for my hand. "I'm just teasing you. You're an easy wind-up, did you know that?"

We walked slowly along the sidewalk together. I loved the feel of his hand in mine. It was warm, big and strong. My hand felt dainty and feminine in contrast. It was . . . perfect.

"I've been told that." I smiled, looking up into his eyes. "What are you doing here, anyway?"

He stopped, turned, and looked at me. "Bailey said you finished now. I thought we could grab a coffee together."

I smiled up at him. "I'd like that." He was so good-looking and his hand was so right in mine, I was at serious risk of swooning right there on the street.

He slipped his arm casually around my waist, and we began walking once more. "Good. It can be our first date."

I stopped in my tracks. Our first date? Our *Last* First Date? My mind began to whirr faster and faster until it hit overdrive. Marcus had spoken to Bailey, and now we were going on a date? Could this really be happening?

"Our . . . what?" I asked, almost breathless.

"Our first date." He crinkled his forehead. "Are you okay? You've gone kind of pale. Is the idea of going out with me that hideous?"

"No, this is . . . great. So, you said you talked with Bailey?"

He nodded, looking suddenly uncertain. "Yes."

"And she was okay with this?"

He narrowed his gaze. "With us going for a cup of coffee together?"

I nodded, biting my lip, my hands clenched at my sides in anticipation.

He shrugged, smiling. "Yes."

A potent concoction of relief and exhilaration flooded through me. So, this was my Last First Date! This was momentous! I was about to go out for coffee with the guy my friends had approved as my future husband. *Marcus* was my future husband. My life flashed before my eyes. I wondered how long we would date before he proposed, what our wedding would be like, where we'd live, how many children we'd have.

He squeezed me, bringing me back to earth. "What do you say?"

I beamed at him. "I say, let's do this. Let's go on our first date."

I pulled my phone out of my purse and texted a "thank you!" to Bailey. She responded a few seconds with "you're welcome," and I slid my phone back in my purse, smiling to myself.

And oh, the date with Marcus was wonderful. We went to a café a couple of blocks away—not my cup of tea, all chrome and glass and self-satisfied baristas with ironic beards—ordered coffee and sat talking and laughing and flirting for the rest of the afternoon.

And it felt so good, so *right*. I could hardly believe my luck; my friends had chosen me the perfect guy, and I was like a pig in a large sty of mud.

The coffee turned into a walk along the waterfront, and then into an early dinner at an Ethiopian restaurant Marcus recommended. Although I'd eaten food from around the world, I'd never had Ethiopian food before and was impressed with Marcus's taste and sophistication.

"What did you do before you worked at the Cozy Cottage?" he asked, holding my hand atop the table, what must be Ethiopian music playing in the background. We were sitting so close together, there was no room for uncertainty.

"I used to work at AGD, the telecommunications company."

Confusion crossed his Hollywood handsome face. "Pouring coffee?"

I let out an easy laugh. "No, silly. I'm just helping Bailey out for now, until I find another job. I was in Marketing for years."

He raised his eyebrows, clearly impressed. "Marketing, huh? Nice. I know someone at AGD. I bet you were great at your job, too."

I thought of how I used to turn up late to work, count the hours until the end of the day, of the way in which Helena and I would spend most of our time complaining about Princess Portia. "Absolutely." I crossed my fingers under the table to counter the fib. Although I didn't want to start my relationship with Marcus off on a lie, he didn't need to know I'd hardly been the employee of the year.

"What are your next steps? Got anything lined up?"

"I have a few things on the boil." I smiled at him, hoping my eyes didn't give me away. It was true, I had looked online at the job openings a couple more times over the last few days but still hadn't seen anything that had come close to rousing my interest. It all still seemed so ho-hum, so uninspiring, so *bleh*.

"I can see it now: Auckland's newest power couple. Only you'll have to start wearing large shoulder pads and I'll have to give up on the socks, maybe don a ten-gallon hat."

"You've watched *Dallas*?" I asked, incredulous. Dad used to watch it when he was young, and he subjected me to DVD box sets of the show when I was a teenager. Although it was too cheesy for words, with everyone sleeping together or plotting one another's demise, it was thoroughly addictive, right down to the big hair, big hats, and over-sized earrings.

He laughed. "You too? We must have similarly minded parents or something. My mom is a bit older, thanks to me being the youngest of five kids, and she was addicted to it. She wore an 'I shot J.R.' badge years after it was a thing."

"I would *love* one of those!"

He smiled, playing with my fingers. "I'll get you one."

As I gazed into his eyes, my chest tightened. This was going well, *so* well. Bailey and Marissa had done good.

The waiter delivered our food, and we thanked him. Marcus had ordered for me, promising I would love the dishes he chose.

"This smells amazing," I declared as I took in the aroma from the large platter in front of me. Not realizing how ravenous I was until the aroma hit me, my tummy rumbled loudly.

"Someone's hungry."

My cheeks heated up. "Sorry." I cleared my throat. Pointing at the platter, I asked, "What is that, some sort of pancake?"

He chuckled. "That's called an 'injera.' It's made out of sourdough, I think. It's really good."

"Okay." I liked most food, and this looked and smelled delicious. I was game for anything. I searched for the silverware on the table. Finding none, I said, "I think they forgot our utensils."

"No, you eat with your hands. Well, your right hand, the other one's used for . . . bathroom activities."

Getting his inference and not wanting to detract in any way from the romance of the date, I nodded, eying the mounds of different-colored mush on the oversized pancake, or "injera."

"Bon appétit," I said.

"Shouldn't you say something in Ethiopian?" Marcus asked.

"Umm, I don't know any."

"Let's ask the waiter." Marcus called the waiter over and asked him for the correct expression.

"The language of my country is Amharic. You could say 'bemigibu tedeseti,'" he replied.

We both tried the expression out, me a fraction more successful than Marcus, but we both failed miserably. We chuckled, grinning at one another. *Swoon.*

"I don't think either of us will be invited to the United Nations any time soon," Marcus said quietly after the waiter had gone.

"Well, I'm not sure they have much call for temporary waitresses there."

"No, you're a marketer between jobs," he corrected me.

"So, do we just grab some?" I asked, eying the meal.

"Watch." Marcus tore a piece of the "injera" off, scooped some of the vegetable dish up in it, and placed it in his mouth. He grinned at me. "Delicious."

I smiled back and followed suit, ripping a piece off and collecting some vegetables up inside the fold. I took a bite. The pancake was warm and soft and the vegetables tasty and fresh. "Yum."

"This one is a goat 'wat,'" he said, pointing at the meat stew. "Last time I was here the meat was so tender, it almost melted in my mouth. You should try it."

I nodded, an image of a dissolving goat leaping into my head. I scooped some of the goat "wat" up with another piece of the "injera." I slipped it into my mouth. It was a flavor explosion with multiple herbs and spices. I smiled at him, nodding my appreciation.

And then it began. It was a gentle heat at first, but then began to build and build with every chew. I could handle this. After all, I'd eaten a fair share of vindaloos in my time. Well, okay, I'd had one once and nearly died from the heat, but the point is I'd had one before. This? No biggie.

I sat there, my mouth burning, my lips turning to rubber, as the heat crept into my cheeks and up my face. Even my nostrils felt like they were on fire as little beads of sweat began to form on my upper lip.

"Are you all right?" Marcus asked, concerned, as my eyes began to water.

"Mm-hm." I nodded at him, hoping to look perfectly composed, despite the fact my cheeks were full of the fiery goat stew.

I willed myself to finish chewing so I could swallow and get this agony over with. Though I knew simply swallowing wouldn't end the pain, of course. Oh, no. This date had been going far too well for that.

"Do you need something? You've gone a little . . . pink," Marcus said.

I nodded furiously as I willed myself to swallow that melting goat before it had the chance to melt me. Finally, I swallowed. But, it got caught. *Oh, god!*

You know that moment when you know you're about to choke? It's almost like everything goes into slow motion until your breath runs out and you need to take a new one, but your windpipe is blocked, so you put off the inevitable? Well, with that piece of fiery goat in my throat, I knew I was about to turn purple and sound like a bad imitation of Darth Vadar in an asthma attack.

Only, I didn't think I could breathe *at all*. My eyes darted around the room. I needed to find the Ladies so I could cough my lungs up away from my date, and fast! I pushed back my chair and leapt up.

"Are you all right?" Marcus's eyes looked like they could pop out of their sockets.

Too late, I knew there was no way I could make it to the Ladies. My lungs felt like they were going to explode. I needed to breathe! I gasped for air, clutching my throat, tears streaming down my face. Marcus was out of his chair, patting me forcefully on the back. My hands on my knees, I struggled to breathe as panic spread across my chest, tightening its grip on me.

I'm going to die! I'm going to die on my Last First Date!

Before I knew what was happening, I felt myself being lifted up by two strong arms, wrapped around my middle. The grip was strong, my toes barely touching the floor. *Marcus.* I could feel a body pressed against mine as the arms jolted up once, twice. I was being tossed around like a rag doll, still gasping for air. On the third jolt, something raced up my throat and out of my mouth. I could breathe! I took a deep breath, coughed, and coughed some more. But I knew it was nothing, I knew I could breathe, and whatever was lodged in there was now out, splattered somewhere across the restaurant.

Relief flooded my weary body as I turned to thank him. Only, it wasn't Marcus. It was our waiter, smiling at me, as though he performed the Heimlich maneuver on his customers every day. Perhaps he did. Who knew?

I looked at him, openmouthed, my throat and chest still screaming at me, my breathing shallow as my heart smashed up against my ribs. What do you say to a man had saved your life? "Thank you," I rasped, shocked at how terrible my voice sounded.

He nodded and smiled, catching his breath. "You are very welcome," he replied, in his lyrical accent. "We can't have our patrons choking on our food." He pulled a folded green handkerchief from his pocket and patted his brow.

"No. I . . . You saved my life, and I don't even know your name," I managed, despite the constriction in my throat.

"It's Azmera. I am the owner of this restaurant." He grinned at me, recovering from the sheer physical effort he had put in to saving my life.

I took his hand in mine. "Thank you, Azmera. Without you . . ." I trailed off. Without Azmera, I'd have been in a body bag about now.

"I'm certain your man friend here would have stepped in," Azmera said, nodding at Marcus.

My "man friend" took a step closer to me, putting his hand on my arm. "Yes, of course. I just froze, that's all. I'm so glad you're okay, Paige. That was pretty freaky. Thank you, Azmera."

"Well, I will leave you to it. Can I get you some more water, perhaps?"

"Yes, water would be great, thanks," Marcus said, leading me to my chair.

I plunked down in it, my body slowly returning to normal, my throat still raw.

"That was quite something. I think you managed to hit the back wall." Marcus grinned at me as he sat down in his own chair. He took my hand in his. "Are you sure you're okay?"

I was recovered enough to feel the sting of humiliation. I'd choked, had someone perform the Heimlich maneuver on me, and projected a lump of spicy goat across the room, location unknown—all in front of Marcus.

Cassie had famously punched herself in the face on her One Last First Date, almost breaking her nose. Was this a pact curse or something? Something we all had to go through, some sort of rite of passage? "Thou shalt make a total fool of thyself on thine's One Last First Date." I would laugh if it didn't hurt so much.

I looked down at my food, my appetite gone. "I'm—" I began. What was I? I was torn, that's what I was. I wanted to stay on this amazing date with the guy I knew unequivocally was my future husband, but at the same time, it felt like someone had lit a fire in my trachea and I wanted to just get home and curl up in bed.

Azmera delivered some fresh water, and I drank my glass in three seconds flat, the liquid going some way to soothing my throat as it went down.

"Do you know what?" I croaked. "I think I might like to go home."

He smiled at me. "Sure."

Marcus paid Azmera on our way out, tipping him generously, and I thanked him once again for, you know, that small favor of saving my life.

Not relishing the thought of taking the bus home in my state, I was grateful when Marcus, gentleman that he was, offered to drive me. We walked the handful of blocks to his building where his car was parked in the basement, his arm slung protectively around my shoulders.

Slipping onto the cool leather of his front seat, Marcus flashed me his brilliant smile. "Where do you live?"

I gave him my Dad's address, and he drove us up, out of the basement, and out onto the busy street.

"I'm so sorry about this. I've had a really great time," I croaked.

"Other than the choking part?" Marcus said with a chuckle. "Don't worry about it. I had a great time, too."

Twenty minutes later, Marcus pulled up outside my Dad's house. He switched the ignition off and turned to me. "Can I walk you to your door?"

Was he serious? This guy was totally old school and I liked it, a lot. "Sure," I rasped.

At the front door, we stood awkwardly facing one another.

"Do you want to do this again sometime?" he asked, a half grin plastered across his face.

"Maybe if we skip the choking part next time?" I said with a grin.

"Great plan." He stepped closer so our bodies were almost touching. "I'd like that."

This is it! This was going to be our first kiss, our one last first kiss. The One Direction song of the same name jumped immediately to mind. I braced myself, my belly flip-flopping as he leaned into me. I puckered up, ready, waiting, and more than willing.

But instead of brushing his lips sensuously against mine, he gave me a chaste peck on the cheek, like the sort of kiss you get from your aged auntie with the prickly upper lip, and immediately pulled away.

What?!

"Take care of yourself," he said, giving my arm a squeeze. It felt decidedly brotherly.

"Yes, I . . . thank you."

I didn't know what else to say.

He turned to leave, pausing only to wave at me from the bottom of the path. I stood and watched, dumbfounded, as he got into his car and slipped away into the night.

As he rounded the corner and drove out of sight, my heart hit my belly. Was I wrong to think we had made a connection, we had something? Or was it only fleeting, dealt a fatal blow by my humiliating choking experience? I tried to swallow the rising lump in my throat.

Perhaps this had been our last and only date.

CHAPTER 12

*T*HAT NIGHT, LYING IN my bed, reliving every look, every touch, I let out a heavy sigh. It hadn't felt like an ordinary first date. Bailey and Marissa had given us their blessing after vetting and researching Marcus so thoroughly. I bet they wouldn't have left a single stone unturned in their quest to determine he was the right guy for me. After all, they knew how heartbroken I'd been: they wouldn't have dreamt of putting me through that again.

No, Marcus was clearly the man for me, and although my decision to give up on love was a mere handful of weeks ago, I felt like a different person now. I was someone who was willing and able, someone who wanted to be loved—by Marcus.

Only, after everything that had happened between us tonight, I had absolutely no idea how Marcus felt about me. Was the fact he didn't kiss me that big a deal? What was I thinking? *Of course*, it was. But then, we'd got on so well for the whole run up to The Incident— the one where I almost died from a piece of fiery goat stuck in my throat—and he'd been so affectionate and flirty and . . .

Argh!

I buried my head in my pillow, stifling the urge to scream. I didn't want to alarm Dad, plus screaming would really hurt my poor throat right now.

What did any of this mean? Did he like me? Did he want to see me again? Had I totally blown it? No. I needed to make this work. It *had* to work. I reached down the side of my bed and dragged my laptop up onto the bed, propping myself up. I powered up and went to a sales and marketing position search site. I scrolled through the options. *I can't be a waitress for the rest of my life.* Before I had the chance to back down, I sent my CV off to a recruiter. I snapped my laptop shut. Words like "sensible," "pragmatic," and "career-minded" came to mind.

I was going to win Marcus over, show him what a great catch I was, starting with getting my career back on track, back to Marketing, where I belonged.

* * *

MY ALARM DRAGGED me out of a deep, dreamless sleep some hours later. I squinted at my clock, scrunching my eyes shut when I saw how early it was. On autopilot, I stumbled out of bed and rummaged around in my chest of drawers, looking for something to wear. I swallowed and my hand flew to my neck. Why was my throat . . . ? *Oh, yeah, that's right.*

I chewed the inside of my lip as my new friend, humiliation, made an appearance. God, last night! I squinted in the dim light and scooped my hair up into a ponytail in front of my mirror. I took in the bags under my eyes and my hardened, steely gaze. A bad sleep was inevitable after the way the date had ended, so I could hardly expect to look like a supermodel this morning.

What was that thing Scarlett O'Hara had said? Not the thing about never going hungry again, the one about tomorrow being another day. Except today is tomorrow. So today is another day. *Hmm, maybe it doesn't have quite the same ring to it.*

Whatever it was, I was resolved. I was going to do whatever I could to win Marcus over. After all, he was my vetted, fully sanctioned Last First Date: this was meant to work. It *had* to work.

Throwing on my shoes, a pair of three-quarter length Lycra pants, a baggy T-shirt, and my old, trusty oversized sweatshirt that hides the lumps and bumps, I tiptoed downstairs so as not to wake Dad.

As I rounded the corner at the bottom of the stairs, I noticed a light on in the kitchen. A moment later I stood in the doorway, watching as Dad hummed away to himself, cracking eggs into a bowl.

"Hey, Dad. What are you doing up?"

"Oh, morning, lamb chop. I'm making breakfast." He beamed at me before turning his attention back to his eggs.

"I can see that."

"Do you want some? I'm doing a carb-free breakfast. It's high in protein and healthy fats. It's really good for you."

I raised my eyebrows, noticing a sliced avocado already placed carefully on a plate by the hob. I hadn't thought Dad would know a healthy fat if it jumped out from behind a bush and slapped him on the butt, let alone have anything for breakfast other than half a loaf of bread, slathered with butter and honey.

"Err . . . no, thanks."

"Oh, you should. You want to get yourself into a state where you burn fat for your energy, you see." He smiled at me, looking as proud as punch. "I've gone Paleolithic."

I raised my eyebrows. "You have?"

"Yes! It's all based on the fact we are hunter-gatherers and never ate things like cookies and cakes in the cave."

I chortled. "Unless the cave had an oven."

Dad's face turned serious. "No caves had ovens back then, honey."

"Okay," I replied carefully.

"This is why I'm now eating things like this." He pulled a packet of bars out of the pantry and handed them to me.

I looked down and read the label. "Goji berry, cacao, and chia seed protein bars." I looked back up at Dad. "Are you sure they had this kind of thing in 'the cave'?" I did the air quote with my fingers.

"Of course, they did!" he replied as though I was some sort of imbecile. "Not in packets, though. That would never have happened."

"No, I guess not." I decided to change the subject. Dad's blind enthusiasm for his new diet was a little unnerving. "Hey, Dad. I'm sorry about last night." I was meant to be home, cooking for him, not out with a guy who may or may not be into me. "Something came up at work, and I needed to stay."

I would tell him about Marcus once—if—it became official.

He shook his head. "They work you too hard, you know. You need to put 'you' first from time to time."

Huh?

He pointed at me, nodding sagely, like he was some type of Paleo-hippie-lifestyle guru, wise beyond his years—not an overweight middle-aged man with Type II Diabetes and a penchant for reality cooking shows.

Unsettled by the new, improved version of my father before me, I muttered, "I need to get going actually. I'm meeting someone for a run." I opened the pantry door, grabbed my water bottle, and filled it up at the sink.

"Oh, that's the spirit. Got to keep fit and healthy, don't we? 'Use it or lose it,' right?" Dad whisked his eggs in the bowl and began humming once more.

Twisting the cap closed on my bottle, I furrowed my brow, watching him. "Yeah, that's right, Dad."

What had got into him this morning? He was a happy, chipper kind of person and had been for as long as I remembered, even when Mom decided we weren't for her and left. But "use it or lose it," "high protein," and "healthy fats"? This was all new.

"Everything okay, Dad?" I asked, giving him a sideways glance.

He looked up at me and beamed once more. "Oh, yes. Just great. You go and have a good run. See you tonight." He gave me a peck on the cheek before returning his attention to his meal preparation.

"Okay," I replied uncertainly. I turned to leave, collected my car keys from the key bowl, and glanced back at him. He was spooning a lump of coconut oil onto a pan, still humming, looking like a strange, unfamiliar version of my dad. But happy, definitely happy.

* * *

WHICH WAS MORE than I could say for myself this morning. With conflicting thoughts about my date with Marcus still rolling around my head, I reached The Domain where Josh was waiting for me, as he was each time we ran together. With a sigh, I slipped my keys into the hidden pocket on my pants and jogged over to him.

He greeted me with his habitual smile. "Morning, Paige!" He had one of his legs up on the park bench, stretching down to touch his toes.

"Hey, Josh," I grunted in response, incapable of mustering much more enthusiasm today.

He switched legs and shot me a quizzical look. "That doesn't sound too good. Rough night?"

"Oh, I've got a lot on my mind, that's all, and a sore throat." I bent down to touch my toes, avoiding his inquisitive look.

"Anything I can help with?"

Hanging my head between my knees, I thought about it. I didn't know Josh very well, so telling him about my date disaster seemed . . . too personal. T.M.I., I guessed. So, despite my raw throat being a constant reminder of last night's events, I opted for the career woes conversation, which had also been playing on my mind.

I straightened up and stretched my arms above my head. "I'm trying to work out what to do with the job situation."

"Aren't you happy at the Cozy Cottage? I thought you loved it there. And you're doing that extra design work, right?"

I nodded, thinking about how well the Cozy Cottage website and social media presence had worked out. "I do love it, but I kinda need to get back to my career."

He raised his eyebrows. "Why?"

Why? Was he crazy? "I can't be a waitress all my life."

Josh lowered his leg from the bench and put his hands on his hips. "A waitress who designs incredible websites and comes up with clever marketing plans. Bailey showed me."

I blushed at the compliment—and the fact Bailey was clearly happy enough with my work to share it with others. "Thanks."

"Can you explain the Ryan Gosling thing?"

"The what?" I asked, my cheeks heating up. I knew exactly what he was referring to. I'd stuck an image of Ryan Gosling, looking good enough to eat, on the site as a space filler until I'd had a chance to get all the photos I needed. Bailey had liked it and so had I. Until now.

"Did I get that wrong? Wasn't that a picture of a shirtless Ryan Gosling on the site?" He had a teasing smile on his face. His amusement wasn't helping my blush.

"Look, a girl can have a crush. And if I had to choose, Ryan Gosling is pretty darn good crush material."

He shook his head, his smile broadening. "If you say so. Hey, let's get this thing on the road."

Relieved the attention had been removed from my fantasies about American movie stars, we began to jog, side by side, along the path, past the trees and the rolling grass. Being out in the park was a lot more pleasant than I had anticipated this morning, and I began to enjoy myself.

"Did you like what you did before?" Josh asked as we passed a serious-looking runner going in the opposite direction, a look of sheer determination on his face. And sweat, a lot of sweat.

"Yeah, sure."

He chuckled. "You are a terrible liar, Paige. Did you know that?"

I shrugged, laughing. He was right. I may have perfected the fake smile that could fool anyone, but lying was not exactly in my top five skills. In fact, I was amazed Dad hadn't worked out I wasn't at AGD anymore yet. I guessed it was because of his new Paleo obsession. "Busted."

"But you still think you should go back to it?"

"Yeah. I do. It's what I studied, and I've done it for years." Plus, Marcus was a lot more impressed with Paige-the-marketer than Paige-the-temporary-waitress, for obvious reasons.

"That's not the best reason to do something you hate."

"I don't hate it!" *Did I?*

"You don't?"

"No, it's," I paused, trying to define Email Marketing Assistant in my mind. What was it? Stimulating? Important? Exciting? I settled for "okay." "It's okay."

"'Okay'?" He chuckled. I glanced at him and saw him shaking his head.

"'Okay' is fine. There's nothing wrong with 'okay.' A lot of people out there are in jobs they hate and would be happy with 'okay.' More than happy: ecstatic." I knew I sounded defensive. Plus, he appeared to have picked up the pace, and my breathing had become more labored.

"If you say so."

"Yes, I do," I replied, my voice more than a touch haughty. Anyway, who was he to advise me on my career choices? He was hardly at the top of his career ladder, delivering coffee beans to cafés.

Beside me, Josh came to an abrupt stop, and I ran a few paces before I realized. I turned back and looked at him questioningly. Although I was secretly happy I could take a breather, I was at a complete loss how our conversation had taken such a turn for the worse.

"What?" I asked, taking some deep breaths, my heart beating hard in my chest—and not just from the physical exertion.

"Look, it's your life. You can do whatever you want with it."

"I know. I can, and I will," I replied, indignant. *What was going on here?*

He narrowed his eyes, studying my face for a moment. He nodded, and then, without notice, he sprang back into action, running straight past me. Confused and unsettled, I took off after him along the path. But his pace was faster than before and he was significantly fitter than me, so before long, he was way ahead of me. I was left trailing behind, panting hard, running as fast as I could, and wondering what the heck had just happened.

Eventually, after I'd slogged up the hill, pushing myself to do so, I found him, jogging on the spot beside the imposing neoclassical War Memorial building. I approached him with caution, not knowing quite what to make of recent events.

He glanced at his watch. "You've made good time."

"Yeah, I, ah . . . wanted to see if I could catch up with you." I bit my lip. "What was that all about?"

He let out a puff of air. "I don't know. Got out of bed on the wrong side today?" He shot me his cheeky grin, and although still confused, I melted a little.

"Did I say something?"

He gestured toward a spot on the grass, and we sat down together. As much as I knew the running was good for me—physically as well as mentally—sitting was so much more enjoyable, even if it was in my gross work-out clothes with Josh in a weird mood.

He let out another puff of air. "Not really."

"What is it, then?"

"Would you accept that old saying 'it's not you, it's me'?"

I smiled, relieved I hadn't said anything to upset him. "We can go with that. Want to talk about it?"

As he looked off into the distance, I studied his profile. Without his glasses, which held more than a passing resemblance to Harry Potter's circular specs, he was a good-looking guy. Sharp nose, long lashes, full lips. Actually, from the side, he looked quite a lot like Ryan Gosling in *La La Land*—only without the zoot suit, piano, and Emma Stone, of course.

After a moment or two, he turned back to me, and said, "I guess I don't like seeing someone trying to force themselves into a pigeon hole." He looked away once more. "I did that, mainly to please my dad, and it didn't end too well. You see, I was working in one of those high-flying corporate jobs, throwing my everything into it. And then, something big happened, and I woke up and realized it was slowly killing me."

Killing him? *That's a bit dramatic, isn't it?* "What did you do?"

He shrugged as he played with a blade of grass. "I left. And I haven't looked back."

So, Josh left a big, high-flying job to deliver coffee beans. *Huh. Interesting.*

"My job wasn't killing me." I could feel Josh's eyes searching my

117

face, almost boring into me. I cleared my throat. "I just didn't like my boss and it was a bit dull."

"But you love it at the Cozy Cottage, right?" I nodded. "And it's a really special place, you know that, don't you?" I nodded again.

Mental note: get drunk-from-the-Kool-Aid-Josh on the café promotional team.

"Why don't you take a step back and just let things come to you? That's what I did with my career, and it's worked out brilliantly for me."

Inside, I couldn't help but scoff a little, despite feeling bad I was doing so. It struck me as a touch grandiose to refer to Josh's bean delivery job as a "career." "Okay. I might just do that."

"Cool." He jumped up in one fluid moment.

I, on the other hand, had to use a couple of limbs to push myself up off the grass, back to a standing position, looking about as fluid as a lump of coal. "Cool," I confirmed with a smile. "Race you to the bottom?" I said, not waiting for a response.

"Paige Miller, I'm going to get you!" he yelled as I swooped down the hill and away, feeling somehow lighter, and having no clue as to why.

CHAPTER 13

*I*T WAS SEVERAL HOURS later that day, after the usual café madness of baking, food preparation, customers, endless coffees, and lines of hungry customers, when I spotted Marcus walk through the front door. My heart leapt into my mouth. I was standing next to Bailey, balancing a tray of muffins in my hands, which I hastily stacked into the cabinet and bolted to the relative safety of the kitchen.

What is he doing here? I placed the tray quietly on the kitchen counter and smoothed my hands down my apron, my heart rate picking up a notch or ten. I wasn't sure whether he was here on his own, had come to specifically see me, or what was going on, but I knew in that moment, I wasn't prepared.

I drummed my fingers on the counter, trying to decide what to do. Go out there and act like nothing had happened? Like I hadn't embarrassed myself completely, ruined any chance we'd had at making our date perfect, by choking on that piece of goat? Or stay in here, hiding like some type of fugitive?

Still mulling over my options, I heard the ping of my phone from the pocket of my apron. Welcoming the distraction, I pulled it out and saw I had an email from a recruiter about the marketing role I'd applied for. With trembling fingers, I swiped my phone open and read it, my eyes widening in surprise when I saw the words, "strong contender for the role" and "come in for an interview" on my screen.

They want to interview me for the job?

Without pausing to think, I fired off an email, using the usual platitudes, such as "thank you for the opportunity," "fit for the role," and "eager to discuss." What did I have to lose?

"Paige? Oh, there you are. Someone's here to see you," Bailey said, her head poking around the doorframe.

I slipped my phone back into my pocket and took a deep, steadying breath. Marcus. *Time to face the music, Paige.*

I pasted on a smile I hoped said "I'm fine whether you want to see me again or not" and stepped out of the kitchen. I was met by a vision of Marcus, standing on the other side of the counter. He was handing some cash over to Sophie, and his eyes crinkled into a smile when they met mine.

Oh, be still my beating heart.

He mouthed "Hi," and I smiled back at him, hoping—praying—he was here for a good reason, the *best* reason, and not the alternative.

His change handed over by a gooey-eyed Sophie, he gestured toward a free table in the corner. I nodded at him, pressing my lips together.

"Bailey? Is it okay if I take a quick break? Five minutes?" I couldn't help but look over at Marcus, sitting at a nearby table, watching me.

I noticed Bailey follow my gaze, and I looked down at the floor, embarrassed.

"Sure, go ahead."

I flashed her a brilliant smile. *Of course,* she would let me take five minutes with Marcus. I smoothed my hair behind my ears, walked around the counter, and over to his table.

Marcus smiled up at me. "Hey, you."

I pulled out a chair and sat down opposite him, as nervous as a duck in shooting season. "Hey."

"You look great today." I could almost feel it as his eyes swept over my body, making me tingle from head to toe.

"Thanks, you do too." He could have been wearing a lab coat and goggles for all I cared; he was here, and he wanted to see me.

"I wanted to say I had a great time yesterday. And I'm sorry I had to cut it short."

"Okay. Me too." By "short," did he really mean "not kiss you on the lips"? "Except for the choking part. I'm really sorry about that."

He shook his head, slipping his hand onto mine beneath the table. "Don't worry about it. It could have happened to anyone. Go Azkim, right?"

"It was Azmera," I corrected him, and immediately regretted it. "But it doesn't matter."

"I just wanted to say that."

"Say what, exactly?"

"That I had a good time. You're a pretty cool chick."

I giggled like a schoolgirl. "You, too. Guy, I mean, not chick."

"So," he began, only to be interrupted by Sophie, delivering Marcus's coffee.

"Here you go, Marcus. I put an extra chocolate fish on the saucer for you," she simpered.

I shot her a look. Sophie was flirting with Marcus? And she knew his name?

"Thanks, Sophie. You look after me well."

And he knew *hers*?

Before the green-eyed monster could rear its ugly head in earnest, he returned his attention to me. "Look, I know you're working and don't have much time, but I wondered if you'd like to go out again. Say, Saturday night?" He spoke in a soft, intimate tone that left no uncertainty in my mind this was a second date.

I beamed at him, my heart squeezing. Saturday night was "date night." Or was that Friday? I didn't care, because in that moment, everything was right with the world. "That would be wonderful. Yes."

"Great." He grinned at me, and I could have melted into a giant blob on the floor.

A noisy group of corporate-dressed women entered the café, steeling my attention away from Marcus. I knew I couldn't hide my disappointment at having to cut our chat short, but I also had a job to do.

I stood up and pushed my chair back under the table. "Until Saturday," I breathed.

I floated around in my happy bubble for the rest of my shift, putting smiles on the customers' faces with my jokes and witty repartee, treating them like they were my close and personal friends, not simply random people who had come to the café for their coupons for free coffee. I got a few odd looks, I would admit, but I didn't care. I was getting a second chance. I was going on my second date with Marcus on Saturday. Life was good. No, scratch that, life was *great*.

"You're in a good mood," Bailey commented as I returned to the kitchen, singing One Direction's "Little Things" quietly to myself, a pile of dirty dishes in my hands.

"Oh, you know. Why not?" I replied, adding the dishes to the growing pile next to the sink.

She smiled at me, nodding. "Why not indeed."

I returned to my song and began to stack the plates in the large dishwasher. *I'm in love with you, and all these little things.* Okay, so it was too early for any "I love yous" and I didn't know the "little things" about Marcus yet, but I was excited to find them out.

"Hey, before I forget, Marissa is popping in at close today. We wanted to talk to you about your Last First Date."

A surge of excitement rose in my belly. I turned to face her, grinning from ear to ear. "Sounds good to me."

"Stick around after your shift ends," Bailey said over her shoulder as she walked back out to the counter.

"I wouldn't miss it for the world."

* * *

A COUPLE OF HOURS LATER, all cleaned up after my shift and barely able to contain my anticipation, I unlocked the front doors to let Marissa in.

"Hi, Paige! Are you excited?" she asked as she bustled past me with her laptop, purse, and a couple of paper shopping bags from expensive boutiques in her hands.

"How could I not be?" I bounced from foot to foot, trying to help push my excitement out into the stratosphere. Really, I was more wound up than a six-year-old on Christmas Eve.

Marissa pulled out a manila folder from her laptop bag and slipped her things onto a chair. "I know, right? This is a big moment. *Huge.*"

I nodded at her, trying to bite down on my smile. Failed. It was all about to become official!

"Hi there, Marissa," Bailey said, walking into the café from the kitchen. "Are you ready for this?"

"I sure am. Got the file and everything." She waived a blue manila folder in the air.

"Awesome. Let's sit down and get this thing on the road then, shall we?" Bailey said.

I didn't need to be asked twice. I was ready and waiting, on a chair, fidgeting like an ADHD kid off my meds, before you could say "Last First Date."

My friends followed suit. Marissa placed the folder in front of her on the table, resting her hands on it. I swear I could almost see the name "Marcus Hahn" burning a hole through the cardboard.

Marissa kicked things off. "Paige. The decision we are sharing with you today is going to change the course of your life."

"Yup." I pressed my lips together, my toes doing a Mexican wave in my shoes.

Not helping me feel calm, here.

Bailey picked up the conversation gauntlet. "We didn't take this decision lightly, you know. We both spent considerable time finding out everything we could about this guy. Of course, I already knew him, so we had a good head start."

"Yup." My insides were beginning to feel like I was standing on one of those vibration machines people used to lose weight.

"We spoke directly with him, with some of his friends and work colleagues," Bailey said. "Marissa even tracked down one of his cousins and spoke to her about him!"

"Yup." I nodded furiously at them both, willing them to say his name.

Marissa chortled. "She must have thought I was some kind of weirdo. You see, I pretended I was doing a telephone survey for a large corporation, only when I started asking about family health issues and blood types, she went a little quiet."

Bailey laughed. "Isn't that funny?"

"Yup." I nodded at them again.

Are they doing this on purpose?

"And I had a few eyebrows raised from one or two of his colleagues," Bailey said, shaking her head at the memory, "especially when I asked them about his ex-girlfriends. I think they thought I was some sort of stalker or something."

Get on with it!

"Great. So . . . ?" I lead, placing my palms flat on the table.

But instead of responding to me, Marissa laughed. "Remember that one guy you told me about? What did he say to you exactly?"

Bailey smiled. "He was concerned I was some type of stalker and told me to 'back off, lady' and threatened to call the police! It was like something out of a cop show."

They both laughed.

This is torture! I'd had just about enough.

"All right, you two. I know you enjoyed doing this, and it sounds like you had a few adventures along the way, but can we *please* just get on with it? I'm dying here!"

Just say it! Say it's Marcus!

"Sorry, sorry," Bailey said, shaking her head.

"Yeah, sorry," Marissa echoed. "We got a bit carried away." She picked the folder up from the table and flipped it open.

I could see sheets of paper poking out. I cocked my head, trying to decipher what was written. I could discern the words "held the position of vice president," but nothing further. Marcus was a vice president? Impressive.

Marissa snapped the cover shut, making me jump back in my seat in surprise. "No peeking."

"Well, then. Let me say first up, we both think you and this guy would be great together," Bailey said, nodding at the folder, as though Marcus was hiding inside and would jump out, shouting "Surprise!" at any moment.

"He might not be the most obvious choice for you," Marissa added.

I nodded along. On what planet was Channing-Tatum-look-alike Marcus Hahn, former vice president of some company, not an obvious choice for me? He had the word "perfection" written all over him! *And* he was taking me on a second date on Saturday night.

"But then, you yourself said you're lousy at picking the right guy. So, we figured you'd be open to it," Bailey said. Her eyes darted between Marissa and me. "So, would you like to know who it is?"

Was she freaking *kidding*? "Um, yeah."

"Well," Bailey said, reaching for the folder. Marissa held onto it so that they were both holding it between themselves.

"Hang on. Shouldn't we build it up a bit more, you know, make it more of an announcement, like you see on *American Idol* or something?" Marissa said.

"We could. What did you have in mind?" Bailey asked.

Why were they doing this when we all knew it was Marcus and I'd already been on my sanctioned first date with him? Without waiting to hear Marissa's thoughts on the subject, I reached out, grabbed the folder, and tore it out of both of their grasps. With surprisingly agile fingers, considering how pent up I'd been, I flipped the cover open and pulled the wad of paper out.

"Hey!" Marissa protested, attempting to snatch the paper from me.

As I read the name on the piece of paper, I knitted my eyebrows together. The room fell silent around me, all I could hear was my own heart, beating loudly in my ears. I looked from the paper up at my friends. They were both watching me closely, sitting still enough to be wax figures in a museum.

"But . . . J. E. Bentley? I don't understand," I said. I was suddenly numb, confused, like I had been transplanted into some alternate universe where nothing made sense.

"What don't you understand, exactly, Paige?" Bailey asked.

I looked back down at the sheet in my hand. "Where's Marcus's name?"

"Who's Marcus?" Marissa scoffed.

My eyes almost popped out of my head. "What do you mean, 'who's Marcus?' Marcus Hahn, my Last First Date." I looked from a perplexed Marissa to Bailey. "You told him he had the go-ahead to ask me on a date." A strange feeling spread across my chest. "You even told me to have fun, remember?"

Bailey's eyebrows shot up into her hairline. "You went on a *date*?"

I blinked at her. "Yes! Our Last First Date. You knew!"

Marissa put her hands up in the "surrender" stance. "Back up the bus, here, Paige. You're telling us you went on a date with some guy called Marcus Something-or-other without us agreeing to it?"

I looked at her dumbly, nodding. My belly began to twist into that elaborate rug again.

"When?"

"Last night. It was wonderful, and we got on so well until I started choking and Azmera had to save my life and Marcus didn't kiss me, but then it didn't matter because he came here today and we're going out on Saturday."

"I'm confused. You're going out with someone called Azmera on Saturday?" Marissa asked, her face scrunched up in complete confusion. She looked at Bailey. "What is going on here?"

Bailey put her hand on Marissa's arm while looking at me. "I think we've somehow got our wires crossed. Did you go on a date with Marcus Hahn last night?"

I let out an exasperated puff of air. *Had they not been listening to me?* "Yes. Like I said. You gave him your blessing."

Bailey paused for a moment, opening her mouth to speak, then closed it again without saying a word. Eventually, she said, "What gave you that idea?"

I drummed my fingers on the table. "You did. Don't you remember? You told Marcus he could ask me out, he said you had told him it was okay to do it. You *sanctioned* it."

I watched as Bailey slowly shook her head from side to side. "No, I didn't."

I could feel the hairs stand up on the nape of my neck. "You did. You authorized it. He said so," I repeated with less force, my voice trailing into a whisper. I looked up into Bailey's eyes. She smiled at me, her face soft.

"Ah." Mortification stung. I looked down at my hands, the words on the paper blurring into gray lines before my eyes.

Marcus wasn't my Last First Date?

"Okay, so I have no idea who this Marcus guy is, but I can tell you he's not your Last First Date," Marissa said.

I swallowed. "Who is?"

"J. E. Bentley." Marissa beamed at me as though this was the best news ever. "You read it yourself."

I let out a heavy sigh, resigned. "Okay."

"Paige, I know you were expecting it to be Marcus, and I'm not sure why you think I said you could go on a date with him, but can you please give this guy a chance?"

I shrugged, my dreams of a future as Marcus's loving wife evaporating into the ether. I let out a sigh. I had agreed to let Marissa and Bailey choose my Last First Date, even though it was only because I was convinced it was Marcus. "Sure."

"Good. Because it's Josh." Bailey's face broke out into a broad grin.

I furrowed my brow, my mind too filled with disappointment to connect any dots. "Josh," I repeated, as though on automatic pilot.

"Mm-hmm." Bailey could barely contain her elation.

In a fog, I glanced at Marissa. She too was smiling at me, as though I should be completely ecstatic they'd matched me with some guy called Josh . . .

Click clank clunk. The cogs in my brain turned over. They meant *Josh* Josh?

"Do you mean Josh, the *coffee delivery guy Josh*?"

"Yes!" they both exclaimed in unison.

I looked at them, agog. "But he . . . he looks like Harry Potter!"

Please don't judge me. I was in shock, and it was the first thing that sprang to mind.

Bailey let out a light laugh. "I guess he does, a bit. I'd never thought of him like that before. It must be those glasses of his, don't you think?"

Marissa nodded her agreement. "Well, it's not his cape and wand." She laughed at her own joke as I continued to gawp at my friends, not quite believing what was happening here.

Marissa and Bailey thought *Josh* was my perfect match?

"I can tell you one thing, though," Marissa continued, "he doesn't look like Harry Potter with his shirt off."

"How do you know what he looks like with his shirt off?" My eyes were huge, staring at Marissa.

"Yeah, how do you know that?" Bailey echoed.

Marissa's cheeks colored a pretty shade of pink. "I bumped into him at the beach, that's all. He looked good in his, ah . . . trunks. Nice muscles."

I blinked at her. An image of Josh dressed up as Harry Potter, with bulging muscles painted that weird orange color favored by body builders, sprung before my eyes. I shook my head to dislodge it.

No. Too, too weird.

"Did you, now," Bailey said, leaning back in her chair, examining Marissa's face. "You didn't mention *that* part of the research."

Marissa shifted in her seat. "It wasn't part of the research, *per se*. I just happened to see him there, that's all."

In a daze, I gazed at Bailey. She had a "do you really think I came down in the last rain shower" look on her face. "Is that so?" she said.

Marissa fidgeted some more, looking as guilty as any one woman could. "You mentioned he goes to that beach up the coast to swim sometimes, so I went there to see if I could track him down."

"Which you did," Bailey said.

"Yes. And he was very friendly and err, looked good. I thought it was important to know, for Paige's sake. And he asked after you, in fact, Paige."

Hearing my name pulled me out of my reverie. "He what?"

"He asked after you. I saw it as a very good sign."

I gave her a weak smile. Big deal. Josh wanted to know how I was. As I sat in my chair, the fog began to lift. Marcus wasn't my Last First Date. It was Josh. Josh who delivered coffee beans, Josh who had become my new running partner, Josh who I had no feelings for whatsoever.

"How are we going to deal with the fact you went on a date with that guy Marcus?" Marissa said.

"We could reset the pact?" Bailey suggested.

Marissa shook her head. "We've already done that. And besides, there's a limit to how many times we can huddle around a beach bonfire and make pacts together. I mean, we're grown women, after all."

"Maybe the fact Paige went out with him without our consent renders the date null and void," Bailey said.

Marissa tapped her finger on her chin. "Yeah, I like that idea. We all agreed we'd find her the right guy, Marcus isn't the right guy, so the date meant nothing." She sat back, satisfied she'd solved the dilemma before her.

"Done." Bailey nodded, smiling at me. "Here." She picked up the folder and paper I had all but forgotten in the "Josh is my Last First Date" bombshell, slid the paper inside, and handed it to me. "In this dossier, you'll find everything we know about him: his family, his friends, right through to what he likes on his toast."

"Okay." I looked down at the folder. I bit my lip. This was *not* turning out the way I'd expected it.

"This is so amazing, isn't it? I mean, you already know him and like him, you already go running together. It's perfect. Are you pumped?" Marissa asked, totally missing the fact I was in deep like with Marcus and hadn't even given Josh a second thought.

I spread my palms on the table. The fog had finally lifted, and I knew what I had to do. "Not . . . exactly. I know you've done all this work, and you clearly think Josh is a great guy—"

"And perfect for you," Bailey interjected.

"All right. *You* think he's perfect for me. The thing is, I like Marcus.

He came in here to ask me out again just today. And I'm going." I locked my jaw and held my breath. What were they going to say?

After a pause, Bailey launched into what I knew would be her best attempt to get me to change my mind. "He's not the right guy for you, Paige. Trust me. Please?"

I shook my head.

She persisted. "Do you remember how you said you were horrible at choosing the right men?"

I bit my lip, wishing I didn't remember. "But that was before—"

Bailey raised her eyebrows. "Before you chose Marcus?"

I gave a reluctant nod. "He's the right guy for me. He's kind, he's sweet, he's funny, he's made it clear he's interested in me, he's really—"

Marissa interrupted me with, "How do you know Josh isn't interested in you?"

"He's not!" I said in exasperation. "You'll just have to trust me on that." I pushed my chair out from the table and stood up, slipping my purse over my shoulder. "Thank you both for going to the effort to do this for me." I gestured at the folder, lying on the table. "But Josh is not the right guy for me."

"Paige, come on," Bailey said. She picked up the folder and handed it to me.

I took it from her absentmindedly, shaking my head, warmth creeping up my neck. "No. I'm going out with Marcus."

And with that I turned on my heel and walked away. I was determined I knew who was right for me, and there was nothing Marissa or Bailey, or anyone else for that matter, could say to me that would change my mind.

CHAPTER 14

$\mathcal{I}$T WAS HARD TO think of anything else for the rest of that week, so I welcomed the chance to take a break from the mental treadmill for more than half an hour when I met with the recruiter for the Email Marketing Assistant role I'd applied for.

She was a woman called Madison "you can call me Madi with an *i*" O'Donnell, who looked about half my age—which of course she wasn't, as that would make her fourteen and we have laws against child labor in this country. She was, however, possibly the most enthusiastic person I've ever met in my entire life.

"Oh, my god. You are super, *super* perfect for this role, Paigey! Can I call you Paigey?" she said, flicking through my CV in her company's offices in downtown Auckland.

"Sure." Ah, no.

"They are going to L. O. V. E. *love* you over there at Nettco Electricity, really they are." Her voice was loud, it was high, it was shrill. Suddenly, I regretted not bringing earplugs with me.

I smiled at her, feeling about one hundred years old. How did she get so perky? And how could she be so overwhelmingly excited about a job in email marketing at a company that sold electricity? "That's great."

"Oh, it is, Paigey, it is! Now, I see you have a degree in . . ." She scanned the page.

"Marketing," I confirmed.

"Yes! Marketing. Good for you! You go, girl! Which is perfect, because they want a marketing assistant!" She grinned at me, her hands palm up, as though this was some crazy cosmic coincidence and nothing to do with the fact I needed the degree in marketing to have become a marketing professional in the first place.

"Great."

Where did they find this woman?

"So." She pasted on a serious "let's get down to business" face. She now looked like she could be fourteen and a half. "We need to talk about the role. Even though I just know you'll be super awesome in it, I need to ensure that You. Are. The. Best. Possible. Fit." She punctuated each word by stabbing her index finger on the table in front of her before breaking into a broad smile.

She sure was one goofy gal.

"Of course. Well, let me tell you about the campaigns I was involved in at AGD. When we launched the new fiber package last year, I was instrumental in—" I halted when I noticed Madi shaking her head, her glossy lips pursed together into a thin line.

"Uh-ah. That's not what I want to hear about," she trilled.

"It's not?"

"No way. What I want to hear about is *you*. What do you like? What do you *love*? I want to hear your passions, what excites you, what makes Paigey Mills tick."

"Ah, it's 'Miller,' not 'Mills.'"

She slapped her hands down on the table, making my jump. "Whatever. My point is not *what* you've done, it's *who* you are. That's what I'm interested in. I can read all about what you've done in here." She brandished my CV at me before slapping it back onto the table. "That's what's going to make me decide whether to send you to meet those amazing people over at Nettco Electricity. So"—she leaned back in her chair—"tell me about Paigey."

I cleared my throat. It had become obvious to me I needed to turn up my inner cheerleader several notches to get across the line with Madi with an *i*. I knew I could do it, I could meet the challenge. I was a positive person by nature. I'm not proud, but I launched into all the things that made me happy, a long list, including my family and friends, beach bonfires (not the pact), and even my newfound love—okay, mild like—of running.

Madi nodded along, looking singularly unimpressed, despite what I thought was my over-the-top enthusiasm.

"And baking. I especially love to bake."

Madi sat forward in her chair. "Ooh, what do you bake?"

That got her attention.

"Cakes, mainly, but also muffins and cookies. I've been doing it for years at home, and now I'm helping my friend out by baking at her café, as well as waitressing. It's fun." I smiled my first genuine smile of the meeting.

"Which one?"

"The Cozy Cottage Café. Do you know it?"

"Know it? I *love* it!" Madi exclaimed.

Of course, she did.

"I had a slice of white chocolate cheesecake there yesterday. It was out of this world good."

"Was it white chocolate and raspberry?"

She nodded. "Oh yes, that's the one. I forgot about those little raspberries. Delish!"

I grinned. "I baked that."

And from there it was plain sailing. Madi decided on the spot to put me forward for the interview, even calling her contact at Nettco while I sat opposite her, telling them what an out-of-this-world candidate I was and how they simply had to meet with me *immediately*. I'd be lying if I said it didn't stroke my ego, making me feel pretty darn special.

By the end of the meeting, Madi pulled me in for a hug, promised me she'd stop by the café for more of what she referred to as "heaven on a plate," and I left with an interview the following Monday for the Email Marketing Assistant's job at Nettco.

* * *

MEANWHILE, things with Bailey at the café were a little strained, to say the least. Well, they were for me, anyway. She was her usual happy self, getting on with the business of running the Cozy Cottage, as she did every day. Luckily for me, she didn't raise the whole Last First Date debacle, and it became a large Josh-shaped elephant in the room.

I was putting the final touches on a cake with a frosting bag early on Friday morning when there was a knock on the back door. Opening up, I was met by the now habitual sight of a smiling Josh, box of beans held in his arms.

"Morning, Paige!"

"Hey, there . . . Josh." I stood in the doorway, holding the door. My belly did a little flip. This was the first time I'd seen him since my friends had got it all wrong about him and me and it felt . . . uncomfortable.

"Can I come in?" he asked.

"Oh, yes. Sorry." I stood back for him, and he brushed past me, heading to the back of the kitchen.

I waited by the door as he placed the beans in the pantry, not sure quite what to do or say. *Does he know Bailey and Marissa chose him as my One Last First Date?*

"Where were you earlier?" he asked as he walked back into the kitchen, his hands now empty.

I gripped the door with my hand. "What do you mean?"

"Our run. I waited, but you didn't show."

"Oh, I'm so sorry! I totally forgot."

"No worries. How about we go for one tomorrow? I've got some time in the afternoon, if that works for you?"

"Tomorrow's Saturday." My big second date with Marcus. My chest expanded with anticipation.

"I'm aware of that." He grinned at me. "How about it?"

"Oh, I'm not sure." I had a busy afternoon of date preparation planned: waxing, buffing, plucking, the works.

"Isn't your Color Run soon?"

"Yeah, but—"

"No buts. Let's do it. We could do the Tamaki Drive run, along the beaches. It'll be busy, but it's meant to be a stunning day. Good for the soul, and all that malarkey." His grin broadened. Why was he in such a good mood? "See you at the that kayak place at two."

Not wanting to give in to my discomfort of spending time with my would-be Last First Date, I agreed. "Sure."

"Awesome." He flashed me his brilliant smile, and a strange feeling passed across my chest. What was it? Guilt? I wasn't sure. "See you then. It's a nice, flat run, so I'm sure you'll cope just fine. Maybe we could grab a coffee afterward?"

"Oh, I can't, sorry." Going on a run with Josh was one thing, having coffee afterward when I could be preparing for my big date, was quite another.

"Okay, no worries. See you tomorrow."

I closed the door behind him. That wasn't so bad. I could cope with seeing Josh. He was just Josh, after all. It was no big deal.

"You're seeing Josh tomorrow?"

I looked up to see Bailey standing in the entranceway, a quizzical look and a half smile on her face.

"Yes." I stood up straighter and looked her in the eye. "We're going on a run. I'm still in training, remember? We're running, and then I'm going home to get ready for my date with *Marcus*."

She crossed her arms over her chest, her half smile still in evidence. "Sounds great."

"It is." I smiled back at her. Two could play this game. "Now, if you'll excuse me, I have a cake to decorate."

"Sure," Bailey said before turning away.

I returned to the cake, picked up the frosting bag, and aimed it at the edge where I'd almost finished a row of flowers. In my distracted state, I must have squeezed too hard. A large dollop of frosting landed on the cake, ruining it. I let out a sigh. The cake now looked like a giant footstep had squished a third of the flowers. I'd have to scrape it off and start again.

Oh, and try not to think about how potentially awkward my run with Josh could be tomorrow.

* * *

WE MET at the allotted time by the kayak rental place the following afternoon. I had grown used to running in the cool morning air—and being able to hide behind my appropriately thick and baggy sweat-shirt, hiding any lumps or bumps I didn't want the world to see. But the afternoon was warm, so I'd been forced to dust off an old pair of running shorts and a T-shirt.

As I stood, waiting for Josh to arrive, I noticed the elastic waist-band on the shorts wasn't quite as tight as I'd expected it to be. *Huh.* Perhaps I had started to lose some of that muffin top I'd been adding to so diligently for the last few months—or longer? Josh and I had got into a regular routine of running in the mornings, so it was possible. And I'd noticed my regular clothes hadn't felt quite as uncomfortable lately. I warmed at the thought.

I spotted a man running toward me and knew by his gait it was Josh. A moment later, he was by my side, panting but with his charac-teristic smile on his face.

"Gorgeous day for a run, right?" I said.

"So gorgeous. Hey, you look cute." He bounced from foot to foot.

I glanced down at my ensemble. I was wearing one of the few outfits I'd bought new because who wants to wear someone's old work-out clothes? Layer upon layer of someone else's dried sweat. *Eww.* "Thanks."

"Shall we get going? I figured you could easily do the five kilome-ters now. I've got the route mapped out, and we can measure it on this." He brandished his watch at me, some sort of black plastic fitness device, I assumed. "Shall we give it a shot?"

I thought about how I wanted to look and feel the best I could for my date with Marcus. Running that far now may ultimately help me look better, but it might also might make me tired for tonight. And I needed to be on my game.

"How about we see how we go? I'm not sure I'm ready."

Josh was still bouncing from foot to foot as though he needed an urgent bathroom break. "Are you chicken?" he goaded.

"No!" I put my hands on my hips. *How dare he!*

"Yeah, you are. You're chicken." He shot me a cheeky grin.

"No, I'm not."

"Well, if you're not chicken, what are you, then?"

My heart clanged in my chest. "I have a date tonight, and I . . . I don't want to be tired."

What was I doing?

Josh ceased bouncing from foot to foot. "A date, huh? I thought—" he stopped mid-sentence and looked at me.

A knot began to form in my tummy as heat crawled up my face. "You thought what?" I pressed my lips together, looking at him from behind my lashes. What would he say? Did he know Marissa and Bailey had singled him out him as my Last First Date?

He shook his head, his ever-present smile returning. "Nothing. Let's get going."

We began to jog along, side by side. I glanced at him, trying to gauge his reaction. If he was bothered, he hid it well. Perhaps my friends hadn't told him, after all?

After running in silence along the path beside the sparkling blue Hauraki Gulf for a few minutes, I began to feel bad about what I'd done. I'd baited him, and it hadn't been a fair—or kind—thing to do. I decided I needed to make up for it as best I could, so I turned to Chatty Paige, the version of me most people seemed to like.

"What are you up to this weekend?" I asked, my tone bright and light.

"Not a lot. I'm going to shoot some pool with a couple of friends tonight, but I generally like to have a quiet Sunday to recover from the week."

"Do you do that a lot?"

"Well, yes. Every Sunday."

I laughed between taking in enough air. "I mean, do you shoot pool a lot?"

"I've got a regular thing going with some guys, yeah."

"I love pool." I'd grown up playing pool with my Dad. We had an old secondhand table in the garage, and we used to go out there and play after dinner most nights. Since moving back home after Dad's diagnosis, that routine had been replaced with reality TV. I'd like to get the old table out again some time. "I'm a pretty good player, you know."

"Is that a challenge, Paige Miller?" Josh asked, as he turned his head and looked at me. I noticed he was smiling once more. The knot in my belly unraveled.

"Sure. If you want it to be." I grinned back at him.

"All right. How about tomorrow?"

"Tomorrow's Sunday, remember. You don't do anything on Sundays."

"I could make an exception for pool."

"All right." I had begun to pant harder now, so I restricted myself to shorter sentences between breaths. "Max's Pool Hall." *Pant* "Tomorrow at three." *Pant pant.*

"Sure, that sounds fun. I warn you, though, I'm a pretty handy player." Josh was clearly not having the same breathing challenges as me.

"Fighting talk." *Pant.* "We'll see." *Pant.*

We ran in silence for some time, primarily because I needed to concentrate on breathing and putting one foot in front of the other while dodging walkers, runners, and the unpredictable rollerbladers on the path, out enjoying the beautiful afternoon. The surprisingly hot autumn sun was beating down on us. Suddenly thirsty, I looked longingly at a grassy area in the shade of a large tree at Mission Bay, a gorgeous golden sand beach next to Tamaki Drive.

"Josh?" *Pant.* "Can we stop?" *Pant.* I pointed at the tree.

He glanced down at his watch. "Sure. We've been running for over two and a half kilometers, anyway. This can be halfway."

We both jogged—there may have been some staggering on my behalf—over to the shaded area, and I plunked myself down on the ground in relief. Dodging the people and the heat of the sun had all taken its toll. I was used to the relative quiet of early morning, only serious runners—and me—around.

"Here." Josh passed me a bottle of water from the clip on his belt.

"Thanks." I took a large mouthful, feeling instantly better. I handed the bottle back to him and watched as he took a drink. I noticed he didn't wipe the nozzle before drinking. It seemed odd, somehow intimate, almost.

"Gosh, it's lovely here," I commented, looking at the young children splashing about in the pristine knee-deep water, their parents keeping a watchful eye.

"It is, isn't it?"

"Mm-hm." I took a deep breath. "Hey, what did you used to do, before you changed to the coffee bean thing?"

Josh looked out at Rangitoto, the dormant volcano out to sea. "I worked for a big global company."

The words "vice president" from Bailey and Marissa's dossier sprang into my mind. "You were a vice president?"

He nodded. "I was Vice President of Finance." He chuckled. "It seems a million years ago now."

"I bet." I studied his profile, as I'd done that morning he'd behaved strangely with me outside the War Memorial Museum. How had he gone from Vice President of Finance at a large global company to coffee bean delivery guy?

"Should we get going? I figure we could run back and we would have done a decent distance," he said.

"Sure." I stood up next to him, and we began to jog back in the direction we'd come from. Someone caught my eye. I looked at him and looked away, doing a double take. I stopped in my tracks, gawping, my jaw slackening.

"Everything all right?" I could hear Josh say in the distance once he must have realized I was no longer at his side.

I watched as a man, dressed in shorts and a T-shirt, stood laughing with a woman I did not recognize. He reached across and put his hand on her shoulder as they smiled at one another, looking so happy together. She looked up, and before I could even move, they kissed one another.

"That's my . . ." I trailed off. Somehow, I found the ability to move again and walked in a daze toward the couple, like I was a piece of metal being drawn in by a magnet.

"Dad?"

He looked over at me, and his smile dropped. "Paige. Honey. What are you doing here?"

I gawped at him. Instead of answering his question, I posed one of my own. "Who's that?" I nodded at the woman I had just watched him kiss only moments ago.

"This is Gaylene." He wrapped his arm around her shoulders possessively.

She beamed at me. "Hi, Paige. It's great to meet you. Your dad has told me so many great things about you."

I blinked at her. Well, he hadn't breathed a word about *you*. I was so confused. My dad was here, with a woman called Gaylene, laughing and *kissing* her?

I looked up, startled, as Josh slipped his hand into mine. "Hey," he said quietly. "You okay?"

It was what I needed to snap me into action. I smiled at him, feeling the warmth of his hand in mine, grateful for his kindness. "Yes." I swallowed and turned back to Dad and Gaylene. "Dad? Can we have a moment?"

"Sure, lamb chop. Of course."

I loosened my hand from Josh's and walked a few paces away with Dad. "Who's Gaylene?"

"I wanted to tell you about her, but there hasn't been the right time. I'm sorry."

I looked into his eyes and could see just how sorry he was. "Who is she?"

"She's . . . well, I suppose you could say she's my girlfriend." He gave a small shrug, trying to suppress a smile.

"You've got a *girlfriend*?" My eyes bulged out of my head. My dad, who spent every evening in front of the television, who allegedly hadn't so much as looked at another woman since my mother left, had a girlfriend. What was this, a parallel universe where middle-aged dads had girlfriends and I had no career?

"Yes. She's really lovely, you'll like her."

"Why didn't you want to tell me about her? It's not like she's going to be my new mommy, Dad, even if this thing between you is serious. I'm a grown woman, you know."

"I know. And it is. Serious, that is."

What? "How long?"

"How long have I known her? A while, but we only started dating recently. We met through that diabetes support group I mentioned to you."

I watched as he glanced over at Gaylene, who was sitting with Josh on the ground. She waved at us, and I lifted my hand to wave back. Weird. I just waved at Dad's girlfriend.

In the distance, a metaphorical penny dropped. All those healthy fats and proteins he'd been eating, the lack of chocolate bars ferreted away so I wouldn't find them—which I always did—around the house. "Is that why you've gone Paleo on me?"

"Yes, it's all part of it. Gaylene and I agreed to do it together, you see. She's a wonderful support."

I ignored the uncomfortable twist in my belly. *She's achieved what I couldn't.*

We both looked over at her again. This time she was deep in conversation with Josh about something. What on earth did they find to talk about?

I smiled at Dad and drew him in for a hug.

"What's that for?" he asked over my shoulder.

"Because I love you," I replied, shocked when my voice caught.

"Oh, lamb chop." Dad squeezed me tighter. "Would you like to meet her properly?"

"Sure. I'd like that." I gave him a watery smile.

He wrapped his arm around my shoulder, and we walked together over to Josh and Gaylene. They both stood up to greet us, Josh in his usual bound-up-in-one-fluid-motion kind of way.

"Paige, honey, this is Gaylene."

I reached my hand out and we shook.

"It's so lovely to meet you, Paige." Gaylene's face creased into a kind smile.

"You too," I muttered.

"And you must be Paige's . . . friend?" He glanced at me out of the corner of my eye. "I'm Rob," Dad said to Josh.

"Yes, I am. I'm Josh Bentley, pleased to meet you, Rob."

The men shook hands. I smiled weakly at them all. This was surreal. My dad and his girlfriend—I was still nowhere near being used to that one—and my would-be Last First Date, standing together on the grass at Mission Bay.

"So, how do you know my Paige? Are you at AGD, too? That place works my girl too hard, you know," Dad said to Josh.

I shot a look at Josh, giving a small shake of my head, my eyes pleading with him not to mention that he knows me as a temporary waitress at the Cozy Cottage.

"They do, Rob, they really do. We've done some work together, but I'm actually out on my own in the coffee business these days."

"Oh, I know who you are, now!" Gaylene exclaimed. "I saw you on TV. You run Ned's Coffee."

I opened my mouth to explain she must have been mistaken, that Josh was the delivery guy, and the only way he'd be on TV would be if he was at a rugby match and they filmed the crowd, when Josh said, "Yeah, that's me. Did you see that thing on local businesses on *Your News* last week?"

My mouth slackened, and my eyes could have popped out of my head as I listened to Gaylene and Josh discussing how much his recent television appearance had done for his business. Apparently, Ned's profits were up and he was even considering expanding his operation to meet the upturn in demand. Or something like that. I was too gobsmacked to catch the details.

"But . . . but you deliver the beans," I said to him when I had gained the ability to speak once more.

Josh smiled at me and winked. "Only for special customers."

"Oh, I see," I replied, not seeing in the slightest. Did he mean Bailey? Was Bailey his "special customer"? Did Josh have a thing for Bailey? An odd sensation I couldn't identify passed over my chest.

"We really should get on with this run. Haven't you got somewhere to be tonight?" Josh said once we'd reached the path.

Given recent developments, my date with Marcus had completely slipped my mind.

"You're right. Gaylene, it was . . ." What was it? Good? Weird? In the end, I settled on that platitude, "nice to meet you. And Dad, I'll see you at home tomorrow. I'm out tonight."

After everyone had said goodbye and told one another how great it was to meet each other once more, Josh and I turned back and followed the path we had come. This time, though, I barely noticed I was running, so occupied was my mind with my thoughts. Dad had a girlfriend, who he looked totally in love with, and Josh was the owner and operator of Ned's Coffee, one of the city's most successful food companies. I felt like I was in a Salvador Dali painting, it was all so surreal.

We reached the kayak rental place where we had met earlier on in the afternoon.

"Hey, great pace on the way back here," Josh said, checking his watch. "We smashed our time from the run on the way there."

I chortled. "It must be the fact I just met my dad's girlfriend for the first time."

"About that." Josh's voice was soft. "Was that weird for you? I mean, you clearly had no idea your dad was in a relationship with anyone, right?"

"Ah, no." That was the understatement of the day.

"He's not married?"

"God, no! His wife hasn't been on the scene for many years."

He raised his eyebrows. "Would that be your mother?"

"Ah, yes."

I noticed Josh had an inquisitive look on his face, and I knew exactly why. I'd encountered it from other people many times before. I knew it was weird that I didn't often think of my dad's ex-wife as my mother. Only on Mother's Day and perhaps my birthday every once in a while. She'd been gone so long, she didn't really enter my consciousness any more. And I didn't feel bad about it. It was simply the way it was. I mean, how could you miss something you never really had in the first place? And besides, Dad and I were a tight unit and always had been.

Only, neither of us had been particularly honest with one another lately. I chewed the inside of my lip.

Josh smiled at me. "I know you need to get going for this big date of yours, but if you want to talk about it . . ."

My big date! He was right; I needed to get home to get ready. "No, I'm fine. Really. And thanks."

"No worries. See you tomorrow for that pool game?"

"I'm going to whip your ass, you know that, right?"

He chuckled, shaking his head. "We'll see."

CHAPTER 15

*a*T HOME, I SCRUBBED and plucked and shaved and buffed until I was shiny and raw. I wanted to look my best for Marcus, and as the saying goes, "no pain, no gain." And oh, my, was there pain. I peered in the mirror after giving myself a particularly brutal brow pluck. My skin was all pink and puffy, thanks to stray hairs being wrenched from their comfortable homes. Ice. I needed ice. I'd read somewhere that Hollywood stars submerged their faces in tubs of ice to tighten the skin and make them look camera-ready. Even though I wasn't expecting any paparazzi on my date tonight, I figured looking as good as a movie star wasn't a bad idea.

Let me preface this by saying, if you haven't ever dunked your head in a bowl of iced water, I recommend you do, if only to feel how darn painful it is. All the ice from the trays in the freezer piled into the bathroom sink, I took a deep breath and lowered my head.

Within seconds, my face began to sting like it had been attacked by a swarm of wasps intent on causing maximum pain. Before long, the headache set in, a doozey, right across my forehead. I had to pull out. It was too horrendous. I dried my face off and peered in the bathroom mirror. All the ice seemed to achieve was to make me look as red as a strawberry, the front of my hair hanging limply around my face.

Note to self: find another way to achieve movie star looks without the risk of frostbite.

I glanced at the time. Six thirty-seven? My tummy lurched. All this Arctic head dipping had taken my eye off the time. I needed to get a move on, stat! I patted my poor, pink face with moisturizer and dried off my hair. Next up was makeup. I'm not big on a lot of makeup, preferring to try to enhance rather than disguise. I applied some loose powder and blush, a wisp of eyeliner and some mascara. A sweep of red lipstick to contrast with my light blue eyes finished off the look.

Satisfied I'd hit the right balance, I zipped up my dark blue, sleeveless tunic dress with a sparkly silver pattern and slipped on a pair of gorgeous navy patent leather heels that provided me with a good few inches to my frame. Marcus was tall; we'd look great together.

One final inspection in my full-length mirror and I was ready for my big date. On our first date, I didn't have time to get nervous because, let's face it, I didn't know it was going to happen. But this one? Let's just say the butterflies in my belly were so numerous, they threatened to burst out *en masse*.

I had no idea what was going through Marcus's mind. Yes, he'd asked me out on a second date, and yes, he'd been flirty with me when he came to see me in the café. But our first date had ended so weirdly, I really had no clue what to think.

And then there was Josh, the guy I was *supposed* to be dating, according to my well-meaning friends. Why had I told him about my date tonight? I let out a sigh. Josh was a nice guy and he seemed more than happy to help me out with training for The Color Run. But there was no spark, no excitement the way there was with Marcus. You can't make that sort of thing happen; in my opinion, it's either there or it's not. And with Josh, quite simply, it was not.

A heaviness settled in my belly. I knew I was breaking the beach pact with my friends. Hell, I'd even made up a story about the pact being in the presence of the Goddess of the Beach, just to get them to take it seriously. And here I was, about to go out with someone my friends hadn't sanctioned. Pact or no pact, I knew they were wrong, and tonight was going to prove it, once and for all.

We had agreed to meet at The Salon, a trendy new restaurant in the city I had heard about but never been to. A well-dressed couple pushed through the door, and I stood back for them, holding the door open for them as they left, chatting among themselves. I entered the restaurant, taking in the music, the conversation, the buzz of the place. It was popular, that was for certain, the place was packed to the gills with diners and people at the bar.

I stood waiting for the *maître d'*, a man probably ten or so years older than me who was speaking with the couple in what had to be a fake French accent, it was so thick. There were so many "zes" and "zis" and "sank you vely much" it was a surprise he didn't trip over his own tongue. I chuckled to myself. Just then, I felt a hand on my waist. I turned and looked straight up into Marcus's eyes.

"Hi, Paige." He leaned down and gave me a kiss on the cheek, only this time it didn't feel like my spiky aunt's chaste peck. It was slow and lingering, his warm breath tickling me. "You look gorgeous."

I smiled self-consciously at him. I've always been attracted to self-confident people. I guess it was something lacking in me. I mean, it wasn't like I was completely devoid of confidence, but I'm not like people like Marcus or Marissa. They seem to be effortlessly confident in a way I could only dream of. By being around them it would rub off on me somehow.

"Thanks," I say, basking in his attention. I took in his striped, collared shirt and slim-fitting pants. He may be dressed like your average twenty-something guy but his physique did something to the clothes, making him stand out from the crowd.

"I'm sorry I couldn't pick you up from home to bring you here like a proper date. Next time, okay?"

The ever-present butterflies whenever I was near him beat their wings in my tummy. Marcus was already talking about our next date?

The couple in front of us dispensed with, the *maître d'* turned and smiled at us. "Bonsoir. Welcome to Le Salon, zee restaurant of zee year. My name is Jean-Luc. 'Ow may I 'elp you?" he simpered.

"We have a reservation for two under the name Marcus Hahn."

I watched as fake Jean-Luc ran his finger down the reservations book on the podium in front of him. "Ah! Voila! Zer you are. Ah, we 'ave ze Louis room reserved for you. It is ze very special place. You are ze very lucky couple zis evening."

"Sure, great. Thanks." Marcus widened his eyes in my direction, and I had to stifle a giggle. I knew exactly what he was thinking. Was this guy for real?

"I bet his actual name is John Smith, and I'd bet my bottom dollar he's from Hamilton," I whispered in Marcus's ear, and he laughed softly.

We followed the *maître d'* through the tables, past all the people laughing and talking at the bar, and into an area separated from the rest of the restaurant by some thick dark red curtains. It was a beautifully decorated room with a floral centerpiece and a collection of pale pink candles placed on a plate of glass on top of a crisp white tablecloth, bouncing the light around the room. Jean-Luc may very well be a bit of a fraud, but he was right, this place was very special.

Once seated, Jean-Luc handed us two large leather-bound menus. "Your waiter will be wis you vely soon. You will ave ze exquisite dinner."

"Sank you"—Marcus shook his head—"I mean, thank you."

Jean-Luc narrowed his eyes at us before he turned on his heel and sashayed away back to his podium at the front of house. "*A bientot.*"

I let out a giggle. "I can't believe you did that."

"I couldn't help myself," he said with a shrug. "That accent was more fake than Pamela Anderson's boobs."

I laughed, trying not to think of Pamela Anderson's chest. I already felt so close to Marcus on this date. We were laughing and having fun. It felt different from our first date, the one that had gone so horribly wrong at the end.

"This room is gorgeous," I said, looking around.

Marcus reached out and took his hand in mine, playing with my fingers. "Actually, Paige, I think you're the gorgeous one. I'm so glad we're doing this tonight."

I beamed at him. "Me too."

"You know, I have a good feeling about us." His eyes were electric.

He felt it, too.

He picked up the menu and opened it. "Now, let me guess what you want to order." I watched, smiling, as he scanned the page. "Aha, I think you'll go for the salmon to start, followed by the fish or . . . no, definitely the fish."

I opened my own menu to look at the options. Although I could eat it all, pan-fried Terakihi with couscous and asparagus was indeed my preference.

"How did you do that?"

He opened his arms, palms up. "It's a gift."

Our waiter arrived, and we placed our orders: a hot smoked salmon to start with, followed by pork belly with apple fritters on a bed of wilted spinach for Marcus, and the pan-fried Terakihi with couscous and asparagus for me.

"Would you like to share a bottle of white?" I nodded at him, smiling. A bottle of wine would make this evening even more romantic.

Marcus discussed wine options with the waiter and placed his order before returning his attention to me.

"Tell me about your day," he said.

"Oh, I went on a run with . . . someone. It was nice."

He arched his eyebrows. "A guy someone?"

Was Marcus jealous? "What if it was?" I teased.

"I might have to kill him, that's all."

I laughed, enjoying our light and fun conversation—even if it was about murdering poor Josh.

After a while, I excused myself to "freshen up"—girl-code for have a pee and check my makeup. I walked out of the velvet-curtained sanctuary and into the restaurant, scanning the room for the sign. Spotting it at the back, I made my way around the tables, impressed with how busy this place was.

I pulled the door open to the Ladies and came face-to-face with a glamorously dressed woman with cropped hair, big blue eyes, and red, glossy lips. My heart leapt into my mouth. It was my old boss, Princess Portia de Havilland.

"Paige! Oh, how lovely to see you. You look"—her eyes ran over my outfit, making me want to wrap my arms around myself and hide from her judgemental eyes—"well, you look the same. How are things with you?"

"Great! Amazing, in fact! Yes, that's what they are, *a*-mazing."

She arched an eyebrow. I've always wanted to be able to do that, arch just one brow. That one gesture says so much, don't you think? Of course, Portia could arch one of her perfectly groomed brows at me, questioning me, judging me, telling me she didn't believe a word I was saying, all with one, simple gesture.

Where was Helena and her Tarantino-style attitude when I needed her?

I was still holding the door open, wishing I wasn't here, when a woman behind me said, "Pardon me." I stood back, muttering an apology, and Portia followed me out into the foyer.

"Now, tell me, do you have another job yet?" she asked, her head cocked to the side, her face a study in concern—totally fake, of course.

"Yes, I'm helping a friend out right now, doing some marketing work for her business, and I have an interview for another job next week, so lots of things going on for me."

"Oh, and here I was thinking you were working in a café. I must have got that wrong."

"Yes, yes, you must." I smiled at her, half hoping the floor would open and swallow me whole. Being digested by a floor monster was preferable to this Portia-induced hell.

"Well, *I* got engaged." Portia bandied her left hand at me. I had to blink to take in the size of the rock on her ring finger.

"Wow. Well, congratulations." Poor guy. I wondered whether I should let him know what he was getting himself in to?

"Thanks. I'm here drinking champagne with the girls to celebrate. Cristal, of course."

I nodded at her. "Of course." Wasn't Cristal the pimps' champagne? Or was that something else? Only getting to drink the stuff occasionally myself, I wouldn't have a clue.

"Well, I must get back to them. We've decided to dine here, after all. Jean-Luc, the *maître d'* is a dear, sweet friend, and he sneaked us in. Isn't that marvelous?"

"Yes, it's . . . marvelous." God, was I thankful for our private dining room. Having to look at Portia sip champagne and name-drop all night with her equally vacuous gal pals would be enough to put me off my food.

"Good luck with that job of yours, Paige. Ciao-ciao." She air-kissed me.

"Ciao," I echoed, hating myself for it, as I watched Portia saunter away, her heels clicking on the hardwood floors, her sequined skirt glinting in the light.

I shuddered, thankful the encounter was over and I could now visit the Ladies in peace.

When I returned to the table, Marcus was scanning his phone, a half-drunk glass of wine in front of him.

"Sorry, sorry," I said as I sat down in my seat.

He raised his glass. "To us."

I followed suit, clinking my glass against his, our eyes locked. "To us." I took a sip, the cool liquid slipping down my throat and warming my belly, thoughts of Patronizing Portia vanishing from my mind.

We ate our appetizers and talked about a whole host of things: from his law practice to his love of yachting, from his family (one of four boys, all very competitive and high achieving) to his boarding school (missed his mother but "made him into the man he is today"). He was very open and happy to talk about anything, making me feel relaxed and comfortable in his presence.

By the time the waiter delivered our main course, conversation turned to my career once more.

"Have you made any progress on the job front?" Marcus asked before taking a bite of his pork. "Oh, this is good. Try it." He sliced off a piece and offered it to me. I wrapped my lips around his fork, enjoying the flavors, and the intimacy.

"Mm, so good. Here, try mine." I followed suit, offering up a forkful.

"Wow, now I have order envy."

We ate our meals, enjoying one another's company, the food delicious, the environment divine. After my final mouthful, I said, "Oh, I forgot to tell you. When I went to the Ladies before I had the worst experience. My old *boss* is here, and she's just as ghastly as she always was. Portia de Havilland. God, she makes me want to hit something."

"Portia de Havilland?"

He said it in such a way as to make me wonder if he knew her. "Yes. Do you know her?"

"No, no. It's just quite a name, isn't it? She could be a character in a book."

"Or better yet, a Tarantino movie where a couple of gangsters track her down and torture her, dumping her body in the harbor."

Marcus laughed. "You don't like her much, do you?"

"Sorry. I went a little too far, didn't I?" I scrunched up my face, and Marcus nodded. "But to be fair, she's a pretty horrible person. You know how people say someone 'upwardly manages'? Well, I think the term was invented for her, she spent so much time sucking up to the bosses. She brandished her gaudy ring in my face."

Marcus finished what was left of his dinner. "She's engaged?"

"Of course. A rock the size of a small country in Europe. She's having dinner here with a bunch of girlfriends."

"Are you all done there?"

I placed my silverware together in the middle of my plate, the way Dad had taught me when I was a kid. "Yes, thank you. It was delicious."

"How about we go get dessert at that place on Fort Street?"

"Sure." I liked the idea of walking through the city streets on Marcus's arm.

"Okay. How about I settle up and I'll meet you out front?"

When I got outside, my dream of going for a walk was spoiled by the rain, monsoon-like in its intensity. That's the thing about Auckland: it can start out cold, warm up to hot during the day, then rain clouds roll in out of nowhere. You have to carry three different outfits with you at all times to deal with it.

I stood under the restaurant's canopy, waiting for Marcus, wishing

I had some sort of tiny umbrella in my clutch that could unfold into a golf-sized one for us both to huddle under. It would be so romantic to wander the streets of Auckland together.

"Darn it, it's raining," Marcus said, pointing out the obvious. "Let's drive, my car's on the other side of the road." He took my hand in his, and we dashed across the street together, me holding my small clutch up over my head in a completely vain attempt to stop my hair from getting wet.

Once in the car—a sleek, black European model of some sort, low to the ground—the doors safely closing the rain out, Marcus switched on the ignition and turned and smiled at me. "Let me guess your favorite dessert."

"Bet you can't."

"I did pretty well on the dinner, don't you think?"

"True. But maybe your psychic powers are limited to the savory," I teased.

He put the car in gear. "I would say you're a chocolate girl. Anything with chocolate, preferably some sort of mousse with chocolate wafers."

Wrong. "Actually, I'm more of a lemon-y dessert girl. And my favorite cake is carrot. But nice try."

"I like your style, Paige Miller." Marcus checked his mirrors and pulled out from the curb. Pressing the accelerator hard, I was pushed back in the leather bucket seat of his expensive car, giggling with sudden excitement.

A few blocks later, he reversed the car into a parallel park not far from Sugar Plum, the most mouth-watering dessert-only restaurant in the city. I've had their self-saucing lemon cake approximately a hundred times, and it was always so light and fluffy, with a hint of sourness in the sauce that set your taste buds humming.

I put my hand on the door handle to push the door open when Marcus placed his hand on my shoulder. I turned back to look at him, and before I knew what was happening, he leaned across, his face so close to mine I could feel his breath against my cheek.

"Paige," he said, his voice low.

I swallowed as I looked into his eyes, my mouth suddenly dry, all thoughts of lemon-y desserts floating off into the ether. This was it. This was our first kiss. This was going to be the kiss we would talk about for years to come: the night we went for dessert at Sugar Plum and ended up kissing in the rain. *So* romantic. I closed my eyes and leaned in, knowing what was coming next.

As his lips brushed against mine, I breathed in his scent, my insides turning to jelly. And, wow. Wow! It had been about a year since I had kissed a guy—that was seven whole years in dog years. Seven years! And the kiss? I mean, oh, my. What a way to break the drought. Tender but firm, slow but insistent, it had everything you could ever want in a first kiss.

Marcus pulled away from me and gazed into my eyes. "Did you want to continue this somewhere else?" He ran his fingers through my hair, making it hard to concentrate on what he was saying.

My eyes darted to the brightly lit Sugar Plum sign behind his head. "Dessert?"

He chuckled. It was low and sexy and rumbled right through me.

"Or not," I offered as an alternative as he pressed his lips against mine once more. Kissing Marcus was even more incredible than eating the self-saucing lemon cake at Sugar Plum.

"I've got a hotel room not far from here," he said between kisses.

I pulled away from him, searching his face. He wanted me to go to some hotel room with him? Alarm bells began to clang so loudly in my head, I could have sworn a herd of cows were wandering past the car. "I, ah . . ."

"I'm having my place redecorated right now, you see, so I'm living at The Royal. It's just down the road from here."

"Oh, I see," I replied, letting out a relieved chortle. At least it wasn't a charge-by-the-hour motel, it was a proper hotel room, booked for a legitimate reason.

But still. My relief was short-lived. He wanted me to go to a hotel room with him on our second date? I wasn't stupid, I knew that meant sex. And it was way too early for sex with Marcus.

He brushed his lips against mine, making my mind go hazy once more. "What do you say?"

What would I say? On the one hand, I wanted him oh-so much. He was charming, he was sexy, and from what I could tell through his shirt, his face wasn't the only thing that looked like Channing Tatum. On the other hand, I didn't want a quick fling, over before it had even begun. I wanted a real relationship, one that grew and deepened each time we saw one another. One that would last. I had agreed to the pact with my friends because I wanted to find The One. Going to his hotel room with him right now was about a million miles away from helping me reach that goal.

"Marcus, I'd love to, but let's take this slow, okay? There's no need to rush things."

Damn him if he didn't kiss me again, this time slipping his fingers up the nape of my neck into my hair, sending tingles down my spine.

"But I want you, Paige," he murmured into my ear, his breath hot on my neck.

"Marcus." My voice came out unnaturally high. I cleared my throat and tried again as he began to dot kisses down my neck. Man, he wasn't playing fair! "Please."

He pulled away and looked into my eyes. "Sorry, sorry. I was getting a bit carried away, wasn't I?"

I smiled. "Yeah."

"I guess I can't help myself. But I respect you and your wishes, so we can take it slow, if that's what you want?"

I bit my lip, barely believing how strong I was being—and also kind of regretting it. I mean, it wasn't every day a hot guy asked you to his swanky hotel room, was it? Well, it wasn't for me, anyway. "It is. Thanks."

He let out a long sigh as he slid back into his seat. "Can I drive you home?"

And he did just that, no self-saucing lemon cake and no more kisses.

CHAPTER 16

*T*HE FOLLOWING AFTERNOON AT our agreed time, I arrived at Max's Pool Hall in downtown Auckland to meet Josh for our game of pool. The place was busy for a Sunday afternoon, full of groups of mainly men, with the odd woman thrown in for good measure, bottles of beer sitting on the bar leaners, waiting for them to make their shots. I spotted Josh at the bar, talking with the barmaid, who was busy explaining something to him, gesticulating with her hands.

I sidled up to him.

"That's what I was telling you! He so did it," the barmaid said, shaking her head for emphasis.

"Who did what?" I asked, taking a seat next to Josh.

"Oh, hey, Paige. Sal here is putting forward her argument as to why O. J. was the killer."

I scrunched up my face. "O. J. Simpson?"

"The very same," Sal said. "Guilty as sin."

"Isn't that pretty universally accepted?" I said, looking from a vehemently nodding Sal to Josh.

"Exactly," Sal said. "Only, Josh here thinks maybe not."

"Hold on there. I didn't say that. All I said was the evidence is not conclusive, that's all." Josh held his hands palm up in supplication.

"Why are you talking about this, anyway? Wasn't this, like, when we were kids?" I asked, wondering what all the fuss was about.

"I just finished watching that show, *The People Versus O. J. Simpson.* Have you seen it?" Josh asked.

"No." I laughed. I preferred happy, feel-good shows, like reruns of *Gilmore Girls, Downton Abbey, This is Us,* and, of course, Dad's and my much-loved reality cooking shows. Not real-life crime documentaries.

"You should," Sal replied, nodding her head sagely at me. "It's nice to meet you, Paige." She extended her hand, and I shook it.

"You too."

"I hope you know what you're up against, taking on this guy in pool."

I raised my eyebrows at Josh. "Been talking yourself up, have you?"

"Me? Never." He grinned, and an unexpected warmth spread through my belly. "What would you like to drink?"

I placed my order with Sal, Josh collected his half-drunk bottle of beer, and we claimed the pool table he'd reserved.

"May the best man win," he said as he offered me a cue.

"She will," I replied with a smirk, selecting my own cue from the rack on the wall.

"Oh, I see. It's like that, is it?" Josh asked. He took a swig of his beer.

"Don't say I didn't warn you." I bent over the table and sized up the break. I liked to take a firm first shot, showing my opponent what I was made of. Traditionally, when I played with Dad, I had a lot of success with the high balls. I liked them, and not just because the stripes on them made them prettier than the plain lows, although it helped.

Concentrating on my target, I drew my cue stick back and stabbed, hearing the satisfying *crack* of a good break. I held my breath, waiting for one of the high balls to drop nicely into a pocket. The ten-ball rolled, heading directly toward the back left, slowing, slowing, and then *plop*, straight into the pocket.

"Nice shot. I can see I've got my work cut out for me this afternoon," Josh said, and I couldn't help but smile, try as I might not to let his compliment distract me from my game.

I flashed him my smile and walked around the table, sizing up my options. I could feel Josh's eyes on me the whole time. I tried to ignore him; I knew he was merely trying to put me off and that was the last thing I was going to let happen.

The thirteen-ball was my best bet. It was about two feet away from the middle right pocket, but I had a clean line of sight to it, and I felt confident I could make it. I got myself into position once more, preparing for my shot. Pulling my cue stick back, I stabbed the white ball once more, it *clunked* into the thirteen, which went hurtling toward the pocket and right down into it.

"Two down." I was enjoying myself, thoughts of Marcus pushed to the back of my mind.

Josh shook his head, smiling. "Lucky shot." He took another swig of his beer, finishing the bottle off.

"Lucky? Ha! Just watch this." I already knew which ball I was going for next: the number twelve. It was a tricky shot, hiding behind one of Josh's balls, but it was close to the right pocket, and I knew I could take it. It was a shot Dad taught me years ago, and I was kind of an expert at it.

I got myself into position, which meant balancing my left butt cheek awkwardly on the edge of the pool table. I thanked my earlier self, who had chosen a pair of slim-fitting cropped pants and lace-up flats over the A-line skirt and wedges ensemble I had initially picked out. I leaned back, my cue held behind my back, ready to take my shot.

"Oh, my god," Josh said.

I harrumphed. The oldest trick in the book: trying to distract a player when she's cleaning you up on the pool table. So not good sportsmanship.

"Is that . . . ? No, it couldn't be," he continued.

Without moving, I stole a glance at him for a second. He was looking intently at something on the other side of the room. I wasn't falling for it. "I'm sure it's nothing."

"If you say so. Only, it looks a lot like that guy you like."

My heart jumped into my mouth. *Marcus is here?* Then, thankfully, my rational brain kicked in. He wasn't here. He said he had a thing today, and besides, Josh didn't even know Marcus. I returned my attention to the table and drew my cue stick back to take the shot.

"Paige, I'm serious. I really do think that's Ryan Gosling."

Ryan Gosling? I snapped my head up and peered at Josh. His mouth was open, and he was gawping at the other side of the pool hall. *Could Ryan Gosling really be here?* I swiveled my head to see what Josh was looking at. I searched frantically. Only, there was no Ryan Gosling, there wasn't even a C-lister from the local soap. Immediately, I lost my balance, wobbling precariously on the edge of the pool table, trying my best to right myself. I fell flat on my face, knocking the balls in all directions across the table.

How embarrassing.

"Paige, are you all right?" Josh said, rushing over to the table from his spot by the bar leaner. His voice had an undeniable note of amusement to it.

I pushed myself up, knocking the balls around the table, a couple pinging off the edges and back at me. I glared at Josh. *How dare he play that trick on me!* "You did that on purpose."

He pressed his lips together, trying to suppress a smile, threatening to turn into a full-blown laugh. "That was very funny."

"There's no Ryan Gosling, is there?"

He shook his head, chuckling.

I was so angry with him I almost growled at him. "Help me up."

He put his hand out. I took it—only because I needed to get out of this humiliating position as quickly as possible—and he pulled me up into a sitting position.

"Sorry." He chuckled, clearly not sorry in the least. "You fell for that one: hook, line, and sinker."

From my spot on the table, I shot him a death stare. "Do you think it's funny to play tricks on people? First the running off ahead of me at the speed of light and now this? Not funny, Josh."

He scrunched his nose. "It kind of is."

I scooted across the table until my legs were hanging over the edge, then I pushed myself off, landing on the sticky floor with a thud, right in front of Josh. He didn't move, instead he stood there, grinning at me. We were so close we were almost touching. My heart began to beat faster and my eyes drifted to his lips. I opened my own. *I wonder what those lips would be like to kiss?*

I blinked, snapping myself out of . . . whatever this was. I cleared my throat and took a step back from him, pressing myself up against the pool table. Kissing one man last night and thinking about kissing another now? What had gotten into me?

"We . . . ah . . . need to start the game again." I slunk along the side of the table for a couple of paces, looking down at the ground. This feeling was too strange, too out of the blue. We needed to focus on something—anything—else.

"Sure. You get the rack and I'll gather up all the, ah . . . balls."

Was it just me, or did he say that suggestively?

Instead of answering *that* question, I busied myself with taking the rack off the wall and placing it on the dot at the end of the table. As Josh arranged the balls inside the rack, I offered him another drink. With his order for another bottle of beer, I leaned across the bar, more than a little relieved to be a good twenty feet away from the confusing situation at our pool table.

"That was quite a spill," Sal said once she'd finished serving the two men in front of me.

"You saw that?" I cringed.

"Sweetheart, *everyone* saw that."

"Ah." I chewed the inside of my lip. "Well, Josh tricked me. He said Ryan Gosling was here."

"Ryan Gosling? Really?" Her eyes got huge. "How likely do you think it is that a Hollywood A-lister would walk into this pool hall on a Sunday afternoon?"

"I know. It's a good point."

"And you fell for that old trick?" Sal let out a laugh.

I shook my head at my own stupidity. I'd been played, well and truly. I glanced over at Josh. I wondered whether the moment we'd just shared was part of the ruse—or something else entirely.

* * *

WHAT WAS it with men and their confusing messages? On the one hand, there was my Mr. Dream Guy Marcus. He was clearly interested in me, and he treated me like a princess on both our dates. But then he didn't want to come near me with a ten-foot barge pole at the end of our first date, and on the second? He propositioned me like I was a cheap one-night stand.

And then there was Josh. Not my Mr. Dream Guy, but there was something about him I couldn't quite put my finger on. That moment at the pool hall where it felt like we could have kissed? I didn't know what to think of *that* in the cold light of Monday morning.

For the rest of the afternoon at the pool hall, Josh had carried on as though nothing had happened between us, as though we hadn't had the moment that was now rattling around inside my head. In our games of pool, we'd been evenly matched: I won the first game, much to his disgust, and he'd won the next two, with me bringing up the fourth and final game with a famous victory I happily lauded over him. Then, we'd said goodbye, agreed to meet for a run Tuesday, and gone our separate ways.

In the end, I guessed it was all in my head, something to do with being confused over Marcus and the mixed messages I was getting from him.

I was standing at the kitchen counter, buttering a piece of toast that bore more than a passing resemblance to a wedge of concrete, when Dad waltzed into the room. He was humming a familiar-sounding song I couldn't quite put a name to, dressed in his new work-out gear.

"Good morning, honey! Beautiful day!" He pecked me on the cheek.

"Hey, Dad." I smiled at him. Taking a bite of my toast, I looked out at the gray morning outside. Not quite my idea of beautiful, but then I guess I wasn't smitten with a Paleo-devotee called Gaylene. Absentmindedly, I chewed the toast. And chewed. And chewed. It was like having a lump of silly putty in my mouth—not that I actually knew what that was like, but I think I had a pretty clear idea now.

"Oh, I see you're eating the new paleo bread. Good, isn't it? No grains, just protein and healthy fats."

I swallowed, feeling it travel down my esophagus like an elderly snail with a dodgy hip, landing with a *thud* in my belly. "Mm. It's delicious."

"It's so good for you. None of those evil grains and additives you get in regular bread. Gaylene made it."

I gave him a weak smile. Since when did Dad think grains were "evil"? I tried to think of something positive to say about the lump of horrible-ness on my plate. "I bet it's full of roughage."

"Oh, yes. And protein and vitamins and minerals. Eat that every morning, and you'll be doing yourself a big favor."

I looked down at the concrete slice on my plate. "Okay."

Not done with extolling its virtues, Dad added, "Plus, you'll be full up until lunch. No need to snack on those high-calorie, nutritionally devoid snacks."

"Wow, Dad, you're really into this whole diet thing," I replied, willing myself to take another bite. I didn't want to offend Dad, so I picked up the toast, took a mouse-sized nibble, and smiled at him. "Mm, yummy."

"Oh, it's not just a diet, it's a way of life. Gaylene said . . ."

I zoned out while he launched into the nutritional value of this food and the sheer evil of that food. He had clearly drunk about a gallon of Gaylene's Kool-Aid—although, shouldn't it be coconut water or hemp juice or something? I was quite certain Kool-Aid should fall under the "evil" category. I suppressed a chuckle.

"So, you and Gaylene?" I led, keen to talk about something— anything—else. I mean, I hadn't even had my first coffee of the day!

Dad got that goofy, happy look people in the flush of new relation-ships get. "It's good."

I raised my eyebrows at him in expectation.

He caved in an instant. "Okay, it's great. But I didn't want to get your hopes up or anything."

"My hopes up? For what, a new mom?" I shook my head. "Dad, we talked about this. And anyway, I'm twenty-eight."

"I know, honey. It's just with your mother and all, I didn't want you to think I was rushing things."

I harrumphed. Like Marcus had wanted to "rush things" with me on Saturday night. "No, it's good. So? Tell me about it." I poured a couple of cups of coffee and sat down at the kitchen table, the concrete slab masquerading as food left on the counter.

Dad took the seat opposite me, his face rosy. "Well, Gaylene is . . . incredible, perfect. Well, not perfect, but she's as close to it as I could imagine. And she's really helped me. My pants are looser, see?" He stood up and pulled on his elasticate waistband. There was enough room in there to fit a small child. Weird image.

"Yeah, I do. That's awesome."

Dad eating better, losing weight, and getting healthy were exactly what I'd been trying to get him to do since his diagnosis. This was a good thing, a very good thing. So, why did I feel deflated?

"And it's all down to Gaylene." His eyes shone bright. He put his hand on mine. "Honey? I think I'm in love."

My eyes got huge. "In *love?*"

He nodded, his grin widening until it almost reached his ears. "I hope you're okay with that."

"Oh, Dad! Of course, I am." I leaped up and hugged him over the table, knocking my full cup of coffee over, its contents spilling and dripping down onto the floor. "Oh, bummer."

I grabbed the kitchen cloth and began sponging up the mess. "At least I didn't get one of us."

Dad gestured toward my skirt. "I think you did."

I looked down at the brown splatter marks all over the floral dress I had put on this morning for my Email Marketing Assistant interview later in the day. Great, that's just what I needed. I let out a defeated sigh.

"Why don't you go and change. I'll clean this up."

"Sure, thanks." I walked toward the staircase, dodging the coffee puddle on my way.

"And honey?"

I turned to look at Dad holding the cloth in his hand.

"Thank you for . . . you know."

"Of course," I replied, shooting him a smile.

My Dad was in love with a Paleo enthusiast called Gaylene, and what did I have? I thought of Marcus, inviting me up to his hotel room and let out a sigh. Not a whole lot, that's what.

CHAPTER 17

$\mathcal{J}$ODAY WAS THE DAY of the interview with Nettco Electricity "Madi with an *i*" O'Donnell thought I would "L. O. V. E. love." Or was it that they would love me? I had forgotten amidst all the "super" and "fabulous" and other over-the-top adjectives Madi had used to describe me and the company. I would classify myself as an enthusiastic person, positive thinking, and happy—or at least, I used to be a lot more than I had been lately—but some people took it just too far, like they swallowed a pep rally for breakfast, or something.

As I sized myself up in my bedroom mirror—the same brown and orange checked wrap dress I had worn on my last day at AGD—I took a deep breath. That famous nuns' song from *The Sound of Music* popped into my head. *"How do you solve a problem like* Marcus . . ." I chewed the inside of my lip. How indeed? *"How do you catch a cloud and pin it down?"* Was Marcus a cloud? An image of a fluffy white cloud with Marcus's face floated through my mind.

Even though I knew it was imperative he contact me first after Saturday night, I'd cracked under the sheer pressure, texting him late last night. I had aimed for a light and breezy tone and had spent at least an hour agonizing over what to say. In the end, all my deliberations and pacing around my room had resulted in "Serious dish abuse occurring. Call immediately," which I had thought was totally cute and I was certain would bring a smile to his face.

But had he texted me back? Had he shown any appreciation for the work that went into composing those six words, of hitting the right balance between being cheeky and playful and showing I was still interested in him? That would be a big fat "no."

I swept my hair up into a loose ponytail, allowing my dark hair to fall about my face. No, I had to ignore those pesky singing nuns and push the problem that was Marcus out of my mind, at least for the next few hours.

A quick glance at my phone as I slipped it into my purse showed me there was still no response from him. I locked my jaw. I'd deal with that later, once I'd nailed this job interview and got my life back on track.

After saying farewell to my happy, loved-up, anti-carb dad, checking my phone at least another hundred times on my way into the city, despite my resolution not to do so, I arrived at Nettco five minutes before my allotted interview time.

I approached the white, glossy reception desk, where a woman was talking into an earpiece with a clipped, efficient voice that had a very nasal quality to it. She had severe black tattooed eyebrows and dark hair, which was pulled back into such a tight bun her eyes had taken on a cat-like appearance. That had to hurt.

Her voice reminded me of Janice from *Friends*. I only hoped she didn't have a sinus attack while I was here. That would be a sound to behold. I waited for "Janice" to finish her call, perusing the framed photographs on the walls. There were photos of happy families playing in fields, of pretty women laughing together as they shopped, of a group of workers in hard hats smiling as they looked at plans on a large sheet of paper laid out on a table. They were all lovely, positive images, but what they had to do with electricity was a complete mystery to me. Maybe they were all happy their microwaves worked or they got to watch *MasterChef* on TV?

I thought of the Cozy Cottage website. We had happy, smiley people on it, enjoying their coffee and food, but the images were completely relevant to the business. After all, a café is a place where happy, smiley people are likely to go, not an electricity company. And the Cozy Cottage had been full to the brim since we'd gone live, with no time to even think, a steady stream of customers toting their coffee coupons.

Bailey had run the numbers and told me how successful the coupon promo had been and how she was now thinking of employing not one, but two new members of staff to replace me when I left. I'd beamed with pride, knowing what I'd done for her and her special café.

"Welcome to Nettco Electricity, Auckland's favorite electricity company. How may I help you today?" "Janice" the receptionist said in her foghorn voice behind me.

I turned and smiled at her, not one hundred percent certain she was talking to me or into her earpiece. She was smiling back at me in such a way as it looked almost painful for her, like arranging her facial features like that was the last thing in the world she wanted to do.

Still not clear she was talking to me, I took a step closer to the counter. I put my hand on my chest and mouthed "me?" She nodded at me, and I think she knitted her eyebrows together, but it was hard to tell. "Hi there," I began, putting my hands on the counter in front of her. "I'm Paige Miller. I have an interview with Roger Barnett."

"Janice" stood up and pushed an electronic device toward me. She was so skeletal she could be mistaken for a toothpick, the leopard-print shirt and skirt combo she was wearing making her look like a stick insect at a costume party. If I'd had a Cozy Cottage cake in my purse, I'd have pulled it out and made her eat it, there and then. "Write your name here."

"Sure." I picked up the stylus and wrote on the screen. In an instant, a name tag popped out of the device. I ripped it off, peeled it away from the backing, and stuck it to my top.

With an audible sniff, "Janice" picked up the paper backing, screwed it up in her hand, and pointed to an uncomfortable-looking red sofa by a glass table. "Take a seat." It was an instruction, not a request.

"Sure. Thanks, Ja—" I stopped before I said the name, turned, and did as I was told. The sofa was as uncomfortable as it looked.

"Roger, I have your ten o'clock here," I heard her say into her headset. "Yes . . . No . . . She might be." She peered at me from her seat. I couldn't help but listen in. What could they have been talking about? "I'm quite sure. Yes."

"Janice" finished up their conversation, pressing her earpiece with her finger, like Uhura from *Star Trek*. She turned her feline eyes on me. "Mr. Barnett will be out shortly."

"Oh, right. Thanks a lot."

Almost before I'd had a chance to finish my sentence, someone burst through the glass doors to my right. "Paige Miller! How fantastic to meet you!" a booming voice said.

I stood up and turned to meet him and my hands were instantly grabbed by a short, wide man with a big grin and rosy cheeks. He looked like a bald Santa, and I felt a ping of disappointment that he wasn't dressed in head-to-toe red.

"Hi. You're Mr. Barnett?"

"I surely am! But you have to call me Roger, or else!" He shook both my hands with such vigor I was in serious fear for my rotator cuffs.

"Well, it's great to meet you, too . . . Roger." My voice reverberated with the hand shaking. I wondered if any of my organs could get dislodged.

"Madi said such great things, great things!" He still had both my hands in his, still shaking. My palms were starting to sweat, clamped between his warm mitts, my head bobbing up and down with his firm shake.

To my relief, he let go of my hands. I almost staggered back, righting myself just in time.

"Whoa, there! Looks like you need a sit-you-down in old Roger Rabbit's office."

Roger Rabbit? I smiled at the bald, tubby man in front of me. He did not look anything like Roger Rabbit. Stick a hunting hat on his head and rifle in his hands, however, and he'd be the spitting image of Elmer Fudd.

"Come with me." He put his hand on the small of my back. "Thank you for your continued excellent work, Janet," he said to the receptionist as we passed by.

Almost Janice. It suited her. She either smiled at us or grimaced. I still couldn't tell which.

Roger-Rabbit-slash-Elmer-Fudd walked me through the doors and down the corridor into an office with a large oak door. I glanced around the room, taking in the big Nettco logo and photographs of yachts on the walls. He had one of those adjustable desks you could stand at. He'd clearly got the "sitting is the new smoking" message.

"Take a seat, Paigey," he said, indicating red leather chairs that matched the sofa in the reception area.

I tried not to curse Madi for adding the *y* to my name. Why did people do that? Paige is a perfectly good name. It's one syllable, it doesn't require a nickname. Although Will had called me "Millsey," after my last name, Miller, and I'd loved that. *Why am I thinking about Will?*

Roger sat down opposite me, my CV in his big, warm hands. "Now, let me have a look-see here." He ran one of his pudgy fingers down the page until he found what he was looking for. "Aha! You worked at AGD for a long time. Good for you!"

I didn't know quite what to say. "Err, thanks?"

"I've heard it's a really demanding company. For you to have survived that long, you must have been an awesome employee."

I thought about my frequent trips to the Cozy Cottage, my counting the minutes to the end of the day. "I don't like to brag, Roger, but I did okay there."

He raised his fingers in quotation marks. "'Okay'? Ha! Madi said you'd be humble and I love that, *love* that!"

I smiled at him. He was so upbeat, he rivaled Madi in the perkiness stakes. In an attempt to be professional, I tried to steer the conversation back to my work achievements. "Let me tell you a little bit about my responsibilities at AGD. As you see, I worked there for a long time, and I achieved a lot there. I was involved in many, many email marketing campaigns. One that sticks out clearly in my mind is the one . . . we . . ." I stopped when I noticed Roger shaking his head at me, his grin still firmly in place.

"I don't need to hear about that, Paigey. I've got that all in here." He waved my CV around in front of my face. "And you know what? I don't need any more of the work stuff. What I need to know is what Paigey Miller is made of."

I swallowed. "What I'm made of?" This was beginning to feel a little familiar.

"Yes. Is she the type of person to join a posse and go after the bad guy, or would she stay at home and tend to the cattle?"

Posse? Cattle? What was Roger Rabbit *on*? "I . . . err . . ."

"Would she get that golden ticket, go to that factory, and dance with the Oompa Loompas?"

I thought of the little orange men from that movie. Paint Roger orange, shrink him down to size, and we'd have a party on our hands. "Well, I don't really . . ."

He bounced out of his chair, his eyes wild. "Would she climb the tallest mountain and rappel down it?"

I blinked at him. Rappelling? All this for a lousy email marketing job?

Roger took a step closer so that he was standing over me. "Would she?" He stared at me in expectation, his face only about a foot from mine. I could see the beads of sweat forming on his forehead, the whites of his eyes bright and shining. I could smell his breath, a mixture of coffee and oatmeal.

I clutched onto the armrests of the chair, fighting my instinct to arch away from him and his enthusiasm. "Yes . . . ?" I held my breath. Was that the right answer? Should I be joining the Oompa Loompas in a posse to the top of Mount Everest? In that moment, I just did not know.

Roger let out a puff of air and stood up straight. "I thought you'd say that." His tone was solemn. He nodded at the photographs on the wall. "Do you sail?"

Was this part of the interview? If I gave him the truthful response that no, I don't, would I fail? In fact, the complete truth was that I was terrified of being out there on the ocean, with all those fish and sharks and who-knows-what-else out there, lurking around, waiting for stray humans to land in their wake. I gave an involuntary shudder at the thought.

Should I lie to try to get the job? Looking at all the photographs of yachts on the wall, it was clear to me Roger was a bit of a sailor. Half of Auckland sailed—it wasn't called the "City of Sails" because we all loved to rock climb, after all. On a beautiful day, the harbor was dotted with a multitude of yachts. The fact I'd managed to live here all my life and get away with only even having sailed once when I was about seven years old was quite miraculous, really.

In the end, I plumped for the truth. "No."

His eyes bulged. "No?"

I chewed the inside of my lip. Was that the wrong thing to say? Should I be gushing about my (fake) yachting experiences, garnering Roger's approval? "Well, I did once, but . . . I didn't really like it."

What? Was I trying to sabotage myself here?

Roger looked at me in shock. "You didn't like it?"

I had to do some quick thinking. Even though I really had no clearer idea about this job than when I had walked through Nettco's front door, I needed to at least *try.* "Well, I . . . err . . . what I mean is, I'm not sure I gave it a good enough shot to like it."

He narrowed his eyes. "You know what, Paigey? I admire you for that. You live in a place where every man, his dog, and his dog's friend's sister's teacher sails. But what do you do? You say no." He nodded at me, crossing his arms across his chest. "Oh yes. I like the cut of your jib."

"I'm pleased you do, Roger." *What else could I say?*

He tapped his chin, looking me straight in the eye. "Yes, yes. My daughter got it right."

I raised my eyebrows. What did his daughter have to do with my "jib," or anything else, for that matter? "Who's your daughter, if you don't mind me asking?"

Roger threw his plump head back and roared with laughter. I smiled, trying to laugh along with him, secretly scoping the room for an escape route. I calculated we were on the ground floor, so if I could unlatch the window I could probably get out successfully, ninja roll over the grass, and make my escape.

Roger interrupted my plans. "Madi. She's my girl. Didn't you know that?"

He turned a framed photo on his desk around, and I peered at it. It was of him and Madi, with Santa hats on their heads, dressed in matching Christmas sweaters—although hers was about ten sizes smaller than his—grinning at the camera as they both gave enthusiastic thumbs-up. Naturally.

Nepotism was alive and kicking in Auckland, it would appear, and it wore cheesy, matching holiday clothes.

"Oh. I had no idea Madi was your daughter. Her last name is O'Donnell, isn't it?"

"Of course, you didn't know. She's like me: serious and professional at work. Out of work? Well, that's another story. We're a couple of mad hatters, I can tell you."

Mad hatters: yes. Serious and professional? Ah, that would be a "no." More like a couple of friendly lunatics, but maybe that was just me? Despite my concerns, I smiled at him, not exactly sure what to think right now. "I bet."

"And she's married and changed her name, you see. Are you married?"

I shook my head. "No." Madi was married? Wow, she looked so young; she would have had to have been in high school when *that* happened.

"Well, Paigey." He sucked his lips, making a weird *smacking* sound at the end. "I think I've seen everything I need to see."

He had?

"Okay," I replied uncertainly. "Look, I'm sorry about the yachting thing."

"Why?"

"Because I said I don't like it, although I might if I gave it a decent try." Which was a lie.

"Oh, I know that." He nodded at me sagely, as though anyone who tried yachting would instantly succumb to its charms. "Do you have any questions for me?"

"Well, maybe some things about the job? Like, what my responsibilities would be if I got it, where I'd be working, who I'd be working with? Those sorts of things." Not whether he would choose the red or blue pill, or any other bizarre question he may have wanted to throw at me. I was still reeling from the Oompa Loompa ordeal.

Roger launched into a spiel about how the company was an electricity retailer who sold electricity over a fixed line network to residential and business customers, and how they needed someone to replace someone called Wolf (really?) in their marketing team, helping to run their email campaigns.

I tried not to let my eyes glaze over as he took me through the stats from their most recent campaign. Their results were good, but I knew AGD did better. I told him as much, hopefully without offending him.

"So, with those few tweaks you were able to increase response rate by over nine percent?"

I nodded. "Yes. It was really so easy to do as well."

He shook his head. "Paigey, do you know what?"

Having no clue what to expect from this loose cannon of a man, I replied, "No."

"Just as well I do," he replied before laughing at his own joke. "I'm going to offer you the job. Right here, right now. I do not care to see anyone else. You are it for me. You've got it. What do you have to say about that, hmm?"

I looked at him, my jaw slack. "You're offering me the job?"

He beamed at me. "Yes, I am. What do you say?"

You know how people say to go with your gut when you're forced to make a quick decision? That without giving it any real thought, you will instinctively know what the right thing to do is? Well, my gut had a tantrum right there and then in Roger Rabbit's office. It gave me it's message loud and clear.

I stood up and faced him. Roger may be on the wrong end of the loop-de-loop spectrum, but he was a picnic in comparison with Portia de Havilland. "I say, yes, Roger. Thank you."

He pumped the air with two fists, his belly bobbing up and down. "Awesomesauce!"

Up until that moment, I didn't think I had heard anyone over the age of about eleven use that expression, but somehow it suited Mr. Possibly-A-Little-Crazy-But-Certainly-Very-Happy Roger Barnett.

We shook hands, and he escorted me out of his office and back out to reception, where Janet was once again talking like Uhura into her earpiece with her charmingly nasal voice, looking like she'd rather be anywhere but here. It was funny, Roger and Janet were just about as polar opposite as any two people could get, in looks as well as in personality. Maybe if you put them together, you'd have a normal, balanced human being?

"So, I'll let Madi know, and we'll see you on the *Pacific Princess* next week."

Confused, I asked, "The Pacific what?"

Roger laughed. Again. "You must have been thinking of *The Love Boat*. Ha!"

Ah, no, I wasn't.

"It's not *that Pacific Princess*. There's no Gopher or Captain Stubing or Julie McCoy, although she was a cutie in her day." He chuckled some more. "You are so funny, Paigey. You're going to fit in well. We're all a little mad, here, you know."

You don't say.

He made his eyes cross to show me just how mad they all were. I wanted to tell him I didn't need any convincing.

"Okay. Great. So, this *Pacific Princess*, not the one on *The Love Boat*."

"Right?" He pointed at me. "You're onto it."

"Thank you. Um, what is it, exactly?" *Please don't be a yacht, please don't be a yacht.*

"My yacht, of course." My heart sank. "You can meet the team and come for a sail. You'll love it!"

My eyes bulged as I tried to swallow a rising lump in my throat. "Great. Yachting. How . . . wonderful."

CHAPTER 18

"YOU HAVE TO GO *YACHTING?*"

I nodded grimly. I was sitting on the sofa with Marissa at Cassie's place, having a glass of wine before I headed home to my loved-up dad and the paleo-tastic dinner he'd promised to make. Eggs with steak and chia seeds, sprinkled with protein powder, or something.

"But aren't you scared of the ocean?" Cassie asked, topping up my wineglass on the coffee table in front of us.

Again, I gave a grim nod, tightness spreading across my chest. This was quickly becoming a disaster-in-the-making. After my interview on Monday, true to his word, Roger had sent over an employment contract with a formal offer for the job. He'd attached a note with a date, time, and location for the dreaded sail.

I buried my head in my hands. "God, how do I get myself into these situations?"

"It's no big deal. Just go, sail, and it'll be over," Marissa said in her pragmatic way.

I looked up at her from my bent-over position. "Do you not remember how I was on the ferry to Waiheke that time?"

Last summer, the three of us had been invited to a wedding at a vineyard on Waiheke, an island off the east coast of Auckland city in the Hauraki Gulf. There was a regular ferry service to and from the island, and, although I had always been freaked out by the ocean, I figured I would be fine on a boat as large as a ferry. I wasn't. While the others enjoyed the brilliant summer sun outside, I spent the entire return journey inside, looking at the floor, clutching onto my seat, trying my best not to think of the terrifying sea life that lay beneath my feet.

"Yes, but I'm sure you'll be fine. How big is the yacht?" Cassie asked.

I shrugged. "Big enough to take the whole team, I guess." Madi had told me her dad had a group of about seven employees in the marketing team. All of them "completely bonkers," apparently.

"And you'll have a life jacket on," Marissa added.

I sat bolt upright. "A lifejacket?"

"Yeah, in case you go over . . . board . . ." Marissa trailed off. "Sorry." She pressed her lips together and knitted her brow when she saw the look of sheer horror on my face. "It's only a safeguard, nothing to worry about, right, Cassie?"

"Absolutely," she said with conviction. "Maybe you need to do a practice run? So you don't get so freaked out."

I chortled. "Spread the panic?"

Cassie shook her head. "I mean, if you go out for a sail before you go with your new boss, it won't seem so bad. Do you know anyone with a yacht?"

"Sure, all my friends have yachts. They keep them at their multi-million-dollar seaside mansions along with their classic car collection and their butler's quarters," I deadpanned.

"Cute. Here's a fresh glass of wine." Cassie handed me my glass. I knew it was a diversion tactic and I didn't care. Being diverted from my certain watery death was fine with me. I took a sip, hoping the alcohol would quell my nerves. It did not.

"Well, I think it's fantastic you got this new job. Cheers!" Cassie raised her glass and the three of us clinked. "When do you start?"

"They want me to start as soon as I can. This guy, Wolf, had to leave in a hurry, so the team is down one."

Cassie raised her eyebrows. "Wolf? What did he have to do, go on a hunting expedition with the pack?"

I laughed.

"I know!" Marissa exclaimed, suddenly excited. Cassie and I looked at her in expectation. "Josh. He sails."

We were back on that? I shook my head. Mr. Action Man sailed yachts: why did that not surprise me? He did pretty much everything, that guy. Not quite beat me at pool, however. A smile crept across my face. "Huh. I did not know that."

"Who's Josh?" Cassie asked.

"He's the guy Bailey and I want Paige to go on her Last First Date with. Only, she's not exactly on board with the idea."

"Ah. Well, isn't that convenient?" Cassie said, grinning at me, her eyes wide.

I pursed my lips, shooting Marissa a look. "Can we deal with one disaster at a time, please?"

Marissa shook her head. "You haven't read the dossier we gave you on him, have you? If you did, you'd know he sails. It's all in there."

I thought of the blue folder they'd given me that afternoon. When I'd got it home, I'd stuffed it into a drawer full of scarves and hats and hadn't given it a second thought.

"Are you going to go out with him?" Cassie asked eagerly.

"I'm hardly going to go yachting on a Last First Date with the guy," I replied. In fact, I wasn't going to do *anything* with Josh on a date because I wasn't going on a Last First Date with him!

"Not your first date. Perhaps your second?" Marissa suggested and Cassie agreed.

I shook my head in exasperation. "Just drop it, okay?"

Marissa shrugged. "Sure, no problem. But he's the right guy for you, Paige. You just don't know it yet."

I clenched my jaw. "Change of subject, please."

Thankfully, that was all it took. Marissa launched into talking about something that had happened at work, and I sat there, only half listening, my upcoming yachting disaster weighing heavily on my mind.

* * *

DURING MY NEXT shift at the Cozy Cottage, Bailey and I were standing next to one another in the kitchen, frosting and decorating cakes.

"I've got some news," I said as I slathered a final blob of frosting onto a carrot cake, trying not to drool too much. There was something about carrot cake—Bailey's carrot cake, in particular. It was light, moist, and delicious, the hint of sourness from the cream cheese frosting providing a wonderful contrast to the sweetness of the cake. And with healthy carrots in there, it had to be good for you, right? At least, that was what I would always tell myself.

"Oh?" she said, looking up from the apple strudel she was sifting powdered sugar over. Her eyes were shining. "Don't tell me. I think I know. You went out with Josh!"

The memory of the look on Josh's face as we stood, almost touching at the pool hall, shot into my mind. My tummy did an involuntary flip. "No, no. I haven't been on a date with Josh."

"You haven't been on a *what* with Josh?"

I turned to see the man himself, standing in the open doorway, holding his habitual box of coffee beans. He had a questioning look on his face. I swallowed. *Awkward!*

Whatever happened to knocking on the door?

I could feel a flush burst onto my cheeks. How much of our conversation had he heard? "Oh, I . . . I said I haven't gone on a *run* with you." Phew! Quick thinking saved the day. I glanced at Bailey. She was smirking, her arms crossed as she watched me. It didn't help my blush in the slightest. I cleared my throat.

Josh took a step into the kitchen. "Paige, have you lost your mind? We went on a run this morning, remember?"

Dang it! "Oh, right. Yes. You're right, I must be losing my mind." I bobbed my head from side to side, rolling my eyes to show Josh just how much of my mind I had in fact lost.

179

I chanced another glance at Bailey. She was pressing her lips together, trying to hide her smirk, still watching me closely. I glared at her. She wasn't helping the situation in the slightest.

Josh chuckled to himself as he walked past us, saying good morning to Bailey as though I hadn't just totally humiliated myself in front of him.

"Good morning, Josh. How was that seemingly forgettable run this morning?" Bailey asked.

I glared at her once more but it was having no effect. She was clearly enjoying teasing me.

Having delivered his box of beans to the pantry, Josh returned to the kitchen. His six-foot-something presence suddenly made the room feel very small. "It was great. Paige is definitely ready for The Color Run. In fact, I think she could do it with her eyes closed."

Bailey smiled at me. "That's awesome, Paige."

"Thanks." I smiled back. I had really thrown myself into my running. I was fitter, slimmer, faster—almost bionic, really. And most importantly, I felt really good about myself. Leaving AGD, working at the café, and running. They'd all helped me get my mojo back, and it felt great.

"Paige was just about to share some news, weren't you?" Bailey led.

Josh raised his eyebrows. "News?"

"Yes. I got offered a job, so I need to give you notice, Bailey," I said with mixed emotions. Although I knew taking the job at Nettco Electricity was the right thing to do, I'd really miss working in the café with her. I needed to get my career back on track and get serious. After all, I was hurtling toward thirty at an alarming rate. Didn't people in their thirties have their lives totally figured out?

"Wow, that's great, Paige," Bailey said, walking over to me and giving me a hug.

"You didn't mention that on our run this morning," Josh said, furrowing his brow.

"That's because you made us run so fast I could barely grunt, let alone actually form words," I replied.

He let out a chuckle. "You remember the run now, do you?"

I shot him a weak smile.

"So, what's the job?" Bailey asked.

"It's an Email Marketing Assistant role, a lot like the one I did at AGD. Only without the terrible boss." I thought of Roger-Rabbit-slash-Elmer-Fudd and his "we're all crazy here" attitude. He was about as far from uptight, social-climbing, thin-as-a-gazelle Portia de Havilland as any one person could be. "I'll be working for Nettco."

"The electricity company?" Josh questioned. When I nodded, he raised his brows and said, "Interesting choice."

I narrowed my eyes at him. "Why?"

He shook his head. "No reason. Good for you."

"Thanks. I need to get through this thing next week, though. I have to go yachting with my new boss and his team."

"Yachting's great!" Josh said. He took in my expression, which must have been one of sheer dread, no matter how much I tried to appear relaxed. "You're not a fan?"

"You could say that."

"Hey, why don't you take Paige yachting, Josh? That way she can have a practice run beforehand." She smiled sweetly at me, as though getting Josh and I alone together in an enclosed space wouldn't work in nicely with her matchmaking.

I wasn't buying it for a second. "Funny, that's what Marissa suggested."

Her eyes wide, she replied, "Really?"

"I'll take you out. Thursday after work good for you?" Josh asked, clearly oblivious to the coded conversation going on in the kitchen without him.

"That will be fine for Paige. In fact, I'll get someone to cover the afternoon so you can go straight after lunch," Bailey said.

"Awesome!" Josh replied.

"Anything to help you with your new job," Bailey added, patting me on the arm.

My top lip curled. Where was Helena and her Tarantino quotes when I needed her?

"When do you start?" Josh asked.

"Well, that's kind of up to Bailey." Even though I could throttle her right about now, I didn't want to let her down. After all, she'd been good to me, and me to her in return. "I figured I'd work here until you have a replacement."

"Thanks, you're a sweetheart. I've been interviewing and I think I may have a couple of good, experienced waitresses."

My heart dropped. Bailey had people lined up to replace me already? "That's great. Really great." I forced a smile, my lips twitching as tears threatened. Why did that make me suddenly so sad?

"Well, I'd better get going," Josh said as he walked toward the back door. "See you for a run tomorrow morning?" he asked me.

I swallowed the lump in my throat. I was being silly. I loved working here but it was just to help Bailey out and keep me busy while I got back to my real life. "Oh, yes. Thanks."

He closed the door behind himself, and I let out a puff of air.

"You okay?" Bailey questioned, returning to her work.

"Yes, thanks."

Was I okay? I wasn't sure. If I was convinced I was doing the right thing by leaving the Cozy Cottage, why did it feel so hard?

* * *

DURING THE LUNCHTIME madness that had become my way of life at the Cozy Cottage, I noticed a tall man in a black suit walk through the door out of the corner of my eye. I looked over at him, and my heart skipped a beat. It was Marcus. Although I hadn't heard from him since our date on Saturday, I had told myself not to be worried. He was a busy man with an important job, he'd see me when he could see me. I just needed to be patient and wait. The last thing I wanted to do was put him off by being too needy.

And anyway, he was *here*.

He joined the back of the line, and I could feel his eyes on me as I served the customers in front of him. I couldn't help but look over occasionally and smile at him, my heart skipping a beat as he smiled back. Finally, after what felt like an hour of serving customers with time-consuming needs—no pickle with this, mayonnaise on the side with that, half decaf with skim milk and cream—Marcus reached the counter.

"What can I get for you, good sir?" I asked with a grin, the butter-flies in my belly singing *He's here! He's here!*

He rested an elbow on the counter and leaned in, a smile teasing the corners of his lips. "Oh, I don't know. Are *you* on the menu?"

I let out a light laugh. "I could be. Later." I bit my lip, not quite believing how flirtatious he was being in the middle of the lunchtime rush.

He shook his head. "Later is too far away while you're wearing *that.*"

I looked down at my regulation Cozy Cottage red polka dot apron. Was it weird he thought I looked hot in it? Maybe he had some weird chef fantasies? Gawd, I hoped his *mother* hadn't worn aprons when he was a kid.

"Well, it's lunchtime." I indicated the lengthening line behind him. The tables were all full, and Bailey and Sophie were buzzing around me, filling orders and restocking the cabinet shelves. I began to feel guilty I wasn't helping them.

"So? I want to take you somewhere special, Paige. You deserve it."

Somewhere special? I wondered where he meant. A swanky restaurant? A lavish picnic lunch in the Botanical Gardens? My specu-lation was interrupted by the man beside Marcus loudly clearing his throat.

"I'm sorry, sir. I'll be with you in just a moment," I said to him before turning my attention back to Marcus. "I can't right now. Can we meet up later? Say at four?"

His expression changed to disappointment as he straightened up. Our shared moment was over. "I'd like that. Now, can I get a chicken pesto panini and a latte to go?"

"Sure." I smiled at him. We were going "somewhere special" together later, and I couldn't be happier.

Only later came and went with no sign of Marcus. I leaned up against the outside wall of the café, looking up the street. Perhaps I'd missed him? Perhaps he'd come to get me while I was in the kitchen and Bailey had sent him away? Only, why would she do that? She may want me to date Josh, but she wasn't the type of person to deliberately sabotage someone. I let out a sigh. He must have got caught up at work or something. I knew there'd be a perfectly viable explanation for why he hadn't come.

The café door banged next to me, making me jump.

"Paige. What are you still doing here?" Bailey asked as she locked up, the "closed" sign swinging from side to side on its string in the window.

"I'm waiting for someone but they didn't come, so I guess I'm heading home."

"That's a shame. You look dead on your feet, anyway, so perhaps it's a good thing. Hey, thanks for your help again today. Since the coupons went out, we've been so busy. It's just great, don't you think?"

"Yeah, I'm really happy for you."

"For us. It was you who pulled the whole thing together. Without your website and social media postings, I'd still be working out how to add them to the old website I had."

"I guess. But it's your café."

She narrowed her eyes at me. She looked like she was about to say something, then stopped herself, smiling instead. "Well, I'll see you tomorrow."

"See you tomorrow."

I stood and watched her walk down the street, her heels clicking on the footpath as she went. I leaned back up against the café wall and decided to give Marcus five more minutes. I pulled out my phone for the umpteenth time. No messages from him, just one from Dad, asking me to pick up some mineral mountain salt on the way home. Whatever that was.

I fired off a text to Marcus, asking where he was. At this point, I figured I had nothing to lose. He wasn't here, I'd been waiting for forty minutes, I was cold and tired. My heart leapt into my throat when my phone immediately *pinged* with a message from him.

So sorry! Work crazy. Will make it up to you xx

My tummy twisted into a painful knot. Marcus had stood me up. After the flirting and carrying on today, he'd simply either forgotten or something else had been more important.

I let out a puff of air. At least he had apologized and signed his name with kisses. That had to mean something, didn't it?

CHAPTER 19

$\mathcal{T}$HURSDAY SWUNG AROUND FAR too quickly for my liking, and I found myself strapped into a bright orange life jacket over my warm clothes, waiting on a pier beside Josh's boat. I felt like the Michelin Tire man's chubbier sister. It was not a good feeling.

To distract myself from my rising panic, I read the name of the boat: "Knot Working." Josh loved a pun, that was for certain. I would have chuckled if it didn't feel like my heart was about to leap out of my mouth with anxiety.

"Here. Let me help you," Josh said, holding his hand out for me.

I shot him a grateful smile. Stepping aboard Josh's yacht while clutching onto his hand like it was my only lifeline, my legs began to wobble—much more from fear than anything to do with the gently lapping water.

I tried to take my mind off the fact I was now on a floating death trap by looking around the boat as Josh busied himself with whatever you had to do to get a yacht ready to go. It looked old-fashioned to me in a lived-in, homey way, as though it had been lovingly restored, the wood a beautiful oak color, the trim and folded sails pristine white. I could imagine Katharine Hepburn and Spencer Tracey perched on it, their hair moving in the breeze. I took a deep breath. If famous Hollywood stars could do it, I could too.

An image of Kate Winslet and Leonardo DiCaprio at the front of the Titanic sprung to mind. Oh, god. The Titanic sunk and nearly everyone died! I swallowed, my mouth drier than the Sahara. What was I doing here?

My eyes darted around the boat until I spotted a cabin down a ladder. I could always stand in there and close my eyes, clutching onto the rail, pretending I was somewhere else—anywhere else—if it all became too much.

To be honest, I had held out a small hope Josh had one of those luxury superyachts you see in magazines sometimes, the ones with famous people lounging on recliners in the sun, sipping martinis. The fact I knew they cost hundreds of millions of dollars should have told me to forget that hope—Ned's Coffee might be a successful business, but there was no way it was doing *that* well.

"Paige! Catch!"

I looked up in time to see a dark object hurtling toward me. I put my hands out and a light bag landed in my arms. "A little more notice next time, please," I snapped.

Josh chuckled, stepping onto the boat himself. "It's just towels. So, what do you think?"

"It's . . . lovely." My belly was so twisted up with anxiety I was finding it hard not to think about my impending demise on board this death trap.

"Thanks. She's a beauty. Built in nineteen fifty-two, can you believe?"

I looked at him in alarm. "Nineteen fifty-two? Isn't that a little old?" For some reason, I'd assumed the boat had merely been made to *look* old, not that it actually was. "I mean, are you sure it's safe? No holes or anything?"

Josh laughed again. "Holes?" He shook his head. "It's fine. Just relax, okay? I promise, you're going to enjoy this once we get moving. I've been sailing this boat since I was a kid. You're in good hands."

I harrumphed. "Enjoyment" wasn't exactly at the top of my list this afternoon. Survival? Survival most certainly was. "So, you didn't name it?"

He smiled. "No, that was my Dad's idea."

"I see." Josh's whole family had a pun problem, by the sounds of things. They needed family pun-therapy. I would have laughed if I wasn't feeling so uptight.

"See the cabin? You can take this baby out and sleep in there. We did it a lot as a family when I was a kid, although it was pretty cramped. We didn't care; it was an awesome adventure."

"That must have been"—I wanted to say "hell," but instead went with—"fun."

"Oh, it was. That's how I learned to sail, with my parents and brother. We spent a lot of time on this boat." He patted the railing as though it were a dog, a whimsical look on his face. "Right, let's get out there, shall we? It would be a shame to waste this beautiful afternoon." Josh turned a key, and the engine spluttered and coughed as it started up.

This was *not* a good sign. I sat down on one of the cushioned seats at the front of the boat—the hull?— and clasped my hands nervously.

"She always takes a while to warm up," Josh explained.

"Okay . . ." *Not okay! This thing should work perfectly every time!* "I thought when you went yachting you used the sail?"

"Yes, we'll do that once we're out of the mooring. For now, you get to sit back, relax, and enjoy the show." He winked at me. Was he meaning *he* was the show? He did look good in his cap and shades, although the lifejacket kind of ruined any yachting fashion statement he may have been aiming for.

"Relax. Sure." I knew *that* wasn't going to happen until we were back on dry land. At least the thing had a motor, in case we got stuck out there. I tried to push the thought of being stranded at sea for days on end from my mind. What was that movie, with Tom Hanks in it, the one where he got stranded on a desert island for years? I knew we were only going for an afternoon's sail around the Hauraki Gulf, but it *could* happen.

The engine now running smoothly, Josh turned the wheel and

drove—is that what you do with a yacht?—away from the pier and out onto the open water. To distract myself, I concentrated on the masts of all the neighboring yachts, listening to the clinking sound they made in the gentle breeze. After a while, we powered away from them —and dry, safe land—and out into the harbor.

"Isn't it fantastic out here? Wait until I turn the engine off. You'll see just how serene it is, like the city is on mute or something."

I looked longingly back at Auckland, holding onto the railing for dear, sweet life. What I wouldn't do to be in the thick of the noisy city right now.

"It's going to take us about fifteen or twenty minutes, maybe longer with the lack of wind, to get out past North Head, over there," Josh said, pointing at the entrance to the harbor.

Anxiety slammed into me. "You mean, we're leaving the harbor?" I gawped at him. I hadn't signed up to open-water yachting, with all those sharks and killer whales and colossal squids out there.

"Of course. What did you think we were going to do? We'll wait until we're a little further out, then we'll put the sail up." He smiled at me, adding, "It'll be all right, Paige. Don't worry."

I nodded and forced a smile, reminding myself I was doing this so I wouldn't make a total idiot of myself in front of Roger and the Nettco marketing team next week. In a roundabout kind of way, this was helping me get back to my career. Although, suddenly, that didn't seem quite so important to me now as staying alive.

I checked the clasps on my lifejacket, tightening them so my boobs were squished uncomfortably against my ribcage—a small price to pay for survival in my eyes. After we'd been chugging along out of the marina and into the harbor for a while, with Josh rabbiting on about winching, tacking, jibbing, and other things I never wanted to know about, I began to feel more comfortable. The sun was shining, the breeze was light and refreshing, and the water sparkled around us. Every time we passed another boat, Josh would wave and they would wave back. I leaned back in my seat, unclasping my hand from the railing for the first time since I'd boarded the yacht. I began to feel I could do this. Today, maybe, I wasn't going to die.

And then "it" happened. Looking back, I don't even know quite how. With Josh steering, the motor propelling us through the calm waters, the boat flat and firm, I decided to chance it and stand up. Josh shot me an encouraging smile as I walked around the back of the boat —I knew that was not what it was called, but I didn't care—resisting the urge to clutch onto the railing. Even though I had enough adrenaline pumping around my body to power an East German weightlifter in the seventies, I had my pride and wanted to at least *look* confident in front of Josh—even if I wasn't feeling it all that much.

I shimmied around the side, heading to the front of the boat, keeping my butt in close contact with the cabin with every side step. I knew there was room to walk like an actual human being, but there was no way I was ready for that just yet with the moving water only a handful of feet away. I reached the front of the boat, holding onto the railing with white-knuckled hands. I could almost hear Celine Dion, telling everyone her heart will go on once Leo DiCaprio was dead and gone.

I swallowed, trying not to think about his fate when Josh called out, "Can you see the dolphins?"

Other sea creatures may have scared the living bejesus out of me, but dolphins were different. Perhaps it was growing up watching them on TV, the almost human laughing sound they made, or the fact they seemed so friendly. I scanned the water, but no sign. "Where?"

"Alongside the boat, port side."

"You'll have to use regular person's language, Josh."

"On the left."

Holding the railing, I did my best crab impression, sidestepping around to the left of the boat. Dolphins swimming alongside the boat seemed such a romantic notion, I was determined to see them. With my legs pressed up against the wire of the railing for support, I peered down to look for Flipper and his buddies, but still no sign. "I can't see them."

"They're still there. There's three of them. They're incredible."

My confidence up—this wasn't so bad, after all—I leaned over to take a better look at this trio of incredible dolphins. Before I knew what was happening, I lost my footing and must have gone head first into the harbor as the next thing I knew, I was under the water, the only sound the dull drone of the boat motor fading. The shock of the cold hit me like a massive body punch. Almost immediately, I bobbed back up to the surface, my life jacket doing its job. Although I must have only been under for a matter of seconds, I gasped for air, gulping it in greedily as I flailed my arms and legs, struggling to find something to grab onto.

Realizing there was nothing to grab a hold of—I was bobbing about in the harbor, after all—I looked around in a panic until I spotted Josh's yacht, moving steadily away from me. In a total panic, I called out, remembering how Kate Winslet's voice had failed her when the Titanic went down. Did I have a whistle? "Josh! Josh! Help!"

I watched as the yacht turned in a wide circle, hoping Josh had seen me fall and was heading back to save me. I flailed my hands around so he could spot me, still yelling at the top of my lungs. There was no sign of Flipper and his cronies, and, if Flipper was out here, he was definitely not interested in rescuing me. So much for those kids' movies I used to love.

After what felt like an hour of waving my arms and trying not to think of shark attacks, Josh pulled the boat up near me and yelled, "Here!" as he threw me a life ring. I clutched onto it, taking in a mouthful of salty water.

"Paige! What happened?" Josh asked as he hauled me out of the water and onto the boat where I sat, barely believing what had just happened to me.

"I . . . I don't know." My teeth began to chatter, my whole body shaking.

"We need to get you out of those wet clothes. Here." He took me by the arm and hauled me up, helping me down the ladder into the cabin like I was an old lady.

He unhooked my lifejacket and helped me slip it off each arm, dropping it on the floor. Then, he pulled my shoes and socks off. All the while I sat there, my teeth chattering so hard I wondered if I'd need dental work, my breathing short and sharp as I imagined myself still in the water.

"Paige? Paige, look at me," I heard Josh say through a thick fog.

I looked at him, watching his lips as I heard his voice, somewhere in the distance, saying, "You've had a shock, and we need to warm you up."

I nodded my head, licking my salty lips. Warming up sounded good to me.

"Lift your arms."

I did as instructed. Josh pulled my sweater and T-shirt up over my head. Wearing nothing but my bra, I watched as he pulled a towel from the bag he'd chucked at me by the pier and wrapped it around me, rubbing my arms. "Here, this will help."

"Th . . . thank y-you."

"We need to get these wet jeans off." He reached under the towel and unzipped my jeans. "Lift your hips."

With shaking arms, I pushed my butt up off the padded bench, and Josh pulled my heavy, wet jeans down my legs. It took him several attempts, the jeans so stiff and heavy with salty water. My legs were shaking almost uncontrollably, and I watched dumbly as Josh got another towel and rubbed my legs down before wrapping me up in it.

He got up and walked away from me, over to the tiny kitchenette, returning a moment later with a flask of something and a metal cup. "Here, this'll help with the shock. Head back, down in one."

He held the small metal cup to my trembling lips. I took it from him and threw my head back, the liquid slipping down my throat, warming me up immediately. I let out a cough, my throat burning. "What is that?" I croaked.

"Brandy. Consider me your own, personal Saint Bernard."

I looked into his smiling eyes, half thinking of him as an oversized, fluffy dog with a miniature barrel of brandy tied around his neck.

"I could have died," I croaked. Tears welled in my eyes, making them sting. I blinked them away, the brandy beginning to do its job.

He pushed my wet hair away from my face. The action was so

tender, so unexpected, I lost the tear battle and they began to roll down my face, big, fat, and hot.

"You had your lifejacket on, and I got back to you in time," he said, crouching down next to me, his hand on my thigh.

There was something in his look that made me feel so safe. Maybe it was the fact I'd thought I was going to die, or maybe it was just Josh. In an instant, everything I'd been holding in for all this time came flooding out: Marcus and his confusing messages, losing my job, not being honest with Dad, pretending I was still working at AGD.

Josh sat next to me, listening and nodding along, shooting me understanding looks. I told him about Portia, about how I'd completely ignored my gut, screaming at me not to take the job at Nettco. I told him about how I'd chosen to listen to my head instead, trying to do what I ought.

"I've worked hard to get where I am. Well, not particularly hard in my final months at AGD, but up until that point." I smiled, the brandy warming my belly, the shaking finally abating.

"Can I say something?" he asked, scrunching up his nose.

"Why not? I've told you pretty much every secret I've ever had."

"All of it means nothing unless you're happy. Believe me, I know."

"Is that why you left that big company to roast beans, because you weren't happy?"

"Yeah, it was. Something happened, something big, and I realized life was too short. I know it's a total cliché, but it's true. I wasn't happy. So, I left, and I made sure I got happy."

"But I've said I'll take the job."

"Have you signed a contract?"

I thought of the white envelope sitting on my nightstand. I hadn't even read through it, let alone signed it. Shouldn't that have told me something? I shook my head.

"Well, then you've got an out, haven't you?"

I nodded, the thought of not working as an Email Marketing Assistant with loop-de-loop Roger Rabbit warming my belly.

"As for your dad? I only met him once, but I think I know the type of man he is. I bet he could handle the truth."

Jack Nicholson's famous line in that movie, "You can't handle the truth!" sprang to mind. Could Dad handle the truth? Would knowing I'd been pushed out of my team for, let's face it, doing a lousy job for a long, long time, affect the way he saw his daughter? The daughter he was always so impressed with, the daughter he helped put through college, who he had always supported, had always wanted to succeed? The warmth gone, my belly tied into a knot. "I guess."

"Hey, why don't you talk to Bailey?"

"About what?"

"Just talk to her, okay?"

I shrugged, at a total loss as to what I was meant to talk to her about. Staying on as a waitress? That was a darn sight more appealing than going back to email marketing, even if it paid beans and wasn't exactly a career in my eyes. "Sure. I will."

"Okay, next topic. This guy you're dating. It sounds pretty complicated. Can't you just walk away?"

My eyes bulged, aghast. "No! It *has* to work."

"Why? Why is it so important it works out with him?"

I looked across at him in exasperation. Why was he playing dumb? He knew exactly why. "Because he's my Last First Date, that's why."

His face creased into a smile. "Your what?"

"My Last First Date." *Geez, make me spell it out, why don't you?*

"Isn't that a song by that boy band, you know, the British one that broke up?"

I let out a heavy sigh. "That's my 'One Last First *Kiss.*'"

"Oh, big difference." He chuckled. "It still doesn't explain what you're talking about."

I crossed my arms. He might have just saved my life, but he was beginning to get on my nerves. "You know, so cut it out."

He shook his head. "Cut what out? Paige, you're not making any sense."

"We took a pact, my friends and me, that we would each get One Last First Date, meaning we would marry the next guy we dated, only I thought I'd gone on a date with Will, but he was in love with Cassie all along, so we reset the pact and I got back to zero, even though I decided I didn't want to go out with *anyone*, and then I went on my One Last First Date with Marcus' and now I'm not sure what's going on, and it was meant to be you all along, but it's not: you're Josh. And . . . and you're *Josh*, you know?" I buried my wet head in my hands, knowing I'd babbled on. The brandy must have gone to my head.

Josh put his hands up in the stop sign. "Whoa! That's a lot of information."

"I know." My voice was muffled in my hands.

"I'm meant to be this last date of yours?"

I looked up at him and nodded from my bent over position.

"Why?"

"Because you are. Because Bailey and Marissa chose you for me, as you well know, only I went out with Marcus, so it has to work with him."

Josh's eyes were huge. "They *chose* me for you?"

"You know all this." I'd just had a near-death experience, couldn't the guy let up with this playing dumb?

He pressed his lips together and shook his head.

I sat up straight. "You do. Why else would you be doing this for me? Helping me train for The Color Run, taking me yachting, being so nice to me?"

He blinked at me. "Maybe because I like you?"

I swallowed, the atmosphere in the cabin suddenly changing. "You do?"

His face creased into a smile. "Yeah, I do."

I looked at him out of the corner of my eye. Against my will, my eyes slid down his face and landed on his lips. They were moist and slightly parted. And they were nice lips. I could almost feel them touching mine. Immediately, I looked away, choosing to study my hands in my lap instead, a much safer option.

"Even though, I need to say, I'm having some serious second thoughts right now." He laughed, his eyes dancing with playfulness.

I laughed along with him for a moment, until we both fell silent, the waves slapping against the sides of the boat the only sound.

"Shall we go back to the pier and get you into some dry clothes? I assume you don't want to do any actual yachting now."

Suddenly aware I was sitting in not much more than a couple of towels, alone with a man who had just told me he liked me (liked or *liked*, I wondered?), I shifted in my seat, tightening the towel around my chest. "That would be great."

"Okay. Good." Josh stood up and started to rearrange things in the hull.

"Hey, Josh?"

He looked over at me, a towel in his hand. "Yup?"

"Thanks for . . . everything."

"Sure. No problem. I'll flick the engine back on to take us back in. You just sit there and . . . dry out."

I opened my mouth to respond but he had already started climbing the steps back up to the deck. After only a short moment, Josh called out to me from the deck. "Paige? Can I get you up here to help out?"

"Up in a second." I slipped on my lifejacket—there was no freakin' way I was going up there without it after what had happened—tightened my towel around me, and climbed the steps.

Josh asked me to help him dock the boat, which we did together, in silence but for his clipped instructions. Once we'd collected our things and Josh had secured his yacht in its mooring, we walked along the pier together, my wet clothes in a bag, slung over my shoulder.

We reached my car, and I threw my wet clothes in the trunk. I turned to Josh and smiled at him, ignoring the strange feeling spreading across my chest. "Thanks a lot for taking me out there today."

He returned my smile. "My pleasure. Not that we got to do any actual yachting."

"No." I shuddered as I recalled how it felt to be in the water. "See you for my final run before the big one on Saturday?"

He grinned at me. "Sure. Same bat time—"

"Same bat channel," I finished for him.

He nodded and began to walk away. I turned and opened my door, exhausted, and more than happy to be heading home.

"Hey, Paige?"

I looked over at Josh, standing in the parking lot. "For the record, if you'd asked me on that Last First Date of yours, I'd have definitely gone."

I looked over at him, that strange feeling in my chest intensifying. "Thanks," I replied, but he'd already turned and walked away.

CHAPTER 20

"*L*ADIES," WILL SAID AS he slid into our booth at Jono's, a fifties-inspired American diner Cassie and Will had promised served the best burgers in town. He greeted Cassie with a kiss, slinging his arm around her shoulder. "Sorry I'm late. We had to wait for this group of old guys at virtually every hole, and The Joffster insisted we stay for a beer after."

"That sounds like The Joffster," Cassie replied.

"So, what's good here, guys?" Marissa asked as she perused the oversized leather-bound menu.

"The Tex Mex, the Double Cheese, the Bacon and Avocado, and the Cajun Chicken," Cassie replied immediately.

"So, basically everything on the menu," Marissa said with a laugh.

"Well, we haven't had the vegetarian, so we can't pass judgment on that one, can we, Will?" Cassie said.

"No. And I'm unlikely to ever try it. Me man, me eat meat." He beat his chest and grunted for effect, Cassie's shoulders shaking with laughter as she rolled her eyes next to him.

It had been a while since I'd last seen Will—since the photographic session for the café website, in fact—and I'd noticed my tummy hadn't lurched quite as much at the sight of him as it had in the past. Perhaps

I'd had time to get used to him being with Cassie, and perhaps having a new, burgeoning relationship with Marcus had helped too.

"I would try the vegetarian if I didn't like the look of the Kiwi Extravaganza so much," Bailey said, reading her menu. "One hundred percent prime beef patty with beets, fried egg, lettuce, tomato, topped off with smoked chili tomato relish? If it's as good as it sounds, how could I not have *that*?"

"Yeah, that's a great choice. I've not had one of those for a while." Will snapped his menu shut and put it on the table. "I'm going for that with a beer and curly fries."

"Me too," I said, also closing my menu and resting my elbows on it. "Except I'm going to have a vanilla-coconut shake."

We placed our orders with the waiter, everyone catching up on one another's news. As the only guy at the table, you'd think Will would be completely talked over by us three women, but he held his own, sharing news of his new job, telling stories about some of his more colorful colleagues.

And those burgers lived up to their hype: succulent, tasty, perfectly cooked, with light and fluffy ciabatta buns, crispy fries, and a sweet and tasty milkshake for me. There was something so satisfying about simple food done well.

Inevitably, the spotlight of attention turned to me when Marissa said, "How did the yachting go with *Josh*?" adding particular emphasis to his name, her eyes dancing with mischief.

"Who's Josh, then?" Will asked, his eyebrows raised.

"No one," I replied, and instantly regretted it. Josh may not be my Last First Date, but he wasn't "no one." I cleared my throat, feeling my cheeks heating up. "What I mean to say is, Josh is a nice guy who kindly took me yachting yesterday so I wouldn't freak out too much when I go out on my new boss's boat next week."

I thought of the unsigned contract in my bedroom and how Josh had asked if taking the new job would make me happy.

"He sounds like a *really* nice guy," Cassie said, shooting me a meaningful look.

Cassie hadn't been involved in the whole Josh dossier building, so all she knew about him was that he was meant to be my Last First Date. The last thing I wanted was any discussion about that when that position had already been filled by Marcus. So, when Marissa began with, "Well, he's more than that, he's also—" I cut her off faster than The Road Runner.

"He saved me from a near-death experience!" I blurted to divert everyone's attention. It worked beautifully, as stories of escaping the jaws of death often do. I launched into how I had fallen into the water, nearly drowned, and how Josh had helped me out. They made all the right noises about how scary it must have been for me and how happy they were I was still alive and not in my watery grave at the bottom of the Hauraki Gulf. I nodded along with them, adding in salient details about how I'd stared death in the eyes and lived to tell the tale.

"Okay, I'll admit it probably wasn't *certain* death, but I was fully clothed and as you know, I'm scared of the water, so it sure did feel pretty darn terrifying to me."

"And Josh saved you," Bailey said with her hand on her heart. "How romantic."

"Oh, yeah," Cassie said, nodding along.

"That's knight in shining armor stuff, right there," Marissa agreed.

"It was his fault!" I protested, even though I knew it wasn't. I had may as well have been whispering into the wind, anyway. All three of them were practically swooning over what a big hero Josh was. I crossed my arms and chewed the inside of my lip. I guess he had *saved* me, if they wanted to put it like that, and he had looked after me very well afterward. But it was no big deal. He was Josh, that's the kind of guy he was. It didn't mean I should be falling at his feet, asking him to be with me for the rest of my life.

Thankfully, conversation moved onto other people's yachting disasters—really, it was a terribly dangerous sport and more people needed to be aware of this fact—and we finished up our burgers and drinks.

As we were splitting the check five ways, I heard a familiar laugh close by. It couldn't be, could it? I searched the room until my eyes landed on her: Portia de Havilland, my old boss and one of my least favorite people. She was gazing lovingly at a man across the table from her. All I could see was the back of his head.

That must be her fiancé, the poor sucker.

I nudged Marissa in the ribs and nodded at the doting couple. "Look, it's Princess Portia."

She followed my gaze. "Oh, yeah. That's her. Oh, and that's her fiancé, too. He was at Friday drinks at O'Dowd's last week."

"You can tell from the back of his head?" I said with a laugh.

"Who else would she be out for dinner with, looking like that?" She nodded over at Portia's table, and as her fiancé turned, I caught sight of his face. *No, it can't be!* I blinked and blinked again. Were my eyes playing some kind of sick trick on me? My jaw dropped open as my heart hit the floor, the world slowing around me. It was Marcus. *My* Marcus. Only, he wasn't my Marcus at all.

Everything and everyone blurred around him as I stared at him, not quite believing what lay so blatantly before my eyes. I was rooted to the spot, my belly twisting painfully with anxiety. Marcus was completely oblivious to my eyes, boring holes in the side of his head, so busy was he laughing with Portia, holding his hand in hers—just like he had with me.

"See? He's kissing her," Marissa said.

With eyes that refused to focus, I nodded dumbly. Marcus was Portia's Marcus, Portia's *fiancé.*

"Paige? Are you all right?" I heard Marissa ask.

I nodded through the fog. "Yes, I . . ."

Marissa wrapped an arm around my shoulders and gave me a squeeze. "Don't let Portia bother you. You've moved on, you've got this great new job, it'll all be okay."

I didn't—couldn't—take my eyes from Marcus. As the shock began to morph into a cocktail of other emotions—sadness, anger, confusion—Marcus stood up from his seat and looked over in my direction. The smile dropped from his face in an instant.

I pressed my trembling lips together in a vain attempt to stem the flow of tears, threatening to engulf me. *How could he do this to me?*

"What's going on?" Bailey asked.

I tore my eyes away from Marcus to look at her. I knew, the moment she saw Marcus, she would know *everything*.

"That's Paige's old boss over there, Portia de Havilland. Paige is just a little upset seeing her, that's all," Marissa explained.

Panic shot through me as I saw Bailey glance over at Marcus and Portia and then back at me. A cloud passed over her features, before she returned to her characteristic smile.

"Well, best we leave, then." Bailey hooked her arm through mine and lead me out of the restaurant into the cool night air.

I smiled at her gratefully, guilt twisting in my belly. As my friends bid one another goodnight with hugs and kisses and "see you soon," all I wanted to do was get home as fast as I could.

I thought of Marcus, standing there, looking at me, his contented fiancée sitting at their table. How could I not have known? How did I not see this when it was so sickeningly obvious to me now? Marcus never wanted a relationship with me. I was just some sort of booty call to him—although, not at all successful from his point of view. I let out a sardonic laugh, stifling it when Bailey shot me a suspicious look.

God, I was such an idiot! Turning off me when I had that coughing fit; inviting me up to his hotel room—*a hotel room!*—on our second date; turning up at the café out of the blue, probably looking for a quickie out back.

That knot in my belly twisted tighter. I felt like I might vomit.

And why did his fiancée have to be *Portia de Havilland*? Portia, the most insincere, self-absorbed woman I'd ever met. She was, quite possibly, the single most detestable person on the face of the planet. I let out a sigh. As much as I may have despised Portia, it wasn't Portia who had broken my heart. It was her two-timing bastard of a fiancé.

"I'm taking you home," Bailey announced in a no-nonsense tone.

I swallowed, knowing I was in for a grilling. "Okay."

Once in her car, she started the engine and pulled out, joining the long stream of traffic back into the city.

"That was such a great burger, wasn't it? The trip out here was totally worth it," she said.

"Mmm," I agreed, not trusting myself to speak without bursting into tears.

"And it's hard to believe you're finishing up at the café so soon," she continued as I looked out the window.

"Yeah."

"Do you want to talk about it?"

"About leaving the café?"

"Ah, no."

I knew she was talking about Marcus. I knew we'd been totally busted—not that there was a "we" anymore. Or ever. I hung my head. "Not really."

"You've been seeing him, haven't you?"

I nodded, biting my lip.

"And you didn't know he was engaged, did you?" Bailey's tone was soft.

"No." My chest tightened as tears stung my eyes.

"Oh, honey," Bailey said, patting me on the back.

"I've been such an idiot."

"I hate to say it, honey, but you weren't the first woman to be played and you won't be the last."

"I was just so sure he was the guy for me. He made me feel special."

"Marcus Hahn is a very charming man. He's also a total slimeball."

"But I thought you liked him? I saw you talking with him one day." I thought about how I'd been so sure Bailey and Marissa were lining Marcus up as my Last First Date—and how I'd felt when I found out it was Josh, instead.

"He was giving me some legal advice on something, that's all. I didn't take it."

"Oh."

We drove for some time in silence until Bailey said, "We may have to reset the pact."

Despite myself, I laughed. "There has to be a limit to how many times we can do *that*."

"You're right. It was worth a shot. But then, Cassie went on her One Last First Date with Parker and ended up with Will."

I let out a watery laugh. "I could still end up with your choice for me, is that what you're saying?"

"Or whomever you choose. But I do hope it'll be Josh. I thought he'd be the right guy for you. But if you're not feeling it, then that's your choice." She pulled her car up outside Dad's house.

My phone had pinged a few times throughout the trip, and when I pulled it out of my purse to check it, I saw they were from that two-timing ass, Marcus.

"Forget about him," Bailey said, eyeing my phone.

I nodded, swallowing down the rising lump in my throat. "I'll try."

Once inside, I closed the front door and leaned up against it, my chest as deflated as a flat tire.

"Is that you, lamb chop?" Dad called from down the hallway.

I tried to force a bright and breezy tone, as though my heart hadn't just been ripped out and thoroughly stomped on. "Hi, Dad. Be there in a second." I pulled a tissue out of my purse and dabbed at my eyes, my smudged mascara blotting the tissue black. I took a few deep breaths to steady myself before walking down the hall into the living room. I didn't want to make Dad worry about me.

It was all in vain. As soon as I saw him, my face creased up and the tears flowed.

"Honey!" he said, pushing himself out of his recliner and collecting me up in one of his famous hugs.

I sobbed into his shoulder, deep, shuddering tears. I'd been holding so much in, keeping so much from my dear old dad. He shushed me, holding me close. I felt like a little girl, crying over a cut or scrape as he held me.

"I've made your shirt all gross," I said as I tried to wipe the mascara smudges from his white polo.

"Don't you go worrying about a thing like that," he said with a smile. "It could be my new 'fashion forward' look."

I let out a watery—and a little snotty—laugh. "I never thought I'd hear you use the term 'fashion forward,' Dad."

"Well, I'm glad your old dad can still surprise you every now and then."

I thought about the way in which he'd been surprising me lately: Gaylene, going Paleo. Using an expression he had picked up from E! Television was a tiny minnow in comparison with those great, hulking fish.

"Did you want to talk about it?" he asked.

I nodded. It was time; I needed to come clean with him. We sat down together on our old sofa with the cat claw rips on the arms from many cats ago.

"I don't know where to start," I said once I'd blown my nose and was feeling marginally more in control.

"The beginning is usually a good place."

So that's what I did. I went all-in, telling Dad everything from top to toe. I told him all about how I'd quit my job at AGD under a dark cloud; how I'd been working for Bailey as a waitress these past weeks; how I'd got another job but wasn't sure I even wanted it.

"Why would you take a job you didn't want?" he asked.

"Because it's my career, Dad."

"Honey, let me tell you something. Do you know why I work at the supermarket?" I shook my head. "Because I love it. I love the people, the way it's so busy, being around all that wonderful produce."

I let out a chortle. "Only if it's what the cavemen ate, right?"

He grinned. "Laugh if you like, but it's working out great for me." He pulled on his jean's waistband to show how much weight he'd lost.

"Dad, that's awesome." I smiled at him through my tears. Although it made me happy to see him taking control of his health the way he was, it still troubled me it was Gaylene who got him to do it, not me.

"I know. Gaylene has changed my life."

I couldn't help but harrumph. Loudly.

Dad's face showed his alarm. "Don't you like her?"

"No, it's not that. It's just . . . I guess, I tried for ages to get you to take care of yourself better, and then Gaylene sailed in and *bam!* you started doing all the things I'd been asking you to do."

It was Dad's turn to hang his head. "I know, and I'm sorry. You feel betrayed."

I nodded at him as he labeled the indistinct feeling I'd been carrying around with me.

"I know what. Why don't we say you loosened the jar so she could open it?"

I furrowed my brow. "What?"

"What I mean is, you laid all the groundwork so that when Gaylene and I got to talking about things, I was already halfway there."

I let out a light laugh. "Let's say that, then."

"Anyway," he said, widening his eyes in mock frustration, "My point about working at the supermarket is I could have worked somewhere else, made some more money. Who knows? But I didn't because I was happy. Honey, you need to do what makes *you* happy, not what anyone else wants you to do."

I thought about what Josh had said on the yacht. Two men in my life seemed to have their heads screwed on right—and seemed to know me better than I knew myself.

I bit my lip. "So, are you saying it would be okay with you if I didn't work as an Email Marketing Assistant anymore?"

"Of course!" He collected me into another hug. "Do what's right for you, that's what I'm trying to tell you. And you know I'll always be proud of you."

Fresh tears welled in my eyes. "I know." A surge of excitement hit me at the thought of "doing what was right for me," but I came back to earth with a splat when I realized I had no idea what the right thing for me was.

"What does that lovely boyfriend of yours think?"

My heart sank at the thought of Marcus. "He's not my boyfriend anymore."

"You broke up with Josh? What happened? He seemed like such a great guy."

"I wasn't dating Josh, Dad. I was seeing a guy called Marcus and . . . well, it's over now."

"Huh. Here I was thinking you were dating Josh."

No, he just rescued me from the ocean, trained me for my run, and gave me career advice—advice that was totally on the money, as it turned out. Oh, and he liked me. He *liked* me. Which was a lot more than I could say for Marcus Hahn.

Suddenly tired, my head heavy, I stood up, and said, "I'm going to bed. I've had enough of today." I leaned down and pecked Dad on the cheek. "Night."

"Night, lamb chop. And thanks for telling me about everything that's been going on. I'm sorry you've been having such a tough time of it."

I shrugged, a small shadow of guilt still lying across my chest. "Sorry."

"It's nothing to worry about."

I ambled slowly toward the door, turning back when Dad said, "Everything will be okay. You know that, don't you?"

I looked at his smiling, upturned face. With no career, no boyfriend, and no direction, I wished with all my heart I could believe him.

CHAPTER 21

*J*ARRIVED AT THE Cozy Cottage the following morning, literally dragging my feet along the ground. Okay, not literally dragging my feet, but I was feeling as low as I'd felt in a very long time. Betrayal and a near-death experience could do that to a gal.

I tapped on the front door, and Bailey appeared from the kitchen to unlock and let me in.

"Good morning. I hope you're feeling better today?" she asked in her usual bright and breezy tone.

I summoned every last bit of energy to form a smile. "Morning. I'm working on it."

"Good. Come and drop your purse. I need you to finish off the breakfast muffins, if that's okay?"

Usually, the thought of Bailey's delicious cream cheese, bacon, and spinach breakfast muffins had my mouth watering. Not today. My taste buds were clearly as down in the dumps as I was.

I followed Bailey out to the kitchen. When I walked through the entranceway, I spotted Josh, glancing in my direction and shooting me a brief smile as he slipped out the back door. A strange feeling passed over me. In my current state of mind, I couldn't identify it.

Bailey turned to me, her eyes shining. "Actually, this can't wait. Can we sit down and have a talk?"

I wondered what was going on. "Of course. But didn't you want me to do the muffins?"

Her face was bright. "Yes, but I have something I need to tell you first. Something to talk to you about. Let's grab a coffee and sit down. Latte?"

"Sure." I dropped my purse out back as Bailey ground the beans and fired up the coffee machine. I was finding it nearly impossible to get excited about anything today, but she had my interest piqued.

Our coffees on the table in front of us, Bailey placed her hands on the table in front of her. She seemed almost nervous.

"What is it?" I asked, knitting my brows together.

"I need to tell you a story. My story."

Out of nowhere, a chill hit me. I nodded.

"You know I've had this place for a while now and I own it with a partner, right?" I nodded. "That's not the whole story." She paused, and I noticed she was now clasping her hands together tight.

I placed one of my hands on hers. "It's okay."

She smiled at me, tears welling in her eyes. "I bought this place with my fiancé."

I blinked at her. Bailey didn't have a fiancé. We'd have known about it if she had. Wouldn't we? "Your fiancé?"

"Daniel. Daniel Bentley."

Josh's last name was Bentley. Coincidence? My mind began to whir. "Any relation to Josh?" I asked uncertainly.

She bit her lip and nodded. "He was Josh's brother. He died." Her voice cracked, and she pressed her lips together.

"I had no idea. My god, Bailey. I'm so sorry."

"Thank you. It was a while ago. It was a biking accident." She looked off into the distance. "He was mad on mountain biking. He and Josh would go on these trips away together. Only, one day just after Dan and I had bought this place, he . . . he didn't come back."

"Oh, Bailey." My heart ached for her. She looked so small, sitting across from me, sharing this awful, awful story of a young man, gone

209

before his time. As I squeezed her hand, tears began to spill down my own cheeks. What had I been so sad about: some guy I barely knew, two-timing me with a woman I hated? That was nothing. This. This was something: the loss of the man you loved.

She pulled a handkerchief out of her sleeve to wipe away the tears, the way my nana used to do. It was quaint and old-fashioned and brought a watery smile to my face.

"I know I may look like I'm not over it, but I am. Well, as much as I'll ever be, I guess. It was hard and it was horrible and I wish with all my heart he was still here, but he's not." She swallowed, then took a deep breath, attempting a smile.

"I'm so sorry. I never knew. And . . . Josh never said anything." Oh, Josh. This must have been so hard on him, too. Something went click in my brain. That was why he had been strange that day on our run: this was the thing he mentioned he had to deal with, the reason he had left his high-flying career as a V.P.

"Don't blame him. I asked him not to say anything to you. It affected him deeply, of course. But for him, out of the ashes came Ned's Coffee, his passion." She let out a puff of air. "You see, Dan's nickname was Ned. It's some weird childhood name, you'll have to ask Josh about it."

I swallowed. Ned's was named after Josh's dead brother, Bailey's dead fiancé. I tried to swallow a lump in my throat the size of Texas. It didn't work.

"So, what happened after Dan passed away is his mother, Meredith, took over his interest in the café. I didn't have the capital to run this place on my own, and it was always Dan's and my dream to do this together." She paused, clearing her throat. "Anyway, to cut a long, unpleasant story short, she's finally agreed to take a step back."

I nodded, watching my friend closely as I tried to take everything in. It was overwhelming for me—I couldn't imagine how all of this was for Bailey. Or for Josh. "That's . . . good?" I chanced.

Her face broke into a smile. "It is good. It means I can call the shots, do what I want to do with the place."

"Bailey, that's great. I'm so happy for you."

"Thanks. I understood what Meredith was doing, of course, trying to keep things the way they were before Dan died. It's good for her she can begin to let go now." She took in a breath of air and her expression changed. "Now, I have a proposition for you, as the new sole owner-operator of the Cozy Cottage Café."

I returned her smile. "That has a nice ring to it."

"It does, doesn't it? I know you want this new job of yours at that electricity company, and you're so talented, I can imagine they're desperate to have you. But, would you like to join me here?" She looked around the café.

"What do you mean?"

"You have so many great ideas, and you've helped me begin to develop this business into what I want it to be. Plus, you're an amazing baker, and I could really use another pair of hands."

"You want me to stay on?"

She bit her lip. "Yes, as my business partner. Help me run this place, make it *our* place." She bit her lip and looked at me, her face full of hope.

This time I didn't need to ignore what my gut instinct was yelling at me. I bounced out my chair and hugged her, tears spilling down my cheeks. "Yes! Oh, my god, yes!"

Bailey let out a laugh. "I'd hoped you'd say that. Josh was right."

I cocked my head to the side. "Josh?"

Bailey nodded. "He told me this needed to become your place now. With me."

"He did?" I thought of Josh on the yacht, telling me to talk to Bailey. I'd assumed it was to stay on as a waitress because he knew I'd loved that so much, not to become Bailey's *partner*.

Somehow, he knew. Somehow, through all this mess, he knew me better than I knew myself. He could tell my heart was here, with Bailey, at the Cozy Cottage Café—not trying in vain to follow some career other people wanted for me, working in a job where my soul was being sucked out of me by some corporate vacuum cleaner each and every day. Here. Doing this.

"You know, it might have been Josh's idea, but the moment he mentioned it, it was like the jigsaw puzzle pieces fell into place. You love this place as much as I do."

A rush of excitement ran through my veins. In an instant, my grin was big and fat. "This is going to be a-mazing!"

"I know! We're really doing this!" Bailey's eyes were the size of the saucers she served her delicious cups of coffee on.

My excitement morphed into a beautiful sense of serenity, the kind of calm you can only achieve when you know deep, deep down in your bones something is right. I looked at Bailey for a moment and took a deep breath. "We are."

CHAPTER 22

*I*T WAS THE DAY of The Color Run, and I was up, ready, and raring to go, my newfound exhilaration at becoming Bailey's Cozy Cottage partner—her *partner!*—threatening to spill right out of me. I wasn't going to let myself waste another second thinking about that love-rat Marcus and had ignored his texts and "please let me explain" voicemail. What would be the point? I didn't need it spelled out that I'd been well and truly played. I knew that already.

I met Marissa and Cassie at the starting point, a cocktail of excitement and nerves running through my veins. We were dressed in our matching white tutus, headbands, and Color Run T-shirts, ready to get majorly "colored" together as we ran through the streets of Auckland. We had cheap reflective sunglasses propped up on our heads, important to keep the colored powder out of our eyes, Marissa had instructed, the only one in our group to have done a Color Run before. We'd agreed to tie our hair up in high pigtails with oversized white ribbons and wear big red dots on our cheeks. We bore more than a passing resemblance to something out of a Britney Spears video from the nineties.

The intensity of the atmosphere, the excitement in the air was almost tangible. I surveyed the crowds of people dressed up in similar outfits to ours. There was a group of people—gender unclear—dressed as large white and black dogs, a bunch of men wearing women's dresses with their fluffy afros and knee-high socks, and even a group of women wearing ball gowns—although how they would ever manage to run five kilometers in those was anyone's guess.

"This is amazing!" I said, shouting over the music blaring from the speakers around us.

"I know, right? So fun," Cassie replied with a grin.

"The atmosphere is electric, isn't it?" Marissa yelled, and we nodded, soaking it all up.

"Well, it *is* the happiest five k's you'll ever run," Cassie added, quoting their catchphrase. "Here, put these on."

She pulled our official numbers out of a bag, and we attached them to our matching tops with safety pins.

"And . . . these." She handed us each a packet of powdered color.

I took mine and looked down at it. "I thought they threw the colors at you, not the other way around."

"This is for your own personal use," she said, her eyes shining. "Line someone up and chuck it at them. The more color, the better."

"Fun!" Now, which of my friends was I going to color bomb first . . . ?

"Hey, look, here's Bailey," Cassie said.

"Geez, it was hard to find you guys!" Dressed in normal people's clothes, no tutu or high pigtails, Bailey greeted us all with her characteristic grin. "You all look awesome! It's almost a shame you're going to get covered in powder. We're here to support you."

"We?" I asked.

"Hey, Paige," a voice said behind me. I turned and came face-to-face with Josh.

"Hi," I said to him, suddenly awkward. I hadn't seen Josh since our "woman overboard" yachting disaster. He looked the same old happy Josh I'd grown to know, but something was different about him, and I couldn't quite put my finger on it. I smiled at him and looked down to read his T-shirt, which had become my habit. It had the words "You are brew-tiful" with a picture of a grinning face on a coffee cup.

I smiled at him. "I haven't seen that one before. Is it a new addition to your extensive collection?"

"Yeah. As a matter of fact, it goes with this one." He held up a smaller white shirt with a picture of a face with long eyelashes on a cup of coffee and the words "I am brew-tiful" emblazoned across the front. "It's for you."

I took the shirt in my hands, gazing down at it, not sure what to think or say.

Marissa elbowed me in the ribs. "Oh, that's so cute! Paige, you *have* to wear that."

I looked from the T-shirt up into Josh's eyes, my heart suddenly inexplicably hammering hard. Our eyes locked and his smile broadened. Something moved in my chest, although I couldn't have named the feeling if you'd paid me a million bucks.

"I hope you'll wear it," he said, an uncertain look on his face.

"There's . . . there's nowhere to change." I tore my eyes from Josh's face and looked around at my friends. All three of them were watching me closely. I felt like a chimpanzee at the zoo.

"Oh, don't be silly," Bailey said. "No one will be looking. We can all crowd around you and you can slip that shirt off and this one on in a flash."

"Just like that," Marissa said.

I bit the inside of my lip. "Okay." I stole a quick glance at Josh. His face was beaming, his eyes dancing. A couple of butterflies batted their wings in my belly. I looked down at my sneakers, not sure quite what to make of what was happening between us right now—but kind of liking it, nonetheless.

"I'll . . . ah . . . just go over here while you do that," Josh said, turning his back and stepping away to give me my privacy. Well, as much privacy as you can get in a field full to the brim with fun runners.

I thought of Josh slipping my wet clothes off me on the yacht after he'd saved me and my tummy began to tingle. He'd already seen me in just my underwear, but this felt different somehow.

As my three friends formed an insufficient human shield, I

changed into my new T-shirt, Josh's face front and center in my mind. I attached the race number and smoothed the shirt down. It fitted me like a glove, the cute coffee mug grinning out at the world.

"You look adorable. Josh obviously really likes you," Cassie said as Marissa and Bailey nodded along, all three of them shooting me meaningful looks.

I looked over at the back of Josh's head. He was standing a few feet away, next to a family group of a mom, a dad, and two kids. And it was then I knew what I wanted to do, what I *needed* to do. Without letting myself even think about it, I took a few short steps over to him and placed my hand gently on his arm. He turned to face me, a smile appearing across his face as he took in my T-shirt. My heart slamming against my ribs, without a word I reached my hand up around his neck and pulled him down to me, brushing my lips lightly against his. After a beat, he wrapped his arms around me and pulled me into him, deepening our kiss, intensifying it so the music, the voices, everything around us disappeared into nothingness. It was just Josh and me, no one else, kissing, knowing. The way he felt, the way he tasted, the scent of him. Everything.

And I'd never known.

He'd been here with me, all this time, and I'd never known.

As I pulled away from him and looked into his eyes, I wondered what I'd been doing with my time when, all along, I could have been doing this, with him.

"Thank you." My voice was breathless, our foreheads touching. "Thank you for this and for talking to Bailey about the café, and . . . well, for everything." I took his hand in mine. It fitted perfectly; it felt right. My heart still thudding, I swallowed, hard. I thought of everything Josh had done for me: helping me train for this race, supporting me with my career, rescuing me when I went overboard—literally as well as figuratively.

And now the T-shirt, one of his special Josh-shirts, customized especially for me.

His eyes were electric, full of the promise of things to come. "For you, anything."

Tears stung my eyes as the enormity of how blind I'd been hit me. "And your brother. Josh, I'm so sorry about him."

I could see the pain written across his face as he said, "Thank you."

I kissed him again, not wanting to let go—ever. "I've been so, so stupid. Can you ever forgive me?" I bit my lip and held my breath, awaiting his response.

A fresh smile spread across his face—a face I had once joked looked like Harry Potter, a face I knew with a deep, unflinching certainty I wanted to see every single day of my life from this day on. Calm pervaded my belly, spreading down my limbs.

Josh. It was Josh.

Why hadn't I seen what was right in front of my eyes?

"There's nothing to forgive," he said, pushing an errant strand of hair away from my face.

"Hey, you two."

I reluctantly tore my eyes from Josh's to see Marissa standing next to us.

"I cannot tell you how sorry I am to have to break this up, really, I can't. I think the race is starting. They just announced it," Marissa said.

I looked at her in shock. "They did?" I had been completely oblivious to anything but Josh. Now, the music, the voices, everything came flying back into my consciousness, like someone had flicked the "on" switch of a massive sound machine.

"Yeah, I think you two were kind of in your love bubble there." Marissa grinned at us and I blushed, looking up at Josh through my lashes. "Love bubble." I liked the sound of that.

Josh squeezed my hand. "Go, run your race. I'll be waiting for you at the finish line."

My belly flip-flopped. "Okay." With reluctance, I let his hand drop to his side. "I guess I'll see you in five kilometers."

He grinned at me and heat spread through my chest. I turned to my friends. All three of them were beaming at me like a bunch of happy teenage delinquents on a day out. I returned their smiles tenfold.

"Shall we go run this race?" Marissa asked.

I nodded, my happiness threatening to bubble over. "Let's do this!"

Bidding a reluctant farewell to Josh and Bailey, Marissa, Cassie, and I walked toward the starting line. My head was abuzz with Josh and that incredible kiss. I couldn't help but turn back to take one final look at him. He was watching me with an intense look on his face, one I hadn't seen before.

"Oh, my god!" Marissa exclaimed. "Did I say you two were perfect together? Let me think. Hmm, why yes, I believe I did!"

I shoved her arm, my happiness almost bursting out of me. "Is that an 'I told you so'?"

"I think it is," Marissa replied with a grin.

We got into position, deep within the large crowd. "Hey, you two, glasses on," Cassie instructed.

We did as she said, slipping our sunglasses into place.

"Now, we need to do this." Marissa ripped open her bag of powdered color and threw it at Cassie and me, my brand-new T-shirt turning pink.

"Oh, no you didn't!" I grabbed my own bag of blue powder and began throwing it at Marissa and Cassie until we all looked like rainbow ballerinas on some kind of bachelorette party in Vegas.

Our bags emptied, we surveyed one another. Marissa's blonde hair had turned blue on one side and pink on the other, with a splash of green thrown in for good measure.

"You look great!" Cassie declared, and we all laughed, having the time of our lives. "And Paige? I'm so happy for you. Josh seems like a great guy."

"Oh, he is," Marissa gushed before I had the chance to respond. "You should read the dossier we put together on him for Paige. He's one impressive guy."

The dossier? I thought of the blue folder, still sitting in my drawer, untouched. I smiled to myself. I didn't need to know what was hidden inside that folder. I had all the time in the world to learn everything I needed to know about Josh. And I liked it that way.

The announcement was made to start the race and we were off, my good friends and me, jogging along together amidst the large pack of runners. I couldn't keep that look on Josh's face as I turned to look at him one last time out of my mind. I knew I was no expert on men—hell, I'd shown how utterly useless I was with them over the Marcus debacle—but that look? It felt different; it felt like something big, something huge. I couldn't wait to see him again, to see what lay ahead for us.

As we reached each color bomb station, we slowed down to ensure we got a decent dousing in color, and by the end of the race, tired and hot, the only white on us was the whites of our eyes, hidden behind our glasses.

As we passed through the finish line, we were each handed a bottle of water by the perky cheerleader officials, congratulating us on a great effort.

"That was amazing!" I said, my hands on my knees, puffing from the exertion of the race. Although it was only five kilometers, we had run the whole way and I had a real sense of achievement. I had set out to do this and I'd done it.

Paige was back!

"Oh, my gosh. Totally!" Cassie said. "Great job, girls!" She raised her hand in the air, and we all high-fived one another, bouncing on the spot, high on the adrenaline, atmosphere, and sheer excitement of the day.

The music was pumping, there were people everywhere, all covered in every color of the rainbow. I unscrewed my water bottle and took a long, cool drink. I scanned the crowd, eager to see Josh again and pick up where we'd left off. I'd felt something for him that had startled me. It was unexpected, and it was very, very nice.

And then there he was, next to me, holding me, kissing me, congratulating me on my run. It felt like a wonderful dream, one I never wanted to wake up from.

CHAPTER 23

I STOOD IN THE Cozy Cottage kitchen, leaning up against Josh, one of his arms wrapped around my middle, the other holding a frosty glass of champagne. It had been nine weeks since The Color Run and we had been getting to know one another and spending a lot of time together. It had been nothing short of blissful.

We had been on our first date together the day of the run, and many, many more since, virtually living in one another's pockets. He'd spent time with Dad, discussing his new Paleo lifestyle and giving him exercise tips, and he'd opened up to me about his brother and how horrible it had all been. We'd even visited Dan's grave together one Sunday afternoon with his mother, Meredith, and Bailey.

We were in that wonderful first flush of a new relationship, and life could not be better.

"I would like to make a toast to my new partner," Bailey said, raising her champagne flute in the air. "Paige, without you, tonight would probably never have happened, so thanks for all your ideas and enthusiasm. I think the Cozy Cottage is a better place with you in it." She grinned at me and a blush climbed up my cheeks. "To Paige."

Cassie, Will, Marissa, and Josh repeated, "To Paige," and we all clinked glasses and took a sip.

"Tonight might have been my brainchild, but without *you*, I would probably be stuck in some job I hated, spending as much time as possible on the other side of the counter here, so here's to you, Bailey." I raised my glass, and everyone toasted Bailey. "And it helped the singer was cute."

"Oh, my! He was," Marissa said, fanning her face.

"Hey!" Josh protested playfully.

I turned to face him. "Not as cute as you, of course."

He grinned at me before planting a kiss, firmly on my lips. "That's good to hear."

I smiled at him, the butterflies still having a party in my tummy every time our eyes locked. Even though he was the same old Josh with the same old puns on his T-shirts—tonight's edition reading "Cool Beans" with a coffee bean in shades—he was *my* Josh. And it had to be just about the best darn feeling in the world.

I raised my glass. "Here's to the first of what we hope will be many more successful 'Cozy Cottage Jams.' Ooh, there's an idea. We could do a line of jellies!" I raised my eyebrows at Bailey.

She shook her head. "Let's just deal with the Friday night concerts first, shall we? Baby steps, remember?" she laughed.

Tonight had been our inaugural "Cozy Cottage Jam," and the café had been packed to the gills, all tickets sold out over a week ago. It could have been because people loved this place almost as much as we did, or because the food here was so good, or it could have been because the acoustic guitar-singer was a fantastic local guy who wrote and played his own songs. The fact he looked a bit like a young Johnny Depp hadn't hurt, either.

Whatever it was, tonight had been a smash hit, Bailey's and my first new venture as Cozy Cottage partners. It was a great start.

"Now, everyone, eat up. We've been slaving away on our new line of pies, and we need you all to be our guinea pigs," Bailey said, uncovering the four pies on the kitchen table she and I had been devising together over the previous weeks. "This one is pumpkin with a cinnamon twist, this one is deep-pan apple and raisin, this one is rhubarb and strawberry, and this one I bet will be the girls' favorite: chocolate mud pie."

"With pleasure," Will said, grabbing a fork and plate from the stack.

"We don't need to be asked twice," Josh added, joining him.

I leaned up against the counter with Bailey as we watched our friends devour the pies, exclaiming each one was better than the last.

"We're good at this, you know," she commented, nudging me in the side.

"I know," I replied, nudging her back.

With only a matter of crumbs left on three of the four pie dishes fifteen minutes later—we may need to revisit the pumpkin pie recipe —Marissa cleared her throat. "I have an announcement to make." She paused for effect. "I've met someone." Her face was shining. "Well, a few *someones*, actually."

We all laughed, Cassie exclaiming, "What?"

"Isn't it meant to be One Last First Date, Marissa? Not *Three* or *Four* Last First Dates?" Bailey asked with a chortle.

"Well, to be fair, we didn't quite manage to get it right first time, did we?" Cassie said to me.

"But we did in the end." I gave Josh a small smile, and he winked back at me.

"Yeah, but not a whole sports team!" Will chimed.

Marissa put her hand in the air. "I know, I know. And it's only three."

"*Only* three?" My eyes were wide.

"Okay, here's the thing. You guys are always going on about how fussy I am about men, right?"

We nodded. "It's true, she is," Cassie said.

"I figured I'd go on Three Last First Dates and pick the best one of the lot. It's a numbers game, don't you see? Plus, I want what you two have got," she said, nodding at Cassie and me. "Well, not Josh and Will, of course. My own guy."

"So, you've decided to take this seriously, huh?" I asked.

"I have," she replied with conviction. "Things have . . . changed for me, and I want to find him."

Cassie shook her head as we all laughed at Marissa's audacity, admirable as it was. "You know what? I think it's a great strategy. Just having One Last First Date didn't work out for us"—she pointed at both me and herself—"so I say why not?"

"Thank you. I will take that as your blessing." Marissa beamed.

"Only you would go on *Three* Last First Dates, Marissa," I commented, shaking my head, wondering exactly what it was that had changed for her.

Before I had the chance to ask, Cassie said, "What about you, Bailey? Are you thinking of looking for your One Last First Date?"

"Or five," Will added with a chuckle.

I glanced at Bailey, hoping the question hadn't upset her. As far as I was aware, the others didn't know about her fiancé. But then, she had agreed to the One Last First Date pact on the beach that night, so perhaps she was ready to move on and meet someone new?

"I might very well be." She had a quiet air of confidence to her, and when she looked at me, we shared a smile. "But right now, we've got a kitchen to clean up and beds to get to. Some of us have work in the morning."

We set to it, cleaning and stacking the dishes and straightening the kitchen up. With everyone gone, Bailey wished Josh and me good night and slipped out the front door.

"You know what?" Josh said, pulling me in for a hug.

I looked up into his eyes, my heart clenching at the sight of him. "What?"

"I think my brother would be happy with the way things turned out." He kissed me on the tip of my nose. "You did good."

"I hope so."

He leaned down and pressed his lips against mine, kissing me so long and so well, I swear I saw stars by the time we were done.

"Come on, you. Let's head home."

As I flicked the light switch off and Josh held the door for us to leave, I took a final look around the Cozy Cottage. The chairs were stacked on the tables, the only light coming from the drinks refrigerator behind the counter. I let out a contented sigh. *This.* This was where I wanted to be. This was my home.

Out on the street, I locked the door behind us. I slipped my hand into Josh's. As he squeezed my hand and smiled at me, the corners of his eyes crinkling the way they did, I knew what I'd known since our very first kiss, what others had seen before I had any clue: Josh was my Last First Date, and I was the luckiest girl in the world.

THE END

ACKNOWLEDGMENTS

Paige's story was one I was looking forward to writing after I'd given her a bit of a tough time in *One Last First Date*. I was glad I could give her a happy ending with a great guy, as well as give her the happiness and self-confidence she had been lacking. Thank you, dear readers, for taking your time to read about Paige and the gang. I hope you got to enjoy a cup of coffee and a slice of cake (or two) while you did so.

As always, I have a host of people to thank for helping me bring this book to publication. First up, thank you to my editor, Chrissy Wolfe from The Every Free Chance Reader. Chrissy, you continue to do a great job for me and you're a pleasure to work with. To my beta reading team of Leanne Mackay, Julie Crengle, Kirsty McManus, and Nicky Willis: thank you once again for your straight-shooting critique and for taking the time out of your busy lives to read my work. I am indebted to you fabulous women.

Thank you to the wonderfully supportive writers I've got to know in both Chick Lit Chat HQ and the Hawke's Bay ladies of the Romance Writers of New Zealand group. I am continually amazed at the support we writers give one another, and so thankful for you all. I especially want to thank fellow author, Geralyn Corcillo who has got to be one of the most positive and supportive people I know, helping me through the rollercoaster of emotions writing a book can bring. Geralyn, you rock!

Thank you to my wonderful son, who is so very proud of his mummy's writing career, doing a school project on me as his "X Factor Person." I love you to the moon and back and back again.

Thank you to my readers. So many of you reach out to me through emails and reviews and on social media. Thanks for being such a huge part of this journey.

And last but never least, thank you to my long-suffering husband, who knows more about my books than any one man should. Without you, I wouldn't be doing this.

ABOUT THE AUTHOR

Kate O'Keeffe is a *USA TODAY* bestselling and award-winning author who writes exactly what she loves to read: laugh-out-loud romantic comedies with swoon-worthy heroes and gorgeous feel-good happily ever afters. She lives and loves in beautiful Hawke's Bay, New Zealand with her family and two scruffy but loveable dogs.

When she's not penning her latest story, Kate can be found hiking up hills (slowly), traveling to different countries around the globe (back when we used to be able to do that), and eating chocolate. A lot of it.